The creature was humanoid, but very far indeed from being human. It had double shoulders and four arms. Its eyes, a flaming red in color, were large and vertically slitted, like a cat's. It was completely hairless, and its bright yellow teeth were clean and sharp.

"You are incompatible with the humanity of our planet and cannot be allowed to stay," it said.

"Suppose we blast you and your jets out of the air and land anyway?" asked Garlock.

"That is perhaps possible," the Arpalone agreed. "We are not invincible. However, it would do you little good. If any one of you leaves this vessel you will surely die. Not quickly, but slowly and with difficulty."

Other Titles in the Ace Great Years Series:

the Galaxy Primes

by

Edward E. "Doc" Smith

ace books

A Division of Charter Communications Inc.

1120 Avenue of the Americas

New York, N.Y. 10036

THE GALAXY PRIMES

Copyright ©, 1965, by Edward E. Smith

Printed in U.S.A.

I

HER HAIR was a brilliant green. So was her spectacularly filled halter. So were her tight short-shorts, her lipstick, and the lacquer on her finger- and toe-nails. As she strolled into the Main of the starship, followed hesitantly by the other girl, she drove a mental probe at the black-haired, powerfully-built man seated at the instrument-banked console.

Blocked.

Then at the other, slenderer man who was rising to his feet from the pilot's bucket seat. His guard was partially down; he was telepathing a pleasant if somewhat reserved greeting to both newcomers.

She turned to her companion and spoke aloud. "So *these* are the system's best." The emphasis was somewhere between condescension and sneer. "Not much to choose between, I'd say . . . 'port me a tenth-piece, Clee? Heads, I take the tow-head."

She flipped the coin dexterously. "Heads it is, Lola, so I get Jim — James James James the Ninth himself. You have the honor of pairing with Clee — or should I say His Learnedness Right the Honorable Director Doctor Cleander Simmsworth Garlock, Doctor of Philosophy, Doctor of Science, Prime Operator, President and First Fellow of the Galaxian Society, First Fellow of the Gunther Society, Fellow of the Institute of Paraphysics, of the Institute of Nuclear Physics, of the College of Mathematics, of the Congress of Psiontists, and of all the other top-bracket brain-gangs you ever heard of. Also, for your information, his men have given him a couple of informal degrees — P.D.Q. and S.O.B."

The big psiontist's expression of saturnine, almost contemptuous amusement had not changed; his voice came flat and cold. "The less you say, Doctor Bellamy, the better. Bitchy, swellheaded women give me an acute rectal pain. Pitching your curves over all the vizzies in space got you aboard, but it won't get you a thing from here on. And for your information, Doctor Bellamy, one more crack like that and I take you over my knee and blister your backside."

"Try it, you clumsy ape!" she jeered. *That* I want to see — any time you want to get both arms broken at the elbows!"

"Now's as good a time as any. I like your spirit, but I can't say a thing for your judgment." He got up and started purposefully toward her, but both noncombatants came between.

"Hold it, Clee!" James protested, both hands against the heavier man's chest. "What the hell kind of show is *that* to put on?" And simultaneously:

"Belle! For godsake — picking a fight already, and with nobody knows how many million people looking on! You know as well as I do that we may have to spend the rest of our lives together, so act like civilized beings — *please* —both of you! And don't . . ."

"Nobody's watching this but us," Garlock interrupted. "When pussy there started using her claws I cut the gun."

"That's what *you* think," James said sharply, "but

Fatso and his number one girl friend are coming in on the tight beam."

"Oh?" Garlock whirled toward the hitherto dark and silent three-dimensional communications instrument. The face of a bossy-looking woman was already bright.

"Garlock! How dare you try to cut Chancellor Ferber off?" she demanded. Her voice was deep-pitched, blatant with authority. "Here you are, sir."

The woman's face shifted to one side and a man's appeared — a face to justify in full his nickname.

" 'Fatso', eh?" Chancellor Ferber snarled. Pale eyes glared from the fat face. "That costs you exactly one thousand credits, James."

"How much will this cost me, Fatso?" Garlock asked.

"Five thousand — and, since nobody can call me that deliberately, demotion three grades and probation for three years. Make a note, Miss Foster."

"Noted, sir."

"Still sure we aren't going anywhere," Garlock said. *"What* a brain!"

"Sure I'm sure!" Ferber gloated. "In a couple of hours I'm going to buy your precious starship in as junk. In the meantime, whether you like it or not, I'm going to watch your expression while you push all those pretty buttons and nothing happens."

"The trouble with you, Fatso," Garlock said dispassionately, as he opened a drawer and took out a pair of cutting pliers, "is that all your strength is in your glands and none in your brain. There are a lot of things — including a lot of tests — you know nothing about. How much will you see after I've cut one wire?"

"You wouldn't dare!" the fat man shouted. "I'd fire you — blacklist you all over the sys —"

Voice and images died away and Garlock turned to

the two women in the Main. He began to smile, but his mental shield did not weaken.

"You've got a point there, Lola," he said, going on as though Ferber's interruption had not occurred. "Not that I blame either Belle or myself. If anything was ever calculated to drive a man nuts, this farce was. As the only female Prime in the system, Belle should have been in automatically — she had no competition. And to anybody with three brain cells working the other place lay between you, Lola, and the other three female Ops in the age group.

"But no. Ferber and the rest of the Board — stupidity *über alles!* — think all us Ops and Primes are psycho and that the ship will never even lift. So they made a Grand Circus of it. But they succeeded in one thing — with such abysmal stupidity so rampant I'm getting more and more reconciled to the idea of our not getting back... at least, not for a long, long time."

"Why, they said we had a very good chance . . ." Lola began.

"Yeah, and they said a lot of even bigger damn lies than that one. Have you read any of my papers?"

"I'm sorry. I'm not a mathematician."

"Our motion will be purely at random. If it isn't, I'll eat this whole ship. We won't get back until Jim and I work out something to steer us with. But they must be wondering no end, outside, what the score is, so I'm willing to call it a draw — temporarily — and let 'em in again. How about it, Belle?"

"A draw it is — temporarily." Neither, however, even offered to shake hands.

"Smile pretty, everybody," Garlock said, and pressed a stud.

". . . the matter? What's the matter? Oh . . . the worried voice of the System's ace newscaster came in. "Power failure *already?*"

"No." Garlock replied. "I figured we had a couple of minutes of privacy coming, if you can understand the meaning of the word. Now all four of us tell everybody who is watching or listening *au revoir* or goodbye, whichever it may turn out to be." He reached for the switch.

"Wait a minute!" the newscaster demanded. "Leave it on until the last poss —" His voice broke off sharply.

"Turn it back on!" Belle ordered.

"No."

"Scared?"

"Exactly. I'm scared purple. So would you be, if you had three brain cells working in that gloryhound's head of yours. Get set, everybody, and we'll take off."

"Stop it, both of you!" Lola exclaimed. "Where do you want us to sit, and do we strap down?"

"You sit here; Belle at that plate beside Jim. Yes, strap down. There probably won't be any shock, and we should land right side up, but there's no sense in taking chances. Sure your stuff's all aboard?"

"Yes, it's in our rooms."

The four secured themselves; the two men checked their instruments for the dozenth time. The pilot donned his scanner. The ship lifted effortlessly, noiselessly. Through the atmosphere; through and far beyond the stratosphere. It stopped.

"Ready, Clee?" James licked his lips.

"As ready as I ever will be, I guess. Shoot."

The pilot's right hand moved unenthusiastically toward a red button on his panel . . . showed . . . stopped. He stared into his scanner at the Earth far below.

"Hit it, Jim!" Garlock snapped. *"Hit* it, for godsake, before we *all* lose our nerve!"

James stabbed convulsively at the button, and in the very instant of contact — instantaneously, without a fractional microsecond of time-lapse — their familiar surroundings disappeared. Without any sensation of motion, of displacement, or of the passage of any time whatsoever, the planet beneath them was no longer their familiar Earth. The plates showed no familiar stars nor patterns of heavenly bodies. The brightly-shining sun was very evidently not Sol.

"Well, we went *somewhere* . . . but not to Alpha Centauri, not much to our surprise." James gulped twice; then went on, speaking almost jauntily now that the attempt had been made and had failed. "So now it's up to you, Clee, as Director of Project Gunther and captain of the good ship *Pleiades,* to boss the more-or-less simple — more, I hope — job of getting us back to Tellus."

Science, both physical and paraphysical, had done its best. Gunther's Theorems, which defined the electromagnetic and electrogravitic parameters pertaining to the annihilation of distance, had been studied, tested, and applied to the full. So had the Psionic Corollaries — which, while not having the status of paraphysical laws, did allow computation of the qualities and magnitudes of the stresses required for any given application of the Gunther Effect.

The planning of the starship *Pleiades* had been difficult in the extreme, its construction almost impossible. While it was practically a foregone conclusion that any man of the requisite caliber would already be a member of the Galaxian Society, the three planets and eight satellites were screened, psiontist by psiontist, to select the two strongest and most versatile of their breed.

These two, Garlock and James, were heads of departments of, and under iron-clad contract to, vast Solar System Enterprises, Inc., the only concern able and willing to attempt the building of the first starship.

However, Alonzo P. Ferber, Chancellor of SSE, would not risk a tenth-piece of the company's money on such a bird-brained scheme. Himself a Gunther First, he believed implicitly that Firsts were in fact tops in Gunther ability; that these few self-styled "Operators" and "Prime Operators" were either charlatans or self-deluded crackpots. Since he could not feel that so-called "Operator Field," no such thing did or could exist. No Gunther starship could ever, possibly, work.

He did loan Garlock and James to the Galaxians, but that was as far as he would go. For salaries and for labor, for research and material, for trials and for errors; the Society paid and paid and paid.

Thus the starship *Pleiades* had cost the Galaxian Society almost a thousand million credits.

Garlock and James had worked on the ship since its inception. They were to be of the crew; for over a year it had been taken for granted that they would be its only crew.

As the *Pleiades* neared compeltion, however, it became clearer and clearer that the displacement-control presented an unsolved, and quite possibly an insoluble, problem. It was mathematically certain that, when the Gunther field went on, the ship would be displaced instantaneously to some location in space having precisely the Gunther coordinates required by that particular field. One impeccably rigorous analysis showed that the ship would shift into the nearest solar system possessing an Earth-type planet — which was believed to be Alpha Centauri and which was close enough to Sol so that orientation would be automatic and the return to Earth a simple matter.

Since the Gunther Effect did in fact annihilate distance, however, another group of mathematicians, led by Garlock and James, proved with equal rigor that the point of destination was no more likely to be any one given Gunther point than any other one of the myriads of billions of equiguntherial points undoubtedly existing throughout our entire normal space-time continuum.

The two men would go anyway, of course. Carefully-calculated pressures would make them go. It was neither necessary nor desirable, however, for them to go alone.

Wherefore the planets and satellites were combed again this time to select two women — the two most highly-gifted psionicists in the eighteen-to-twenty-five age group. Thus, if the *Pleiades* returned successfully to Earth, well and good. If she did not, the four selectees would found, upon some far-off world, a race much abler than the humanity of Earth; since eighty three percent of Earth's dwellers had psionic grades lower than Four.

This search, with its attendant fanfare and studiedly blatant publicity, was so planned and engineered that the selected women did not arrive at the spaceport until a bare fifteen minutes before the scheduled time of take-off. Thus it made no difference whether the women liked the men or not, or vice versa; or whether or not any of them really wanted to make the trip. Pressures were such that each of them had to go, whether he or she wanted to or not.

"Cut the rope, Jim, and let the old bucket drop," Garlock said. "Not too close. Before we make any kind of contact we'll have to do some organizing. These instruments"— he waved at his console —"show that ours is the only Operator Field in this whole region of space. Hence, there are no Operators and no Primes. That means that from now until we get back to Tellus . . ."

"*If* we get back to Tellus," Belle corrected, sweetly.

"Until we get back to Tellus there will be no Gunthering aboard this ship . . ."

"*What?*" Belle broke in again. "Have you lost your mind?"

"There will be little if any lepping, and nothing else at all. At the table, if we want sugar, we will reach for it or have it passed. We will pick up things, such as cigarettes, with our fingers. We will carry lighters and use them. When we go from place to place, we will walk. Is that clear?"

"You seem to be talking English," Belle said, "but the words don't make sense."

"I didn't think you were that stupid." Their eyes locked and held. Then Garlock grinned savagely. "Okay. You tell her, Lola, in words of as few syllables as possible."

"Why, to get used to it, of course," Lola explained, while Belle glared at Garlock. "So as not to reveal anything we don't have to."

"Excellent, Miss Montandon — all monosyllables except two. That should make it clear, even to Miss Bellamy." He paused, glancing calmly at Belle's glare, then said, "In emergencies, of course, anything goes. We will now proceed with business."

"One minute, please!" Belle snapped. "Just why, Lord Director Captain Garlock, are you insisting on oral communication, when lepping is so much faster and better? It's stupid — reactionary. Don't you ever lep?"

"With Jim, on business, yes; with women, no more than I have to. What I think is nobody's business but mine."

"What a way to run a ship! Or a project!"

"Running this project is my business, not yours; and if there's any one thing in the entire universe it does *not* need, it's a female exhibitionist. Besides your obvious qualifications to be one of the Eves in case of Ultimate Contingency . . ." He broke off and stared at her, his contemptuous gaze traveling slowly, dissectingly, from her toes to the topmost wave of her hairdo. "Forty-two, twenty, forty?" he asked.

"You flatter me." Her voice was controlled fury. "Thirty-nine, twenty-two, thirty-nine. Five-seven. One thirty-five. If any of it's any of your business, which it isn't. You should be discussing brains and ability, not vital statistics."

"Brains? Well, yes — as a Prime, you *must* have a brain. What do you think you're good for on this project? What can you do?"

"I can do anything any man ever born can do, and do it better!"

"Okay. Compute a Gunther field that will put us two hundred thousand feet directly above the peak of that mountain."

"That isn't fair and you know it — not that I expected fairness from you. That doesn't take either brains or ability . . ."

"Oh, no?"

"No. Merely highly specialized training that you know I haven't had. Give me a five-tape course on it and I'll come closer than either you or James; for a hundred credits a shot."

"I'll do just that. Something you *are* supposed to know, then. How would you go about making first contact?"

"Well, I wouldn't do it the way *you* would — by knocking down the first native I saw, putting my foot on his face, and yelling, 'Bow down, you stupid beasts, and worship me —'"

14

"Hold it, both of you!" James broke in. "What the *hell* are you trying to prove? How about cutting out this cat-and-dog act and getting some work done?"

"You've got a point there," Garlock admitted, holding his temper by a visible effort. "Sorry, Jim. Belle, what were you briefed for?"

"To understudy you." She, too, fought her temper down. "To learn everything about Project Gunther. I have a whole box of tapes in my room, including advanced Gunther math and first-contact techniques. I'm to study them during all my on-watch time unless you assign other duties."

"No matter what your duties may be, you'll have to have time to study. If you don't find what you want in your own tapes — and you probably won't, since Ferber and his Miss Foster ran the selections — use our library. It's good — designed to carry on our civilization. Miss Montandon? No, that's ridiculous, the way we're fixed. Lola?"

"I'm to learn how to be Doctor James'. . ."

"*Jim*, please Lola," James said. "And call him Clee."

"I'd like that." She smiled winningly. "And my friends call me 'Brownie'."

"I see why they would. It fits like a coat of lacquer."

It did. Her hair was a dark, lustrous brown, as were her eyebrows. Her eyes were brown. Her skin, too — her dark red playsuit left little to the imagination — was a rich and even brown. Originally fairly dark, it had been tanned to a more-than-fashionable depth of color by naked sunbathing and by practically-naked outdoor sports. A couple of inches shorter than the green-haired girl, she too had a figure that would have delighted any sculptor.

"I'm your friend, Brownie, and very glad to be such," James said. "Go ahead."

"I'm to be your assistant. I have about a thousand tapes to study, too. It'll be quite awhile, I'm afraid, before I can be of much use, but I'll do the best I can."

"If we had hit Alpha Centauri that arrangement would have been good, but as we are, it isn't." Garlock frowned in thought, his heavy black eyebrows almost meeting above his finely-chiseled, aquiline nose. "Since neither Jim nor I need an assistant any more than we need tails, it was designed to give you girls something to do. But out here, lost, there's work for a dozen trained specialists and there are only four of us. So we shouldn't duplicate effort. Right? You first, Belle."

"Are you asking me or telling me?" she asked. "And that's a fair question; don't read anything into it that isn't there. With your attitude, I want information."

"I am asking you," he replied, carefully. "For your information, when I know what should be done, I give orders. When I don't know, as now, I ask advice. If I like it, I follow it. Fair enough?"

"Fair enough. We're apt to need any number of specialists."

"Lola?"

"Of course we shouldn't duplicate. What shall I study?"

"That's what we'll have to figure out. We can't do it exactly, of course; all we can do now is set up a rough scheme. Jim's job is the only one that's definite. He'll have to work full time on nebular configurations. If we hit inhabited planets he'll have to add their star-charts to his own. That leaves three of us to do all the other work of a survey. Ideally, we would cover all the factors that would be of use in getting us back to Tellus, but since we don't know what those factors are . . . Found out anything yet, Jim?"

"A little. It's a Tellus-type planet, apparently strictly so. Oceans and continents. Lots of inhabitants — farms, villages, all sizes of cities. We're not close enough to say definitely, but the inhabitants seem to be humanoid, if not human."

"Hold her here. Besides astronomy, which is all yours, what do we need most?"

"We should have enough to classify planets and inhabitants, so as to chart a space-trend if there is any. I'd say the most important ones would be geology, stratigraphy, paleontology, oceanography, xenology, anthropology, ethnology, vertebrate biology, botany, and at least some ecology."

"That's about the list I was afraid of. But there are only three of us."

"Each of you will have to be a lot of specialists in one, then. I'd say the best split would be planetology, xenology, and anthropology—each, of course, stretched all out of shape to cover a dozen related and non-related specialties."

"Good enough. Xenology, of course, is mine. Contacts, liaison, politics, correlation, and so on, as well as studying the non-human life forms—including as many lower animals and plants as possible. I'll make a stab at it. Now, Belle, since you're a Prime and Lola's an Operator, you get the next toughest job. Planetography."

"Why not?" Belle smiled and began to act as one of the party. "All I know about it is a hazy idea of what the word means, but I'll start studying as soon as we get squared away."

"Fine. That leaves anthropology to you, Lola. Besides, that's your line, isn't it?"

"Yes, Sociological Anthropology. I have my M.S. in it, and I was working for my Ph.D. But as Jim said, it isn't only the one specialty. You want me, I take it, to cover humanoid races, too."

"Check. You and Jim both, then, will know what you're doing, while Belle and I are trying to play ours by ear."

"Where do we draw the line between humanoid and non-human?"

"In case of doubt we'll confer. That covers it as much as we can, I think. Take us down, Jim — and be on your toes to take evasive action fast."

The ship dropped rapidly toward an airport just outside a fairly large city. Fifty thousand — forty thousand — thirty thousand feet.

Then a thought-message touched their minds: "Calling strange spaceship — you must be a spaceship, in spite of your incredible mass. Do you read me?"

"I read you clearly. This is the spaceship *Pleiades,* home planet Tellus, Captain Garlock commanding, asking permission to land and information as to landing conventions." He did not have to tell James to stop the ship; James had already done so.

"I was about to ask you to hold position; I thank you for having done so. Hold for inspection and type-test, please. We will not blast unless you fire first. A few minutes, please."

A group of twelve jet fighters took off practically vertically upward and climbed with fantastic speed. They leveled off a thousand feet below the *Pleiades* and made a flying circle. Up and into the ring thus formed there lumbered a large, clumsy-looking helicopter.

"We have no record of any planet named 'Tellus'; nor of any such ship as yours. Of such incredible mass and with no visible or detectable means of support or of propulsion. Not from this part of the galaxy, certainly . . . could it be that intergalactic travel is actually possible? But excuse, Captain Garlock, none of that is any of my business — which is to determine whether or not you four human beings are compatible with, and thus acceptable to, our humanity of Hodell . . . But you do not seem to have a standard televideo testing-box aboard."

"No, sir; only our own tri-di and teevee."

"You must be examined by means of a standard box. I will rise to your level and teleport one across to you. It is self-powered and fully automatic."

"You needn't rise, sir. Just toss the box out of your 'copter into the air. We'll take it from there." Then, to James: "Take it, Jim."

"Oh? You can lift large masses against much gravity?" The alien was all attention. "I have not known that such power existed. I will observe with keen interest."

"I have it," James said. "Here it is."

"Thank you, sir," Garlock said to the alien. Then, to Lola: "You've been reading these — these Hodellians?"

"The officer in the helicopter and those in the fighters, yes. Most of them are Gunther Firsts."

"Good girl. The set's coming to life — watch it."

The likeness of the alien being became clear upon the alien screen, visible from the waist up. While humanoid, the creature was very far indeed from being human. He — at least, it had masculine rudimentary nipples — had double shoulders and four arms. His skin was a vividly intense cobalt blue. His ears were black, long, and highly dirigible. His eyes, a flaming red in color, were large and vertically slitted, like a cat's. He had no hair at all. His nose was large and Roman; his jaw was square, almost jutting; his bright yellow teeth were clean and sharp.

After a minute of study the alien said, "Although your vessel is so entirely alien that nothing even remotely like it is on record, you four are completely human and, if of compatible type, acceptable. Are there any other living beings aboard with you?"

"Excepting micro-organisms, none."

"Such life is of no importance. Approach, please, one of you, and grasp with a hand the projecting metal knob."

With a little trepidation, Garlock did so. He felt no unusual sensation at the contact.

"All four of you are compatible and we accept you. This finding is surprising in the extreme, as you are the first human beings of record who grade higher than what you call Gunther Two ... or Gunther Second?"

"Either one; the terms are interchangeable."

"You have minds of tremendous development and power; definitely superior even to my own. However, there is no doubt that physically you are perfectly compatible with our humanity. Your blood will be of great benefit to it. You may land. Goodbye."

"Wait, please. How about landing conventions? And visiting restrictions and so on? And may we keep this box? We will be glad to trade you something for it, if we have anything you would like to have."

"Ah, I should have realized that your customs would be widely different from ours. Since you have been examined and accepted, there are no restrictions—you will not act against humanity's good. Land where you please, go where you please, do what you please, for as long as you please. Take up permanent residence or leave as soon as you please. Marry if you like, or simply breed—your unions with this planet's humanity will be fertile. Keep the box without payment. As Guardians of Humanity we Arpalones do whatever small favors we can. Have I been clear?"

"Abundantly so. Thank you, sir."

"Now I really must go. Goodbye."

Garlock glanced into his plate. The jets had disappeared, and the helicopter was falling rapidly away. He wiped his brow.

"Well, I'll be damned," he said.

"Damned and blasted," Belle agreed.

"Make it three damns — in spades," said James.

And Lola just sat speechless, staring at the rapidly-vanishing helicopter.

Garlock was the first to recover his poise. "Lola, do you check me that this planet is named Hodell, that it is populated by human beings exactly like us, that these creatures — Arpalones — are, in some way or other, Guardians of Humanity?"

"Exactly, except they aren't 'creatures'. They're humanoids, and very fine people."

"You'd think so, of course ... correction accepted. Well, let's take advantage of their extraordinary hospitable invitation and go down. Cut the rope, Jim."

The airport was very large, and was divided into several sections, each of which was equipped with runways and/or other landing facilities to suit one class of craft — propellor jobs, jets, or helicopters. There were even a few structures that looked like rocket pits.

"Where are you going to sit down, Jim? With the 'copters or over by the blast-pits?"

"With the 'copters, I think. Since I can place her to within a couple of inches, I'll put her squarely into that far corner, where she'll be out of everybody's way."

"No concrete out there," Garlock said, "but the ground seems good and solid."

"We'd better not land on concrete," James grinned. "Unless it's terrific stuff we'd smash it. On bare ground,

21

the worst we can do is sink in a foot or so, and that won't hurt anything."

James pulled out his scanner and stuck his face into it. The immense starship settled downward toward the selected corner. There was no noise, no blast, no flame, no smoke — no slightest visible or detectable sign of whatever force it was that was braking the thousands of tons of the vessel's mass in its miles-long, almost vertical plunge to ground.

When the *Pleiades* struck ground the impact was scarcely to be felt. When she came to rest, after settling into the ground her allotted "foot or so," there was no jar at all.

"Atmosphere, temperature and so on approximately Earth-normal," Garlock said. "Just as our friend said it would be."

James scanned the city and the field. "Our visit is kicking up a lot of excitement. Shall we go out?"

"Not yet!" Belle exclaimed. "I want to see how the women are dressed, first."

"So do I," Lola added, "and some other things besides."

Both women — Lola through her Operator's scanner, Belle by manipulating the ship's tremendous Operator Field by the sheer power of her Prime Operator's mind — stared eagerly at the crowd of people now beginning to stream across the field.

"As an anthropologist," Lola announced, "I'm not only surprised, I am shocked, annoyed, and disgruntled. Why, they're *exactly* like white Tellurian human beings!"

"But *look* at their *clothes!*" Belle insisted. "They're wearing anything and everything, from bikinis to coveralls!"

"Yes, but notice." This was the anthropological scientist speaking now. "Breasts and loins, covered. Faces, uncovered. Heads and feet and hands, either bare or covered. Ditto for legs up to there, backs, arms, necks and shoulders down to here, and torsos clear down to there. We won't violate any conventions by going out as we are. Not even you, Belle. You first, Chief. Yours the high honor of setting first foot — the biggest foot we've got, too — on alien soil."

"To hell with that. We'll go out together."

"Wait a minute," Lola said. "There's a funny-looking automobile just coming through the gate. The Press. Three men and two women. Two cameras, one walkie-talkie, and two microphones. The photog in the purple shirt is really a sharpie at lepping. Class Three, at least — possibly a Two."

"How about screens down enough to lep, boss?" Belle suggested. "Faster. We may need it."

"Check. I'm too busy to record, anyway — I'll log this stuff up tonight."

And thoughts flew.

"Check me, Jim," Garlock flashed. "Telepathy, very good. On Gunther, the guy was right — no signs at all of any First activity, and very few Seconds."

"Check," James agreed.

"And Lola, those 'Guardians' out there. I thought they were the same as the Arpalone we talked to. They aren't. Not even telepathic. Same color scheme, that's all."

"Right. Much more brutish. Much flatter cranium. Long, tearing canine teeth — carnivorous. I'll call them just 'guardians' until we find out what they really are."

The press car arrived and the Tellurians disembarked — and, accidentally or not, it was Belle's green slipper that first touched ground. There was a terrific Babel of thought — even worse than voices would have been, since thoughts came so much faster. The reporters, all of them, wanted to know everything at once. How, what, where, when, and why. Also who. And all about Tellus and the Tellurian solar system. How did the visitors like Hodell? And all about Belle's green hair. And the photographers were prodigal of film, shooting everything from all possible angles.

"Hold it!" Garlock loosed a blast of thought that silenced almost the whole field. "We will have order, please. Lola Montandon, our anthropologist, will take charge. Keep it orderly, Lola, if you have to throw half of them off the field. I'm going over to Administration and check in. One of you reporters can come with me, if you like."

The man in the purple shirt got his bid in first. As the two men walked away together, Garlock noted that the man was in fact a Second — his flow of lucid, cogent thought did not interfere at all with the steady stream of speech going into his portable recorder. Garlock also noticed that in any group of more than a dozen people there was always at least one guardian. They paid no attention whatever to the people, who in turn ignored them completely. Garlock wondered briefly. Guardians? The Arpalones, out in space, yes. But these creatures, naked and unarmed on the ground? The Arpalones were non-human people. These things were — what?

At the door of the Field Office the reporter, after turning Garlock over to a startlingly beautiful, leggy, breasty, blonde receptionist-usherette, hurried away.

He flecked a feeler at her mind and stiffened. How could a Two — a high Two, at that — be working as an usherette? And with her guard down clear to the floor? He probed — and saw.

"Lola!" He flashed a tight-beamed thought. "You

aren't putting out anything about our sexual customs, family life, and so on."

"Of course not. We must know their mores first."

"Good girl. Keep your shield up."

"Oh, we're so glad to see you, Captain Garlock!" The blonde, who was dressed little more heavily than the cigarette girls in Venusberg's Cartier Room, seized his left hand in both of hers and held it considerably longer than was necessary. Her dazzling smile, her laughing eyes, her flashing white teeth, the many exposed inches of her skin, and her completely unshielded mind all waved banners of welcome.

"Captain Garlock, Governor Atterlin has been most anxious to see you ever since you were first detected. This way, please, sir." She turned, brushing her bare hip against his leg in the process, and led him by the hand along a hallway. Her thoughts flowed on. "I've been anxious to see you, too, and I'm simply delighted to see you close up, and I hope to see a lot more of you. You're a wonderfully pleasant surprise, sir; I've never seen a man like you before. I don't think Hodell ever saw a man like you before, sir. With such a really terrific mind and yet so big and strong and well-built and handsome and clean-looking and blackish. You're wonderful — you'll be here a long time, I hope? Here we are, sir."

She opened a door, walked across the room, sat down in an overstuffed chair, and crossed her legs meticulously. Then, still smiling happily, she followed with eager eyes and mind Garlock's every move.

Garlock had been reading Governor Atterlin, so he knew why it was the governor who was in that office instead of the port manager. He knew that Atterlin had been reading him — as much as he had allowed. They had already discussed many things, and were still discussing.

The room was much more like a library than an office. The governor, a middle-aged, red-headed man a trifle inclined to portliness, had been seated in a huge reclining chair facing a teevee screen, but got up to shake hands.

"Welcome, friend Captain Garlock. Now, to continue. As to exchange. Many ships visiting us have nothing we need or can use. For such, all services are free — or rather, are paid by the city. Our currency is based upon platinum, but gold, silver, and copper are valuable. Certain jewels, also . . ."

"That's far enough. We will pay our way — we have plenty of metal. What are your ratios of value for the four metals?"

"Today's quotations are . . ." He glanced at a screen, and his fingers flashed over the keys of a computer beside his chair. "One weight of platinum is equal in value to seven point three four six . . ."

"Decimals are not necessary, sir."

"Seven plus, then, weights of gold. One of gold to eleven of silver. One silver to four of copper."

"Thank you. We'll use platinum. I'll bring some bullion tomorrow morning and exchange it for your currency. Shall I bring it here, or to a bank in the city?"

"Either. Or we can have an armored truck visit your ship."

"That would be better yet. Have them bring about five thousand tanes. Thank you very much, Governor Atterlin, and good afternoon to you, sir."

"And good afternoon to you, sir. Until tomorrow, then."

"Oh, may I go with you to your ship, sir, to take just a little look at it?" the girl asked, winningly.

"Of course, Grand Lady Neldine. I'd like to have your company."

She seized his elbow and hugged it quickly against her breast. Then, taking his hand, she walked — almost skipped — along beside him. "And I want to see Pilot James close up, too, sir — though he's not nearly as wonderful as you are. And I wonder why Planetographer Bellamy's hair is green? Very striking, of course, sir, but I don't think I'd care for it much on me — unless you'd think I should?" And so on.

Belle knew, of course, that they were coming; and Garlock knew that Bell's hackles were very much on the rise. She could not read him, except very superficially, but she was reading the strange girl like a book and was not liking anything she read. Wherefore, when Garlock and his joyous companion reached the great space-ship —

"How come you picked up *that* little man-eating shark?" she sent, venomously, on a tight band.

"It wasn't a case of picking her up. I haven't been able to find any urbane way of scraping her off. First Contact, you know."

"She wants altogether too much Contact for a First — I'll scrape her off even if she is Right the Honorable Grand Lady Claire Vere de Vere Cabot-Lodge . . ." Belle changed her tactics even before Garlock began his reprimand. "I shouldn't have said that, Clee, of course." A light mental laugh came. "It was just the shock; there wasn't anything in any of my First Contact tapes covering what to do about beautiful and enticing girls who try to seduce our men. She doesn't know, though, of course, that she's supposed to be a bug-eyed monster and not human at all. Won't Xenology be in for a rough ride when we check in? Wow!" And for the rest of the day Belle played flawlessly the role of perfect hostess.

It was full dark before the Hodellions could be persuaded to leave the *Pleiades* and the locks were closed.

"I've refused one hundred seventy-eight invitations," Lola reported then. "All of us, individually and collectively, have been invited to eat everything, everywhere in town. To see shows in a dozen different theaters and eighteen night spots. To dance all night in twenty-one different places, ranging from dives to strictly soup-and-fish. I was nice about it, of course — just begged off because we were dead from our belts both ways from our long, hard trip. My thought, of course, is that we'd better eat our own food and take it slowly at first. Check, Clee?

"On the beam, dead center. And you weren't lying much, either. I feel as though I'd done a day's work. After supper there's a thing I've got to discuss with all three of you."

Supper was soon over. Then:

"We've got to make a mighty important decision," Garlock began abruptly. "Grand Lady Neldine — that title isn't exact, but close — wondered why I didn't respond at all, either way. However, she didn't make a point of it, and I let her wonder; but we'll have to decide by tomorrow morning what to do, and it'll have to be airtight. The Hodellians expect Jim and me to impregnate as many as possible of their highest-rated women before we leave. By their Code it's mandatory, since we can't hide the fact that we rate much higher than they do — their highest rating is only Grade Two by our standards — and all the planets hereabouts upgrade themselves with the highest-grade new blood they can find. Ordinarily, they'd expect you two girls to become pregnant by your choices of the top men of the planet; but they know you wouldn't breed down and don't expect you to. But how in all hell can Jim and I refuse to breed them up without dealing out the deadliest insult they know?"

There was a minute of silence. "We can't," James said then. A grin began to spread over his face. "It might not be too bad an idea, at that, come to think of it. That ball of fire they picked out for you would be a blue-ribbon dish in anybody's cookbook. And Grand Lady Lemphi — wow!"

"Is that nice, you back-alley tomcat?" Belle asked plaintively. Then she paused in thought and went on slowly. "I won't pretend to like it, but I won't do any public screaming about it."

"Any anthropologist would say you'll have to," Lola declared without hesitation. "I don't like it, either. I think it's horrible; but it's excellent genetics and we cannot and must not violate systems-wide mores."

"You're all missing the point!" Garlock snapped. He got up, jammed his hands into his pockets, and began to pace the floor. "I didn't think any one of you was *that* stupid! If *that* was all there were to it we'd do it as a matter of course. But *think*, damn it! There's nothing higher than Gunther Two in the humanity of this planet. Telepathy is the only ESP they have. High Gunther uses hitherto unused portions of the brain. It's transmitted through genes, which are dominant, cumulative, and self-multiplying by interaction. Jim and I carry more, stronger, and higher Gunthere genes than any other two men known to live. Can we take the chance of planting such genes where none have ever been known before?"

"My God!" said Belle.

Then there were two full minutes of silence.

"That one has *really* got a bone in it," James said, unhelpfully.

Three minutes more of silence.

"It's up to you, Lola," Garlock said then. "It's your field."

"I was afraid of that. There's a way. Personally, I like it less even than the other, but it's the only one I've been able to think up. First, are you absolutely sure that our refusal — Belle's and mine, I mean — to breed down will be valid with them?"

"Positive."

"Then the whole society from which we come will have to be strictly monogamous, in the narrowest, most literal sense of the term. No exceptions whatever. Adultery, anything illicit, has always been not only unimaginable, but in fact impossible. We pair — or marry, or whatever they do here — once only. For life. Desire and potency can exist only within the pair; never outside it. Like eagles. If a man's wife dies, even, he loses all desire and all potency. That would make it physically impossible for you two to follow the Hodellian Code. You'd both be completely impotent with any women whatever except your mates — Belle and me."

"That will work," Belle said. *"How* it will work!" She paused. Then, suddenly, she laughed — the rich, full-throated laugh which so few women ever allow themselves. "But do you know what you've done, Lola?"

"Nothing, except to suggest a solution. What's so funny about that?"

"You're wonderful, Lola — simply priceless! You've created something brand-new to science — an impotent tomcat! And the more I think about it —" Belle was rocking back and forth with laughter. She could not possibly talk, but her thought flowed on: "An *impotent tomcat,* and he'll have to stay true to me — oh, this is simply *killing* me!"

"It *does* put us on the spot — especially Jim," came Garlock's thought.

He, too, began to laugh; and Lola, as soon as she stopped thinking about the thing only as a problem in anthropology, joined in. James, however, did not think it was very funny.

"And that's less than half of it!" Belle went on. "Think of Clee, Lola. Six two — over two hundred — hard as nails — a perfect hunk of man telling this whole damn cockeyed region of space that he's impotent, too! And with a perfectly straight face! And it ties in so *beautifully* with his making no response, yes or no, when she propositioned him. The poor, innocent, impotent lamb just simply didn't have even the *faintest* inkling of what she meant!"

"Listen — *listen* — *LISTEN!*" James managed finally to break in. "Not that I want to be promiscuous, but —"

"Oh don't worry," Belle soothed him, speaking aloud but with a still-unsteady voice as she held down her mirth. "Us Earthgirls will take care of you two, see if we don't. You won't need any nasty little . . ." Belle could not hold the pose she went off again into whoops of laughter.

"Shut up, will you, and *listen!*" James roared aloud. "There ought to be *some* better way than that."

"Better? Than sheer perfection?"

"If you can think of one, Jim, the meeting is still open," said Garlock. "But it'll have to be a dilly. I'm not exactly enamored of Lola's idea, either, but as the answer it's one hundred percent to as many decimal places as you want to take time to write zeroes."

There was more talk, but no improvement could be made upon Lola's idea.

"Well, we've got until morning," Garlock said, finally. "If anybody comes up with anything by then, let me know.

If not, it goes into effect the minute we open the locks. The meeting is adjourned."

Belle and James left the room; and, a few minutes later, Garlock went out. Lola followed him into his room and closed the door behind her. She sat down on the edge of a chair, lighted a cigarette, and began to smoke in short, nervous puffs. She opened her mouth to say something, but shut it without making a sound.

"You're afraid of me, Lola?" he asked, quietly.

"Oh, I don't . . . Well, that is . . ." She wouldn't lie, and she wouldn't admit the truth. "You see, I've never . . . had very much experience."

"You needn't be afraid of me at all. I'm not going to pair with you."

"You're not?" Her mouth dropped open and the cigarette fell out of it. She took a few seconds to recover it. "Why not? Don't you think I could do a good enough job?"

She stood up and stretched, to show her splendid figure to its best advantage.

Garlock laughed. "Nothing like that, Lola; you have plenty of sex appeal. It's just that I don't like the conditions. I never have paired. I never had had much to do with women, and that little has been urbane, logical, and strictly *en passant;* on the level of mutual physical desire. And I've never taken a virgin. Pairing with one is very definitely not my idea of urbanity and there's altogether too much obligation to suit me. For all of which good reasons I am not going to pair with you, now or ever."

"How do you know whether I'm a virgin or not? You've never read me that deep. Nobody can. Not even you, unless I let you."

"Reading isn't necessary — you flaunt it like a banner."

"I don't know what you mean . . . I certainly don't do

it intentionally. But I *ought* to pair with you, Clee!" Lola had lost all of her nervousness, most of her fear. "It's part of the job I was chosen for. If I'd known, I'd've gone out and got some experience. Really I would have."

"I believe that. I think you would have been silly enough to have done just that. And you have a very high regard for your virginity, too, don't you?"

"Well, I . . . I used to. But we'd better go ahead with it. I've *got* to."

"No such thing. Permissible, but not obligatory."

"But it was assumed. As a matter of course. Anyway . . . well, when that girl started making passes at you, I thought you could have just as much fun, or even more, without pairing with me, and then I had to open my big mouth and be the one to keep you from playing games with *anyone except* me, and I certainly am not going to let you suffer . . ."

"Bunk!" Garlock snorted. "Sheer nonsense! Pure psychological prop-wash, started and maintained by men who are either too weak to direct and control their drives or who haven't any real work to occupy their minds. It applies to many men, of course, possibly to most. It does not, however, apply to all, and it lacks one whole hell of a lot applying to me. Does that make you feel better?"

"Oh, it does . . . it does. Thanks, Clee. You know, I like you, a lot."

"Do you? Kiss me."

She did so.

"See?"

"You *tricked* me!"

"I did not. I want you to see the truth and face it. Your idealism is admirable, permanent, and shatter-proof; but your starry-eyed schoolgirl's mawkishness is none of the three. You'll have to grow up, someday. In my opinion, forcing yourself to give up one of your hardest-held ideals — virginity — merely because of the utter bilge that those idiot headshrinkers stuffed you with, is sheer, plain idiocy. I suppose that makes you like me even less, but I'm laying it right on the line."

"No . . . more. I'll argue with you, when we have time, about some of your points, but the last one — if it's valid — has tremendous force. I didn't know men felt that way. But no matter what my feeling for you really is, I'm really grateful to you for the reprieve . . . and you know, Clee, I'm pretty sure you're going to get us back home."

"I'm going to try to. Even if I can't, it will be Belle, not you, that I'll take for the long pull. And not because you'd rather have Jim — which you would, of course . . ."

"To be honest, I think I would."

"Certainly. He's your type. You're not mine; Belle is. Well, that buttons it up, Brownie, except for one thing. To Jim and Belle and everyone else, we're paired."

"Of course. Urbanity, as well as to present a united front to any and all worlds."

"Check, so watch your shield."

"I always do. That stuff is 'way, 'way down. I'm awfully glad you called me 'Brownie,' Clee. I didn't think you ever would."

"I didn't expect to — but I never talked to a woman this way before, either. Maybe it had a mellowing effect."

"You don't *need* mellowing — I do like you a lot, just exactly as you are."

"If true, I'm very glad of it. But don't strain yourself; and I mean that literally, not as sarcasm."

"I know. I'm not straining a bit, and this'll prove it."

She kissed him again, and this time it was a production.

"That was an eminently convincing demonstration,

Brownie, but don't do it too often."

"I won't." She laughed, gaily and happily. "If there's any next time, you'll have to kiss me first."

She paused and sobered. "But remember. If you should change your mind, any time you really want . . . to kiss me, come right in. I wont be as silly and nervous and afraid as I was just now. That's a promise, Goodnight, Clee."

"Goodnight, Brownie."

II

Next morning, Garlock was the last one, by a fraction of a minute, into the Main. "Good morning, all he said, with a slight smile.

"Huh? How come?" James demanded, as all four started toward the dining nook.

Garlock's smile widened. "Lola. She brought me a pot of coffee and wouldn't let me out until I drank it."

"Brought?"

"Yeah. They haven't read their room-tapes yet, so they don't know that room-service is practically unlimited."

"Oh. Why didn't I think of that coffee business a couple of years ago?"

"Well, why didn't I think of it myself, ten years ago?"

Belle's eyes had been going from one man to the other. "Just *what* are you two talking about? If it's anybody's business except your own?"

"He's an early-morning grouch," James explained, as they sat down at the table. "Not fit to associate with man or beast when he first gets up. How come you were smart enough to get the answer so quick, Brownie?"

"Oh, the pattern isn't too rare." She shrugged daintily, sweeping the compliment aside. "Especially among men who work under a lot of pressure."

"Then how about Jim?" Belle asked.

"Clee's the Big Brain, not me," James said.

"You're a much Bigger Brain than any of the men Lola's talking about," Belle insisted.

"That's true," Lola agreed. "But Jim must be an ice-box raider. Eats in the middle of the night. Clee probably doesn't. It's a good bet that he doesn't nibble between meals at all. Check, Clee?"

"Check. But what has an empty stomach got to do with the case? And how?"

"Everything. Nobody knows how. Lots of theories — enzymes, blood sugar, endocrine balance, what have you — but no proof. It isn't always true. However, six or seven hours of empty stomach, in a man who takes his job to bed with him, is very apt to uglify his pre-breakfast disposition."

Breakfast over and out in the Main:

"But when a man's disposition is ugly all the time, how can you tell the difference?" Belle asked, innocently.

"I'll let that pass," Garlock said, "because we've got work to do. Have any of you thought of any improvement on Lola's monogamous society?"

No one had. In fact —

"There may be a loop-hole in it," Lola said thoughtfully. "Did any of you happen to notice whether they know anything about artificial insemination?"

"D'you think I'd stand for *that?*" Belle blazed, before Garlock could begin to search his mind. "If you'd thought of that idea as a woman instead of as a near-Ph.D. in anthropology, you'd've thrown it into the converter before it even hatched!"

"Invasion of privacy? That covers it, of course, but I didn't think it would bother you a bit." Lola paused, studying the other girl intently. "You're quite a problem yourself. Callous — utterly savage humor — yet very sensitive in some ways — fastidious . . ."

"I'm not on the table for dissection!" Belle snapped. "Study me all you please, but keep the notes in your notebook. I'd suggest you study Clee."

"Oh, I have been. He baffles me, too. I'm not very good yet, you—"

"That's the unders —"

"Cut it!" Garlock ordered sharply. "I said we had work to do. Jim, you're hunting up the nearest observatory."

"How about transportation? No teleportation?"

"Out. Rent a car or hire a plane, or both. Fill your wallet — better to have too much money than not enough. If you're too far away tonight to make it feasible to come back here, send me a flash. Brownie, you'll work this town first. Belle and I will have to work in the library for a while. We'll all want to compare notes tonight . . ."

"Yeah," James said into the pause, "I could tune in remote, but I don't know where I'll be, so it might not be so good."

"Check. You can 'port, but be *damn* sure nobody sees or senses you doing it. That buttons it up, I guess."

James and Lola left the ship; Garlock and Belle went into the library.

"If I didn't know you were impotent, Clee," Belle said, laughing, "I'd be scared to death to be alone with you in this spaceship. Lola hasn't realized yet what she really hatched out — the screamingest screamer ever pulled on anybody!"

"It isn't *that* funny. You have got a hostile sense of humor."

"Perhaps." She shrugged her shoulders. "But you were on the receiving end, which makes a big difference. She's a peculiar sort of duck. Brainy, but impersonal — academic. She knows all the words and all their meanings; all the questions and all the answers, but she doesn't apply any of them to herself. She's always the observer, never the participant. Pure egghead . . . pure? *That's* it. She looks, acts, talks, and thinks like a *virgin* . . . Well, if that's all, she isn't any — or is she? Even though you've started calling her 'Brownie,' you might not . . ." She broke off and stared at him.

"Go ahead. Probe."

"Why waste energy trying to crack a Prime's shield? But just out of curiosity, are you two pairing, or not?"

Garlock smiled calmly. "Don't be inurbane. Let's talk about Jim instead. I thought he'd be gibbering."

"No, I'm working under double wraps — full dampers. I don't want him in love with me. You want to know why?"

"I think I know why."

"Because having him mooning around underfoot would weaken the team and I want to get back to Tellus."

"I was wrong, then. I thought you were out after bigger game."

Belle's face went stiff and still. "What do you mean by that?"

"Plain enough, I would think. Wherever you are, you've got to be the Boss. You've never been in any kind of a party for fifteen minutes without taking it over. When you snap the whip everybody jumps — or else — and you swing a wicked knife. For your information I don't jump, I'm familiar with knives, and you will never run this project or any part of it."

Belle's face set; her eyes hardened. "While we're putting out information, take note that I'm just as good with actual knives as with figurative ones. If you're still thinking of blistering my fanny, don't try it. You'll find a rawhide haft sticking up out of one of those muscles you're so proud of."

"Why don't you talk sense, instead of just shooting off your mouth like that?"

"Huh?"

"I know you're a Prime, too, but don't let it go to your head. I've got more stuff than you have, so you can't Gunther me. You weigh one thirty-five to my two seventeen. I'm harder, stronger, and faster than you are. You're probably a bit more limber — not too much — but I've forgotten more judo than you ever will know. So what's the answer?"

Belle was breathing hard. "Then why don't you do it right now?"

"Several reasons. I couldn't brag much about licking anybody I outweigh by eighty-two pounds. I can't figure out your logic — if any — but I'm pretty sure it wouldn't do either of us any good. Just the opposite."

"From your standpoint, would that be bad?"

"What a *hell* of a logic! You've got the finest brain of any woman living. You're stronger than Jim is, by more than the Prime-to-Op ratio. You've got more initiative, more drive, more guts. You know as well as I do what your brain may mean before we get back. Why in all hell don't you start *using* it?"

"*You* are complimenting *me?*"

"No. It's the truth, isn't it?"

"What difference does that make? Clee Garlock, I simply can't understand you at all."

"That makes it mutual. I can't understand a geometry in which the crookedest line between any two given points is the best line. Let's get to work, shall we?"

"Okay. One more bit of information first, though. Any

such idea as taking the project away from you simply *never* entered my mind." She gave him a warm and friendly smile as she walked over to the file-cabinets.

For hours, then, they worked, each scanning tape after tape. At midday they ate a light lunch. Shortly thereafter, Garlock put away his reader and all his loose tapes. "Are you getting anywhere, Belle? I'm not."

"Yes, but of course planets are probably pretty much the same everywhere — Tellus-type ones, anyway. Is all the Xenology as cockeyed as I'm afraid it must be?"

"At least. The one basic assumption was that there are no human beings other than Tellurians. From that they derive the secondary assumption that humanoid types will be scarce. From there they scattered out in all directions. So I'll have to roll my own. I've got to see Atterlin, anyway. I'll be back for supper. So long."

"Be good, — Clee as though you could be anything else! Oh, simon-pure monogamy, how wonderful you are!" She snickered gleefully as Garlock strode out.

At the Port Office, Grand Lady Neldine met him even more enthusiastically than before; taking both his hands and pressing them against her firm, almost-bare breasts. She tried to hold back as Garlock led her along the corridor.

"I have an explanation, and in a sense an apology, for you, Grand Lady Neldine, and for you, Governor Atterlin," he thought carefully. "I would have explained yesterday, but I had no understanding of the situation here until our anthropologist, Lola Montandon, elucidated it very laboriously to me. She herself, a scientist highly trained in that specialty, could grasp it only by referring back to somewhat similar situations which may have existed in the remote past — so remote a past that the concept is known only to specialists and is more than half mythical, even to them."

He went on to give in detail the sexual customs, obligations, and limitations of Lola's purely imaginary civilization.

"Then it isn't that you don't *want* to, but you *can't?*" the lady asked, incredulously.

"Mentally, I can have no desire. Physically, the act is impossible," he assured her.

"What a shame!" Her thought was a peculiar mixture of disappointment and relief: disappointment in that she was not to bear this man's super-child; relief in that, after all, she had not personally failed — if she couldn't have this perfectly wonderful man herself, no other woman except his wife could ever have him, either. But what a shame to waste such a man as that on *any* one woman!

"I see . . . I see — wonderful!" Atterlin's thought was not at all incredulous, but vastly awed. "It is of course logical that as the power of mind increases, physical matters become less and less important. But you will have much to give us; we may perhaps have some small things to give you. If we could visit your Tellus, perhaps . . . ?"

"That also is impossible. We four in the *Pleiades* are lost in space. This is the first planet we have visited on our first trial of a new method — new to us, at least — of interstellar travel. We missed our objective, probably by many millions of parsecs, and it is quite possible that we four will never be able to find our way back. We are trying now, by charting the galaxies throughout billions of cubic parsecs of space, to find merely the direction in which our own galaxy lies."

"What a concept! What stupendous minds! But such immense distances, sir . . . what can you possibly be using for a space-drive?"

"None, as you understand the term. We travel by instantaneous translation, by means of something we call 'Gunther'. I am not at all sure that I can explain it to you satisfactorily, but I will try to do so, if you wish."

"Please do so, sir, by all means."

Garlock opened the highest Gunther cells of his mind. This was nothing as elementary as telepathy, teleportation, telekinesis, or the like — it was the pure, raw Gunther of the Gunther Drive, which even he made no pretense of understanding fully. He opened those cells and pushed that knowledge at the two Hodellian minds.

The result was just as instantaneous and just as catastrophic as Garlock had expected. Both blocks went up almost instantly.

"Oh, no!" Atterlin exclaimed, his face turning white.

The girl shrieked once, covered her face with her hands, and collapsed on the floor.

"Oh, I'm *so* sorry . . . excuse my ignorance, please!" Garlock implored, as he picked the girl up, carried her across the room to a sofa, and assured himself that she had not been really hurt. She recovered quickly. "I'm very sorry, Grand Lady Neldine and Governor Atterlin, but I didn't know . . . that is, I didn't realize . . ."

"You are trying to break it gently." Atterlin was both shocked and despondent. "This being the first planet you have visited, you simply did not realize how feeble our minds really are."

"Oh, not at all, really." Garlock began deftly to repair the morale he had shattered. "Merely younger. With your system of genetics, so much more logical and efficient than our strict monogamy, your race will undoubtedly make more progress in a few centuries than we made in many millenia. And in a few centuries more you will pass us — will master this only partially-known Gunther Drive.

"Esthetically, Lady Neldine, I would like very much to father you a child." He allowed his coldly unmoved gaze to survey her superb body. "I am very sorry indeed that it cannot be. I trust that you, Governor Atterlin, will be kind enough to spread word of our physical shortcoming, and so spare us further embarrassment?"

"Not shortcomings, sir, and, I truly hope, no embarrassment," Atterlin protested. "We are immensely glad to have seen you, since your very existence gives us so much hope for the future. I will spread word, and every Hodellian will do whatever he can to help you in your quest."

"Thank you, sir and lady," Garlock said, and took his leave. "What an act!" came Belle's clear thought, bubbling with unrestrained merriment. "For our revered Doctor Garlock, the Prime Exponent and First Disciple of Truth, *what* an act! *Esthetically,* he'd like to father her a child, it says here in fine print — God, if she only knew! Clee, I *swear* this thing is going to kill me yet!"

"Anything that would do that I'm very much in favor of!" Garlock growled the thought and snapped up his shield.

This one was, quite definitely, Belle's round.

Garlock took the Hodellian equivalent of a bus to the center of the city, then set out aimlessly to walk. The buildings and their arrangement, he noted — not much to his surprise now — were not too different from those of the cities of Earth.

With his guard down to about the sixth level, highly receptive but not at all selective, he strolled up one street and down another. He was not attentive to detail yet; he was trying to get the broad aspects, the "feel" of this hitherto unknown civilization.

He found himself practically saturated with thought. Apparently this was the afternoon rush hour, as the sidewalks were crowded with people and the streets were full of cars. It did not seem as though anyone, whether in the buildings, on the sidewalks, or in the cars, was doing any blocking at all. If there were any such things as secrets on Hodell, they were scarce. Each person, man, woman, or child; went about his own business, radiating full blast. No one paid any attention to the thoughts of anyone else except in the case of couples or groups, the units of which were engaged in conversation. It reminded Garlock of a big Tellurian party when the punch-bowls were running low — everybody talking at the top of his voice and nobody listening.

This whole gale of thought was blowing over Garlock's receptors. He did not address anyone directly and no one addressed him. At first quite a few young women, at sight of his unusual physique, had sent out tentative feelers of thought; and some men had wondered, in the same tentative and indirect fashion, who he was and where he came from. However, when the information he had given Atterlin spread throughout the city — and it did not take long — no one paid any more attention to him than they did to each other.

Probing into and through various buildings, he learned that groups of people were quitting work at intervals of about fifteen minutes. There were thoughts of tidying up desks; of letting the rest of this junk go until tomorrow; of putting away and/or covering up office machines of various sorts. There were thoughts of powdering noses and of repairing makeup. There was one sequence of thought particularly sharp and clear — a high Third — which would have startled Garlock no little if he had received it on Tellus. She wouldn't do it after the show tonight, either, if she had to slug him in the brisket. She'd cancel him tonight anyway, whether he tried to make her or not. She'd quit playing around with both those damn wolves and marry Tomko while she was still a virgin — there was an honest-to-God man . . .

He pulled in his receptors and scanned the crowded ways for guardians — he'd have to call them that until either he or Lola found out their real name. Same as at the airport — the more people, the more guardians. What were they? How? And why?

He probed — carefully but thoroughly. When he had talked to the Arpalone he had read him easily enough, but here there was nothing whatever to read. The creature simply was not thinking at all. But that didn't make sense! Garlock turned, first down, then up; and finally, at the very top of his range, he found something, but he did not at first know what it was. It seemed to be a mass-detector . . . no, two of them, paired and balanced. Oh, that was it! One tuned to humanity, one to the other guardians — balanced across a sort of bridge — *that* was how they kept the ratio so constant! But why? There seemed to be some wide-range receptors there, too, but nothing seemed to be coming in . . .

While he was still studying and still baffled, some kind of stimulus, which was so high and so faint and so alien that he could neither identify nor interpret it, touched the guardian's far-flung receptors. Instantly the creature jumped, his powerful, widely-bowed legs sending him high above the heads of the crowd and, it seemed to Garlock, directly toward him. Simultaneously there was an insistent, low-pitched, whistling scream, somewhat like the noise made by an airplane in a non-power dive; and Garlock saw, out of the corner of one eye, a yellowish something flashing downward through the air.

At the same moment the woman immediately in front of Garlock stifled a scream and jumped backward, bumping into him and almost knocking him down. He staggered, caught his balance, and automatically put his arm around her to keep her from falling to the sidewalk.

In the meantime the guardian, having landed very close to the spot the woman had occupied a moment before, leaped again, this time vertically upward. The thing, whatever it was, was now braking frantically with wings, tail, and body-trying madly to get away. Too late. There was a bone-crushing impact as the two bodies came together in midair, and a jarring thud as the two creatures, inextricably intertwined, struck the pavement as one.

The thing varied in color, Garlock now saw, shading from bright orange at the head to pale yellow at the tail. It had a savagely-tearing curved beak, and tremendously powerful wings; it's short, thick legs ended in hawk-like talons.

The guardian's bowed legs had already immobilized the yellow wings by clamping them solidly against the yellow body. His two lower arms were holding the frightful talons out of action. His third hand gripped the orange throat; his fourth was exerting tremendous force against the jointure of neck and body. The neck, originally short, was beginning to stretch.

For several seconds Garlock had been half-conscious that his accidental companion was trying, with more and more energy, to disengage his encircling left arm from her waist. He wrenched his attention away from the spectacular fight — to which no one else, not even the near-victim, had paid the slightest attention — and now saw that he had his arm around the bare waist of a statuesque matron whose entire costume would have made perhaps half of a

Tellurian sunsuit. He dropped his arm with a quick and abject apology.

"I should apologize to you instead, Captain Garlock," she thought, with a wide and friendly smile, "for knocking you down, and I thank you for catching me before I fell. I should not have been startled, of course. I would not have been, except that this is the first time that I, personally, have been attacked."

"But what *are* they?" Garlock blurted.

"I don't know." The woman turned her head and glanced, in complete disinterest, at the two furiously-battling creatures. Garlock knew now that this was the first time, except for that instantly-dismissed thrill of surprise at being the actual target of an attack, that she had thought of either one of them. "Orange-yellow? It could be a . . . a fumapty, perhaps, but I've no idea, really. You see, such things are none of our business."

She thought at him a half-shrug, half-grimace of mild distaste — not at the personal contact with the man nor at the savage duel, but at even thinking of either the guardian or the yellow monster — and walked away into the crowd.

Garlock's attention flashed back to the fighters. The yellow thing's neck had been stretched to twice its natural length and the guardian had *eaten* almost through it. There was a terrific crunch, a couple of smacking, gobbling swallows, and head parted from body. The orange beak still clashed open and shut, however, and the body thrashed violently.

Shifting his grips, the guardian proceeded to tear a hole into his victim's body, just below its breast-bone. Thrusting two arms into the opening, he yanked out two organs — one of which, Garlock thought, could have been the heart — and ate them both; if not with extreme gusto, at least in a workmanlike and thoroughly competent fashion. He then picked up the head in one hand, grabbed the tip of a wing with another, and marched up the street for half a block, dragging the body behind him.

He lifted a manhole cover with his two unoccupied hands, dropped the remains down the hole, and let the cover slam back into place. He then squatted down, licked himself meticulously clean with a long, black, extremely agile tongue, and went on about his enigmatic business quite as though nothing had happened.

Garlock strolled around a few minutes longer, but could not recapture any interest in the doings of the human beings around him. He had filed away every detail of what had just happened, and it had so many bizarre aspects that he could not think of anything else. Wherefore he flagged down a "taxi" and was taken out to the *Pleiades*. Belle and Lola were in the Main.

"I saw the *damndest* thing, Clee!" Lola exclaimed. "I've been gnawing all my fingernails off clear up to the knuckles, waiting for you!"

Lola's experience had been very similar to Garlock's own, except that her monster was an intense green in color and looked something like a bat about four feet long, with six-inch canine teeth and several stingers. . . .

"Did you find out the name of the thing?" Garlock asked.

"No. I asked half a dozen people, but nobody would even listen to me except one half-grown boy, and the best he could do was that it might be something he had heard another boy say somebody had told him might be a 'lemart'. And as to those lower-case Arpalones, the best I could dig out of anybody was just 'guardians'. Did you do any better?"

"No, I didn't do as well," and he told the girls all about his own experience.

"But I didn't find any detectors or receptors, Clee." Lola frowned. "Where were they?"

" 'Way up — up here." He showed her. "I'll make a full tape tonight on everything I found out about the guardians and the Arpalones — besides my regular report, I mean — since they're yours, and you can make me one about your friend the green bat. Meanwhile, how are you coming, Belle?"

"Nice!" Belle's voracious mind had been so busy absorbing new knowledge that she had temporarily forgotten about her fight with her captain. "I'm just about done here. I'll be ready tomorrow, I think, to visit their library and tape up some planetographical and planetological — notice how insouciantly I toss off those two-credit words? — data on this here planet Hodell."

"Good going. You've been listening to this stuff Lola and I were chewing on. Does any of it make sense to you?"

"It does not. I never heard anything to compare with it."

"Excuse me for changing the subject," Lola said plaintively, "but when, if ever, do we eat? Do we *have* to wait until that confounded James boy gets back from wherever it was he went?"

"If you're hungry, we'll eat now."

"*Hungry?* Look!' Lola turned herself sidewise, placed one hand in the small of her back, and with the other pressed hard against her flat, taut belly. "See? Only a couple of inches from belt-buckle to backbone — dangerously close to the point of utter collapse."

Garlock laughed and all three crossed the room to the

dining alcove. While they were still ordering, James appeared beside them.

"Find out anything?" Garlock asked.

"Yes and no. Yes, in that they have an excellent observatory, with a hundred-eighty-inch reflector, on a mountain only seventy-five miles from here. No, in that I didn't find any duplication of nebulary configurations with the stuff I had with me. However, it was relatively coarse. Tomorrow I'll take a lot of fine stuff along. It'll take some time — a full day, at least."

"I expected that. Good going, Jim."

All four ate heartily, and later they taped up the day's reports. Then, tired from their first real day's work in weeks, all went to their rooms.

A few minutes later, Garlock tapped lightly at Lola's door.

"Come in." She stiffened involuntarily, then relaxed and smiled. "Oh, yes, Clee; of course. You're . . ."

"No, I'm not. I've been doing a lot of thinking about you since last night, and I may have come up with an answer or two. Also, Belle knows we aren't pairing, and if we don't hide behind a screen at least once in a while, she'll know we aren't going to."

"Screen?"

"Screen. Didn't you know these four private rooms are solid? Haven't you read your house-tape yet?"

"No. But do you think Belle would actually peek?"

"Do you think she wouldn't?"

"Well, I don't like her very much, but I wouldn't think she would do anything like that, Clee. It isn't urbane."

"She isn't urbane, either, whenever she thinks it might be advantageous not to be."

"What a *terrible* thing to say!"

"Take it from me, if Belle Bellamy doesn't know everything that goes on it isn't from lack of trying. You wouldn't know about room service, either, then — better scan that tape before you go to sleep tonight. What'll you have in the line of a drink to while away enough time so she'll know we've been playing games?"

"Ginger ale, please. No, make it Chericol."

"We'll make it both, and some ice cubes. I'll have ginger beer. You do it like so." He slid a panel aside, and his fingers played briefly on a typewriter-like keyboard. Drinks and ice appeared. "Anything you want — details on the tape."

He lighted two cigarettes, handed her one, stirred his drink. "Now, fair lady — or should I say beauteous dark lady? — we will follow the precept of that immortal Chinese philosopher, Chin On."

"You *are* a Prime Operator, aren't you?" She laughed, but sobered quickly. "I'm worried. You said I flaunted virginity like a banner, and now Belle . . . *What* am I doing wrong?"

"There's a lot wrong. Not so much what you're doing as what you aren't doing. You're too aloof — detached — eggheadish. You know the score, words and music, but you don't sing; all you do is listen. Belle thinks you're not only a physical virgin, but a psychic-blocked prude. I know better. You're so full of conflict between what you want to do and what you think you ought to do that you've got no more degrees of freedom than a piston-rod. You haven't been yourself for a minute since you came aboard. Right?"

"You have been thinking, haven't you? You may be right; except that it's been longer than that . . . ever since the first preliminaries, I think. But what can I *do* about it, Clee?"

"Contact. Three-quarters full, say; enough for me to

give you what I think is the truth."

"But you said you *never* went screens-down with a woman."

"There's a first time for everything. Come in."

She did so, held contact for almost a minute, then pulled herself loose.

"Ug-gh-gh." She shivered. "I'm glad I haven't got a mind like that."

"And the same from me to you. Of course the real truth may lie somewhere in between. I may be as far off the beam on one side as you are on the other."

"I hope so. But it cleared things up no end — it untied a million knots. Even that other thing — brotherly love? It's a very nice concept — you see, I never had any brothers."

"That's probably one thing that was the matter with you. There's nothing warmer than that, certainly, and there never will be."

"And I suppose you got the thought — it must have jumped up and smacked you"— Lola's hot blush was visible even through her heavy tan —"how many times I've felt like running my fingers up and down your ribs and grabbing a handful of those muscles of yours, just to see if they're as hard as they look?"

"I'm glad you brought that up; I don't know whether I would have dared to or not. You've got to stop acting like a Third instead of an Operator; and you've got to stop acting as though you had never been within ten feet of me. Now's as good a time as any." He took off his shirt. "Come ahead."

"By golly, I'm *going* to!" Then, a moment later, she said, "Why, they're even *harder!* How do you, a scientist, psiontist, and scholar keep in such shape as that?"

"An hour every day in the gym. Many are better —

but a hell of a lot are worse."

"I'll say." She finished her Chericol, picked up the ginger ale, sat down in her chair, leaned back and put her legs up on the bed. "That was a relief of tension if there ever was one. I haven't felt so good since they picked me as home-town candidate — and that was a mighty small town and eight months ago. Bring on your dragons, Clee, and I'll slay 'em far and wide. But I can't actually *be* like she is . . ."

"Thank God for that. Deliver me from *two* such pretzel-benders aboard one ship."

". . . But I could have been a pretty good actress, I think."

"Correction, please. 'Outstanding' is the word."

"Thank you, kind sir. And women, like men, do bring up certain memories, to . . . to . . ."

"To roll 'em around on their tongues and give their taste-buds a treat."

"Exactly. So where I don't have any appropriate actual memories to bring up, I'll make like an actress, Check?"

"Good girl! Well, we've been in screen long enough, I guess. Fare thee well, little sister Brownie, until we meet again." He tossed the remains of their refreshments, trays and all, into the chute, picked up his shirt, and started out.

"Put it *on,* Clee!" she whispered, intensely.

"Why?" He grinned cheerfully. "It'd look still better if I peeled down to the altogether."

"You're incorrigible," she said; but her answering smile was wide and perfectly natural. "You know, if I'd had a brother something like you it would have saved me a lot of wear and tear. I'll see you in the morning before breakfast."

And she did. They strolled together to breakfast — not holding hands, but with hip almost touching hip. Relaxed, friendly, on very cordial and satisfactory terms. Lola punched breakfast orders for them both. Belle drove a probe, which bounced — Lola's screen was tight, although her brown eyes were innocent and bland.

But during the meal, in response to a double-edged, wickedly-barbed remark of Belle's, a memory flashed into being above Lola's shield. It was the veriest flash, instantly supressed. Her eyes held clear and steady; if she blushed at all it did not show.

Belle caught it, of course, and winked triumphantly at Garlock. She knew, now, what she had wanted to know. And, Prime Operator though he was, it was all Garlock could do to make no sign; for that fleetingly-revealed memory was a perfect job. He would not have — *could not have* — questioned it himself, except for one simple fact: it was of an event that had not happened and never would.

And after breakfast, at some distance from the others, he told her, "You're an Operator, all right; Brownie — and it takes a damn good one to lie like that with her mind!"

"Thanks to you, Clee. And thanks a million, really. I'm me again — I think."

Then, since Belle was looking, she took him by both ears, pulled his head down, and kissed him lightly on the lips.

"I know I said you'd have to kiss me next time," Lola said, very low, "but this act needs just this much of an extra touch. Anyway, such little, tiny, sisterly ones as this, and out in public, don't count."

III

Lola and Garlock went to town in the same taxi. As they were about to separate, Garlock said:

"I don't like those hell-divers — yellow, green, or any other color — and you, Brownie, are very definitely not expendable. Are you any good at mind-bombing?"

"I never heard of such a thing."

"You isolate a little energy in the Op field, remembering, of course, that you're handling a hundred thousand gunts. Transpose it into osmium or uranium or anything good and heavy. For one of these monsters you'd need two or three micrograms. For a battleship, up to maybe a gram or so. 'Port it to the exact place you want it to detonate. Reconvert and release instantaneously. One hundred percent conversion atomic bomb, tailored exactly to fit the job. Very effective."

"It would be. My God, Clee, can *you* do that?"

"Sure — so can you. Any Operator can."

"Well, I *won't*. I *never* will. Besides, I'd probably kill too many people, besides the monster. No, I'll 'port back to the Main if anything attacks me. I'm chain lightning at that."

"Do that, then. And if anything unusual happens give me a flash."

"I'll do that. 'Bye, Clee." She turned to the left; he

56

walked straight on toward the business center, to resume his study at the point where he had left off the evening before.

For over an hour he wandered aimlessly about the city receiving, classifying, and filing away information. He saw several duels between guardians and yellow and green-bat monsters, to none of which he paid any more attention than did the people around him. Then a third kind of enemy appeared — two of them at once, flying wing-and-wing — and Garlock stopped and watched.

While they did not really closely resemble flying saber-toothed tigers, that was the first impression that leaped into Garlock's mind. Their bodies were black and yellow and sleek, like a tiger's, but they had almost man-like faces — except for the sharp, beakish noses. They dived swiftly, on great gray wings, tiger's claws extended.

Two bow-legged guardians came leaping as usual, but one of them was a fraction of second too late. That fraction was enough. While the first guardian was still high in air, grappling with one tiger, the other swung on a dime — the blast of air from his right wing buffeting people in the crowd below and knocking four of them flat — and took the guardian's head off his body with one savage swipe of a frightfully-armed paw. Disregarding the carcass, both attackers whirled sharply at the second guardian, meeting him in such a way that he could not come to firm grips with either of them, and that battle was very brief indeed. More guardians were leaping in from all directions, however, and the two tigers were forced to the ground and slaughtered.

Since six guardians had been killed, eight guardians marched up the street, dragging grisly loads. Eight bodies, friend and foe alike, were dumped into a manhole; eight creatures squatted down and cleaned themselves meticulously before resuming their various patrols.

Ten or fifteen minutes later, Garlock felt Lola's half-excited, half-frightened thought: "Clee, do you read me?"

"Loud and clear."

"There's something approaching that's certainly none of my business — maybe not even yours."

"I'm coming," he sent, and with the thought he was beside her. "Where?"

She pointed a thought. He followed it. Far away yet, but coming fast, was an immense flock of the winged tigers!

Lola licked her lips. "I'm going home, if you don't mind."

"Go on."

She disappeared.

Jim!" Garlock thought. "Where are you?"

"Observatory. Need me?"

"Yes. Bombing. Two point four microgram loads. Focus spot on my right — teleport in."

"Coming in on your right."

"And I on your left!" Belle's thought drove in as he had never before felt it driven. Being a Prime, she did not need a focus spot and appeared only an instant later than did James.

"Can you bomb?" Garlock snapped.

"What do *you* think?" Belle snapped back.

A moment of flashing thought and the three Tellurians disappeared, materializing five hundred feet in the air, two hundred feet ahead of the van of that horrible flight of monsters, drifting before it.

Belle got in the first shot. Not only did the victim disappear — a couple of dozen around it were torn to fragments and the force of the blast staggered all three Tellurians.

"Damn it, Belle, cut down or get the hell out!" Garlock said sharply. "I told you two point four *micrograms,* not milligrams. Just kill 'em, don't scatter 'em around all over hell's half acre. Less mess to clean up and I *don't* want you to kill people down below. Especially I don't want you to kill us — not even yourself."

"Sorry — I guess I was a bit enthusiastic in my weighing."

There began a series of muffled explosions along the front, each followed by the plunge of a tiger-striped body to the ground. Faster and faster the explosions came as the Operator and the Primes learned the routine of the job.

Nor were they long alone. The roaring, screaming howl of jets came up from behind them; four Arpalones appeared at their left, strung out along the front. Each held an extraordinarily heavy-duty blaster in each of his four hands; sixteen terrific weapons were hurling death into the flying horde.

"Slide over, Tellurians," came a calm thought. "You three take their left front; we'll take their right and center."

As they obeyed the instructions: *"They* don't give a damn where the pieces fly!" Belle protested. "Why should we be fussy about their street-cleaning department? *I'm* starting to use fives."

"Okay. We'll have to hit 'em harder, anyway, to keep up. Five, or maybe six — just be damn sure not to knock us or the Arpalones out of the air."

Carnage went on. The battlefront, while inside the city limits, was now almost stationary.

"Ha! Help arriveth — I hear footsteps approaching on jetback," Garlock announced. "Give 'em hell, boys!"

A flight of fighter-planes, eight abreast and wing-tips

almost touching, howled close overhead and along the line of invasion. They could not fire, of course, until they reached the city limits. There they opened up as one, and the air below became literally filled with falling monsters. Some had only broken wings; some were dead, but more or less whole; many were blown into unrecognizable bits of scraps of flesh.

Another flight screamed into place immediately behind the first; then another and another and another until six flights had passed. Then came four helicopters, darting and hovering, whose gunners picked off individually whatever survivors had managed to escape all six waves of fighters.

"That's better," came a thought from the Arpalone nearest Garlock. "Situation under control, thanks to you Tellurians. Supposed to be two squads of us gunners, but the other squad was busy on another job. Without you, this could have developed into a fairly nasty little infection. I don't know what you're doing or how you're doing it — we were told that you weren't like any other humans, and how true *that* is — but I'm in favor of it. I thought there were four of you?"

"One of us is not a fighter."

"Oh. You can knock off now, if you like. We'll polish off. Thanks much."

"But don't the boys on the ground need some help?"

"The Arpales? Those idiots you have been thinking of as 'guardians'? Which they are, of course. No. Besides, we're air-fighters. Ground work is none of our business. Also, these guns would raise altogether too much hell down there. Bound to hit some humans."

"Check. Those Arpales aren't very intelligent; you Arpalones are extremely so. Any connection?"

" 'Way back, they say. Common ancestry, and doing

two parts of the same job. Killing those fumapties and lemarts and sencors and what-have-you. I don't know what humanity's job is and don't give a damn. Probably fairly important, though, some way or other, since it's our job to see that the silly, gutless things keep on living. We have nothing to do with 'em, ever. The only reason I'm talking to you is you're not really human at all. You're a fighter, too, and a damn good one."

"I know what you mean," Garlock sent, and the three Tellurians turned their attention downward.

The heaviest fighting had been over a large park at the city's edge, which was now literally a shambles. Very few people were to be seen, and those few were moving unconcernedly away from the center of violence. All over the park thousands of Arpales were fighting furiously and hundreds of them were dying — for hundreds of the sencors had suffered only wing injuries, the long fall to ground had not harmed them farther, and their tremendous fighting ability had been lessened very little if at all.

"But I'd think, that just for efficiency if nothing else," Garlock argued, "you'd support the Arpales *some* way. Lighter guns or something. Why, thousands of them must have been killed, just in this last hour or so."

"Yeah, but that's their business. They breed fast and die fast. Everything has to balance, you know."

"Perhaps so." Garlock was silenced, if not convinced. "Well, it's about over. What happens to the bodies they're dumping down manholes? They can't go down a sewer that way?"

"Oh, you didn't know? Food."

"Food? For what?"

"The Arpales and us, of course."

"What? You don't mean . . . you *can't* mean that they — and you Arpalones, too — are cannibals?"

"Cannibals? Explain, please? Oh, eaters-of-our-own-species. Of course — certainly. Why not?"

"Why, self-respect . . . common decency . . . respect for one's fellowman . . . family ties . . ." Garlock was floundering; to be called upon to explain his ingrained antipathy to such a custom was new to his experience.

"You are silly. Worse, squeamish. Worst, supremely illogical." The Arpalone paused, then went on as though trying to educate a hopelessly illogical inferior. "While we do not kill Arpales purposely — except when they over-breed — why waste good meat as fertilizer? If a diet is wholesome, nutritious, well-balanced and tasty, what shred of difference can it *possibly* make what its ingredients once were?"

"Well, I'll be damned," Garlock quit.

"And blasted," Belle agreed. "This whole deal makes me sick at the stomach and I think my face is turning green too. But I'm devilishly and gleefully glad, Clee, that I was here to hear *somebody* give you cards, spades, and big casino and still beat hell out of you at your own game of coldblooded logic!"

"We gunners must go now. Would you like to come along with us and see the end of this particular breeding-hole of sencors?"

At high speed the seven flew back along the line of advance of the winged tiger horde, across a barren valley, toward and to the side of a mountain.

An area almost a mile square of that mountain's side was a burned, blasted, churned, pocked, cratered and flaming waste; and the four helicopters were still working on it. High-energy beams blasted, fairly volatilizing the ground as they struck in as deep as they could be driven. High-explosive shells bored deep and detonated, hurling shattered rock and soil and yellow smoke far and wide;

establishing new craters by destroying the ones existing a moment before.

While it seemed incredible that any living thing larger than a microbe could emerge under its own power from such a hell of energy, many winged tigers were doing so — apparently being blown aloft with the hirtherto undisturbed volume of soil in which the creatures had been. Most of them were not fully grown; some were so immature as to be unrecognizable to an untrained eye; but from all four helicopters hand-guns snapped and cracked. *Nothing* was leaving that field of carnage alive.

"What are you gunners supposed to be doing here?" Garlock asked.

"Oh, the 'copters will be leaving pretty soon — they've got other places to go. But they won't get them all — some of the hatches are too deep — so we'll stick around for two-three days to kill the late-hatchers as they come out."

"I see." And Garlock probed. "There are four cells that they won't reach. Shall I bomb 'em out?"

"I'll ask." The slitted red eyes widened and he sent out a call. "Commander Knahr, can you hop over here a minute? I want you to meet these things we've been hearing about. They look human, but they really aren't. They're killers, with more stuff and more brains than any of us ever heard of."

Another Arpalone appeared, indistinguishable to Tellurian eyes from any one of the others.

"But why do you want to mix into something that's none of your business?" Knahr was neither officious nor condemnatory. He simply could not understand.

"Since you have no concept of our quality of curiosity, just call it education. The question is, do you or do you not want those four deeply-buried cells blasted out of existence?"

"Of course I do."

"Okay. You've got all of 'em you're going to get. Tell your 'copters to give us about five miles clearance, and we'll all fall back, too."

They drew back, and there were four closely-spaced explosions of such violence that one raggedly mushroom-shaped cloud went up into the stratosphere and one huge, ragged crater yawned where once churned ground had been.

"But that's *atomic!*" Knahr gasped the thought. "Fall-out!"

"No fall-out. Complete conversion. Have you got a counter?"

They had. They tested. There was nothing except the usual background count.

"There's no life left underground, so you needn't keep this squad of gunners tied up here," Garlock told the commander. "Before we go, I want to ask a question. You have visitors once in a while from other solar systems, so you must have a faster-than-light drive. Can you tell me anything about it?"

"No. Nothing like that would be any of my business."

Knahr and the four gunners disappeared; the helicopters began to lumber away.

"Well, *that* helps — I don't think," Garlock thought, glumly. *"What* a world! Back to the Main?"

In the Main, after a long and fruitless discussion, Garlock called Governor Atterlin, who did not know anything about any faster-than-light drive, either. There was one, of course, since it took only a few days or a few weeks to go from one system to another; but Hodell didn't have any such ships. No ordinary planet did. They were owned and operated by people who called themselves "Engineers". He had no idea where these Engineers came from; they didn't say.

Garlock then tried to get in touch with the Arpalone inspector who had checked the *Pleiades* in, and could not find out even who it had been. The inspector then on duty neither knew or cared anything about either faster-than-light drives or Engineers. Such things were none of his business.

"What difference would it make, anyway?" James asked. "No drive that takes 'a few weeks' for an intra-galactic hop is *ever* going to get us back to Tellus."

"True enough; but if there is any such thing I want to know how it works. How are you coming?"

"I'll finish up tomorrow easily enough."

Tomorrow came, and James finished up, but he did not find any familiar pattern of galactic arrangement. The other three watched James set up for another try for Earth.

"You don't think we'll ever get back, do you, Clee?" Belle asked.

"Not right away, no. But someday, yes. I've got the germ of an idea. Maybe three or four more hops will give me something to work on."

"I hope so," James said, "because here goes nothing," and he snapped the red switch.

It was not nothing. Number Two was another Arpalone inspector and another planet very much like Hodell. It proved to be so far away from both Earth and Hodell, however, that no useful similarities were found in any two of the three sets of charts.

Number Three was equally unproductive of helpful results. James did, however, improve his technique of making galactic charts; and he and Garlock designed and built a high-speed comparator. Thus the time required per stop was reduced from days to hours.

Number Four produced a surprise. When Garlock touched the knob of the testing-box he yanked his hand away before it had really made contact. It was like touching a high-voltage wire.

"You are incompatible with our humanity and must not land," the inspector ruled.

"Suppose we blast you and your jets out of the air and land anyway?" Garlock asked.

"That is perhaps possible," the Arpalone agreed, equably enough. "We are not invincible. However, it would do you no good. If any one of you four leaves that so-heavily-insulated vessel in the atmosphere of this planet you will surely die. Not quickly, but slowly and with difficulty."

"But you haven't tested *me!*" Belle said. "Do you mean they'll attack us on sight?"

"There is no need to test more than one. Anyone who could live near any of you could not live on this planet. Nor will anyone attack you. Don't you know what the thought 'incompatible' means?"

"With us it does not mean death."

"Here it does, since it refers to life forces. The types are mutually, irreconcilably antagonistic. Your life forces are very strong. Thus, no matter how peaceable your intentions may be, many of our human beings would die before you would; but you would not live to get back to your ship if you landed it and let its protective insulation."

"Why? What is it? How does it work?" Belle demanded.

"It is not my business to know; only to tell. I have told. You will go away now."

Garlock's eyes narrowed in concentration. "Belle, can you blast? I mean, could you if you wanted to?"

"Certainly . . . but I dont *want* to, Clee!"

"I don't either—and I'll file that one away to chew on some night when I'm hungry, too. Take her up, Jim, and try another shot."

Numbers Five to Nine were neither productive nor eventful. All were, like the others, Hodell all over again, in everything fundamental. One was so far advanced that almost all of its humanity were Seconds; one so backward —or so much younger—that its strongest telepaths were only Fours. The Tellurians became acquainted with, and upon occasion fought with, various types of man-sized monsters in addition to the three varieties they had seen on Hodell.

Every planet they visited had Arpalones and Arpales. Not by those names, of course. Local names for planets, guardians, nations, cities, and persons went into the starship's tapes. Every planet they visited was peopled by *Homo Sapiens,* capable of interbreeding with the Tellurians and eager to do so—especially with the Tellurian men. Their strict monogamy was really tested more than once; but it held. Each had been visited repeatedly by starships; but all Garlock could find out about them was that they probably came from some world somewhere that was inhabited by compatible human beings of Grade Two. He could learn nothing about the faster-than-light drive.

Number Ten was another strange one—the Tellurians were found incompatible.

"Let's go down anyway," Belle suggested. "Overcome this unwillingness of ours and find out. What do you think they've got down there, Clee, that could possibly handle you and me both?"

"I don't think it's a case of 'handling' at all. I don't

know what it is, but I believe it's fatal. We won't go down."

"But it doesn't make sense!" Belle protested.

"Not yet, no; but it's a datum. Enough data and we'll be able to formulate a theory."

"You and your theories! I wish we could get some *facts!*"

"You can call that a fact. But I want you and Jim to do some math. We know that we're making mighty long jumps. Assuming that they're at perfect random and of approximately the same length, the probability is greater than one-half that we're getting farther and farther away from Tellus. Is there a jump number, N, at which the probability is one-half that we land nearer Tellus instead of farther away? My jump-at-conclusions guess is that there isn't—that the first jump set up a bias."

"Ouch. That isn't in any of the books," James said. "In other words, do we or do we not attain a maximum? You're making some poor assumptions—among others that space isn't curved and that the dimensions of the universe are very large compared to the length of our jumps. I'll see if I can put it into shape to feed to Compy. You've always held that these generators work at random—the rest of those assumptions are based on your theory?"

"Check. I'm not getting anywhere studying my alleged Xenology, so I'm going to work full time on designing a generator that will steer."

"You tried it before. So did everybody else."

"I know it, but I've got a lot more data now. And I'm not promising; just trying. Okay?"

"Sure—I'm in favor of anything that has any chance at all of working."

Jumping went on; and Garlock, instead of going abroad on the planets, stayed aboard the *Pleiades* and worked.

At Number Forty Three, their reception was of a new kind. They were compatible with the people of this world, but the Inspector advised them against landing.

"I do not forbid you," he explained carefully. "Our humans are about to destroy themselves with fission and fusion bombs. They send missiles, without warning, against visitors. Thus, the last starship to visit us here disregarded my warning and sent down a sensing device as usual— Engineers do not land on non-telepathic worlds, you know —and it was destroyed."

"You're a Guardian of Humanity," Garlock said. "Can't you straighten your people out?"

"Of course not!" The Arpalone was outraged. "We guard humanity against incompatibles and non-humans; but it is not our business to interfere with humanity if it wishes to destroy itself. That is its privilege and its own business."

Garlock probed downward. "No telepathy, even—not even a Seven. This planet *is* backward—back to Year One. And nothing but firecrackers . . . We're going down."

"Good!" Belle said. "This will break the monotony, at least." And the others agreed.

"You won't object, I take it," Garlock said to the inspector, "if we try to straighten them out. We can postpone the blowup for a few years, at least."

"No objections, of course. In fact, I can say that we Guardians of Humanity would approve such action."

Down the *Pleiades* went, into the air of the nation known as the "Allied Republican Democracies of the World," and an atomic-warheaded rocket came flaming up.

"Hmmm . . . Ingenious little gadget, at that," James reported, after studying it thoroughly. "Filthy thing for fallout, though, if it goes off. Where'll I flip it, Clee? One of their moons?"

"Yes. Third one out—no chance of any contamination from there."

The missile vanished; and had an astronomer been looking at the world's third and outermost moon at the moment, he might have seen a tremendous flare of light, a cloud of dust, and the formation of a new and different crater among the hundreds already there.

"No use waiting for 'em, Jim. All three of you toss everything they've got out onto that same moon, being sure not to hurt anybody—yet. I'll start asking questions."

The captain who had fired the first missile appeared in the Main. He reached for his pistol, to find that he did not have one. He tensed his muscles to leap at Garlock, and found that he could not move.

Garlock drove his probe: "Who is your superior officer?" Before the man could form a mind-shield, that superior stood helpless beside him.

Then three . . . and four. At the fifth:

"Ah, you are the man I want. Prime Minister—euphemism for Dictator—Sovig. Missile launching stations and missile storage? You don't know? Who does?"

Another man appeared, and for twenty minutes the *Pleiades* darted about the continent.

"Now submarines, atomic and otherwise, and all surface vessels capable of launching missiles." Another man appeared.

This job took a little longer, since the crew of each vessel had to be teleported back to its base. An immense scrap-pile, probably visible with a telescope or even moderate power, built up rapidly on the third moon.

"Now a complete list of your uranium-refining plants, your military reactors, heavy-water and heavy-hydrogen plants, and so on." Another man appeared, but the starship did not move.

"Here is a list of plants," said Garlock coldly, and named them. "You will remember them. I will return you to your office and you may—or may not, as you please— order them evacuated. Look at your watch. We start destroying them in exactly seventy-two of your hours from this moment. Any and all persons on the properties will be killed; any within a radius of ten of your miles may be killed. Our explosives are extremely powerful, but there is no radioactivity and no danger from the fallout. The danger is from flash-blindness, flash-burn, sheer heat, shock-wave, concussion, and flying debris of all kinds."

The officer vanished and Garlock turned back to the Prime Minister.

"You have an ally, a nation known as the 'Brotherhood of Peoples' Republics'. Where is its capital? Slide us over there, Jim. Now, Prime Minister Sovig, you and your ally, the second and first most populous nations of your world, are combining to destroy—a pincers movement, let us say?—the third largest nation, or rather, group of nations: the Nations of the North . . . Oh, I see. Third only in population, but first in productive capacity and technology. They should be destroyed because their ideology does not agree with yours. They are too idealistic to strike first, so you will. After you strike, they will not be able to. Whereupon you, personally, will rule the world. I will add to that something you are not thinking, but should: You will rule it until one of your friends puts his pistol to the back of your neck and blows your brains out."

They were now over the ally's capital—which launched three missiles instead of one. Garlock collected four more men and studied them.

"Just as bad. If possible, worse. Who, Lingonor, is the leader of your opposition, if any?" Another man, very evidently of the same race, appeared.

"Idealistic, in a way, but spineless and corrupt," Garlock announced to all. "His administration was one of the most corrupt ever known on this world. We'll disarm them, too."

They did. The operation did not take very long, as this nation, while very high in manpower, was very low in technology.

The starship moved to a station high above the Capitol Building of the Nations of the North and moved slowly downward until it hung poised one scant mile over the building. Missiles, jets, and heavy guns were set and ready, but no attack was made. Therefore Garlock introduced himself to various personages and invited them aboard instead of snatching them; nor did he immobilize them after they had been teleported aboard.

"The president, the chief of staff, the chief justice, the most eminent scientists, the head of a church, the leaders of the legislative body and four political bosses, the biggest business man, biggest labor leader, the biggest gangster. Fourteen men." As Garlock studied them his face hardened. "I thought to leave your Nations armed, to entrust this world's future to you, but no. Only two of you are really concerned about the welfare of your peoples, and one of those two is very weak. Most of you are of no higher motivation than are the two dictators and your gangster Clyden. You are much better than those we have already disarmed, but are not good enough."

Garlock's hard eyes swept over the group for a long thirty seconds before he went on:

"I am opening all of your minds, friend and foe alike, to each other, so that you may all see for yourselves what depths of rottenness exist there and just how unfit your world is to associate with the decent worlds of this or any other galaxy. It would take God Himself to do anything with such material, and I am not God. Therefore, when we have rid your world of atomics we will leave and you will start all over again. If you really try, you can not only kill all animal life on your planet, but make it absolutely uninhabitable for—"

"Stop it, Clee!" Lola jumped up, her eyes flashing. Garlock dropped the tuned group, but Belle took it over. Everyone there understood every thought. "Don't you see you've done enough? That now you're going too far? That these twenty-odd men, having had their minds opened and having been given insight into what is possible, will go forward instead of backward?"

"Forward? With such people as the Prime Ministers, the labor and business leaders, the bosses and the gangsters to cope with? Do you think they've got spines stiff enough for the job?"

"I'm sure of it. Our world did it with no better. Millions and millions of other worlds did it. Why can't this one do it, too?"

"May I ask a couple of questions?" This thought came from the tall, trim, soldierly chief of staff.

"Of course, General Cordeen."

"We have all been taking it for granted that you four belong to some superhuman race—some kind of *Homo Superior*. Do I understand correctly your thought that your race is *Homo Sapiens*, the same as ours?"

"Why, of course it is," Lola answered in surprise. "The only difference is that we are a few thousand years older than you are."

"You said also that there were 'millions and millions' of worlds that have solved the problems facing us. Were all those worlds also peopled by *Homo Sapiens*? It seems incredible."

"True, nevertheless. On any and every world of this type humanity is identical physically; and the mental differences are due only to their being in different stages of development. In fact, every planet we have visited except this one makes a regular custom of breeding its best blood with the best blood of other solar systems. And as to the 'millions and millions,' I meant only a very large but indefinite number. As far as I know, not even a rough estimate has ever been made—has it, Clee?"

"No, but it will probably turn out to be millions *of* millions, instead of millions *and* millions; and squared and then cubed at that. My guess is that it'll take another ten thousand years of preliminary surveying such as we're doing, by all the crews the various Galaxian Societies can put out, before even the roughest kind of an estimate can be made as to how many planets are inhabited by mutually fertile human peoples."

For a moment the group was stunned. Then:

"Do you mean to say," asked the businessman, "that you Galaxians are not the only ones who have interstellar travel?"

"Far from it. In fact, yours is the only world we have seen that does not have it, in one form or another."

"Oh? More than one way? That makes it still worse. Would you be willing to sell us plans, or lease us ships . . . ?"

"So that you could exploit other planets? We will not. You would get nowhere, even if you had an interstellar drive right now. You, personally, are a perfect example of what is wrong with this planet. Rapacious, insatiable—you violate every concept of ethics, common decency, and social responsibility. Your world's technology is so far ahead of its sociology that you not only should be, but actually are being, held in quarantine."

74

"What?"

"Exactly. One race I know of has been inspecting you regularly for several hundred of your years. They will not make contact with you, or allow you to leave your own world, until you grow up to something beyond the irresponsible-baby stage. Thus, about two and a half of your years ago, a starship of that race sent down a sensing element—unmanned, of course—to check your state of development. Brother Sovig volatilized it with an atomic missile."

"We did not do it," the dictator declared. "It was the warmongering capitalists."

"You contemptible idiot," Garlock said. "Are even you actually stupid enough to try to lie with your mind? To minds linked to your own and to mine?"

"We did do it, then, but it was only a flying saucer."

"Just as this ship was, to you, only a flying saucer, I suppose. So here's something else for you to think about, Brother Sovig, with whatever power your alleged brain is able to generate. When you shot down that senser, the starship did not retaliate, but went on without taking any notice of you. When you tried to shoot *us* down, we took some slight action, but did not kill anyone and are now discussing the situation. Listen carefully now, and remember—it is very possible that the next craft you attack in such utterly idiotic fashion will, without any more warning than you give, blow this whole planet into a ball of incandescent gas."

"Can that actually be done?" the scientist asked. For the first time, he became really interested in the proceedings.

"Very easily, Doctor Cheswick," Garlock replied. "We could do it ourselves with scarcely any effort and at very small cost. You are familiar, I suppose, with the phenomenon of ball lightning?"

"Somewhat. Its mechanism has never been elucidated in any very satisfactory mathematics."

"Well, we have at our disposal a field some . . ."

"Hold it, Clee," James warned. "Do you want to put out that kind of stuff around here?

"Ummmm . . . What do you think?"

James studied Cheswick's mind. "Better than I thought," he decided. "He has made two really worthwhile intuitions —a genius type. He's been working on what amounts almost to the Coupler Theory for ten years. He's almost got it, but you know intuitions of that caliber can't be scheduled. He might get it tomorrow—or never. I'd say push him over the hump."

"Okay with me. We'll take a vote—one blackball kills it. Brownie? Just the link, of course. A few hints, perhaps, at application, but no technological data."

"I say give it to him. He's earned it. Besides, he isn't young any more and may die before he gets it, and that would lose them two or three hundred years."

"Belle?"

"In favor. Shall I drop the linkage? No," she answered her own question. "No other minds here will have any idea of what it means, and it may do some of them a bit of good to see one of their own minds firing on more than one barrel."

"Thank you, Galaxians." The scientist's mind had been quivering with eagerness. "I am inexpressibly glad that you have found me worthy of so much help."

Garlock entered Cheswick's mind. First he impressed, indelibly, six symbols and their meanings. Second, a long and intricate equation, which the scientist studied avidly.

During the ensuing pause Garlock cut the president and

chief of staff out of the linkage. "We have just given Cheswick a basic formula. In a couple of hundred years it will give you full telepathy, and then you will really begin to go up. There's nothing secret about it—in fact, I'd advise full purlication—but even so it might be a smart idea to give him both protection and good working conditions. Brains like his are apt to be centuries apart on any world."

"But this is . . . it could be . . . it *must* be!" Cheswick exclaimed. "I *never* would have formulated *that!* It isn't quite implicit, of course, but from this there derives the existence of, and the necessity for, electrogravitics—an entirely new field of reality and experiment in science!"

"There does indeed," Garlock agreed, "and it is far indeed from being implicit. You leaped a tremendous gap. And yes, the resultant is more humanistic than technological."

Belle was smiling and shaking her head at the same time. "How do you like *them* tid-bits, Clee?" she asked. "Two hundred years in seventy eight seconds? You folks will have telepathy by the time your present crop of babies grows up. Clee, ain't you sorry you got mad and blew your top and wanted to pick up your marbles and go home? *Three* such institutions in one man's lifetime beats par even for the genius course."

"It sure does," Garlock admitted ruefully. "I should have studied these minds—particularly his—before jumping at conclusions."

"May I say a few words?" the president asked.

"You may indeed, sir. I was hoping you would."

"We have been discouraged, faced with an insoluble problem. Sovig and Lingonor, knowing that their own lives were forfeit anyway, were perfectly willing to destroy all the life on this world to make us yield. Now, however, with the insight and the encouragement you Galaxians have given us, the situation has changed. Reduced to ordinary high explosives, they cannot conquer us ..."

"Especially without an air-force," Lola put in. "I, personally, will see to it that every bomber and fighter plane they now have goes to the third moon. It will be your responsibility to see to it that they do not rebuild."

"Thank you, Miss Montandon. We will see to it. As for our internal difficulties—I think, under certain conditions, they can be handled. Our lawless element"—he glanced at the gangster—"can be made impotent. The corrupt practices of both capital and labor can be stopped. We have laws"—here he looked at the members of Congress and the judge—"which can be enforced. The conditions I mentioned would be difficult at the moment, since so few of us are here and it is manifest that few if any of our people will believe that such people as you Galaxians really exist. Would it be possible for you, Miss Montandon, to spend a few days—or whatever time you can spare—in showing our Congress, and as many others as possible, what humanity may hope to become?"

"Of course, sir. I was planning on it."

"I'm afraid that is impossible," the chief of staff said.

"Why, General Cordeen?" Lola asked.

"Because you'd be shot," Cordeen said, bluntly. "We have a very good Secret Service, it is true, and we would give you every protection possible; but such an all-out effort as would be made to assassinate you would almost certainly succeed."

"Shot?" Garlock asked in surprise. "What with? You haven't anything that could even begin to crack an Operator's Shield."

"With this, sir." Cordeen held out his automatic pistol for inspection.

"Oh, I hadn't studied it . . . a pellet-projector . . ."

"*Pellet!* Do you call a four-seventy-five slug a pellet?"

"Not much of that, really; it shoots eight times—shoot all eight of them at her—None of them will touch her."

"*What?* I *will* not! One of those slugs will go through three women like her, front to back in line."

"I will, then." The pistol leaped into Garlock's hand. "Hold up one hand, Brownie, and catch 'em. Don't let 'em splash. No deformation, so he can recognize his own pellets."

Holding the unfamiliar weapon in a clumsy, highly unorthodox grip—something like a schoolgirl's first attempt—Garlock glanced once at Lola's upraised palm and eight shots roared out as fast as the gases of explosion could operate the mechanism. The pistol's barrel remained rigidly motionless under all the stress of ultra-rapid fire. Lola's slim, deeply-tanned arm did not even quiver under the impact of that storm of heavy bullets against her apparently unsupported hand. No one saw those bullets strike her palm, but everyone saw them drop into her cupped left hand, like drops of water dripping rapidly from the end of an icicle into a bowl.

"Here are your pellets, General Cordeen." Lola handed them to him with a smile.

"Good God!" the general said.

"You see, I am perfectly safe from being 'shot,' as you call it," Lola said. "So I'll come down and work with you. You might have your news services put out a bulletin, though. I never have killed anyone, and am not going to do so here, but anyone who tries to shoot me or bomb me or anything will lose both hands at the wrists just before he fires. That would keep them from killing anyone standing near me, don't you think?"

"I should *think* it would," General Cordeen thought,

and a pall of awe covered the linked minds. The implications of the naively frank remark just uttered by this apparently inoffensive and defenseless young woman were simply too overwhelming to be discussed.

"Anything else on the agenda, Clee?" Lola asked.

There was not, and the starship's guests were returned, each to his own home place.

And not one of them was exactly the same as he had been.

IV

"I THINK I'll come along with you and bodyguard you, Lola," Belle said the following morning after breakfast. "Clee's going to be seven thousand miles deep in mathematics and Jim's doing his stuff at the observatory, and I can't help either of 'em at the moment. You'd do a better job, wouldn't you, if you could concentrate on it?"

"Of course. Thanks, Belle. But remember, it's already been announced—no death. Just hands. I can't really believe that I'll be attacked, but they seem pretty sure of it."

"I'd like to separate anyone like that from his head instead of his hands, but as it is published so it will be performed."

"How about wearing some kind of halfway comfortable shoes instead of those slippers?" Garlock asked. "That could turn out to be a long, tough brawl, and your feet'll be begging for mercy before you get back here."

"Uh-uh. Very comfortable and a perfect fit. Besides, if I have to suffer just a little bit for good appearance's sake in a matter of intergalactic amity . . ."

"A matter of showing off, you mean."

"Why, Clee!" Belle widened her eyes at him. "How you talk! But they're ready, Lola—let's go."

The two girls disappeared from the Main, to appear on

the speakers' stand in front of the Capitol Building. President Benton was there, with his cabinet, General Cordeen and his staff, and certain other personages.

"Oh, Miss Bellamy, too? I'm *very* glad you are here," Benton said, as he shook hands cordially with both.

"Thank you. I came along as bodyguard. May I meet your Secret Service Chief, please?"

"Why, of course. Miss Bellamy, may I present Mr. Avengord?"

"You have the hospital room ready? . . . Where is it, please?"

"Back of us, in the wing . . ."

"Just think of it, please, and I'll follow your thought . . . ah, yes, there it is. I hope it won't be used. You agree with General Cordeen that there will be one or more attempts at assassination?"

"I'm very much afraid so. This town is literally riddled with enemy agents, and of course we don't know all of them—especially not the best ones. They know that if these meetings go through, they're sunk; so they're desperate. We've got this whole area covered like dew — we've arrested sixteen suspects already this morning — but all the advantage is theirs."

"Not all of it, sir," Belle smiled at him cheerfully. "You have me, and I am a Prime Operator. That is, a wielder of power of no small ability. Oh, you *are* right. There's an attempt now being prepared."

While Belle had been greeting and conversing, she had also been scanning. Her range, her sensitivity, and her power were immensely greater than Lola's—were probably equal to Garlock's own. She scanned by miles against the scant yards covered by the Secret Service.

"Where?"

"Give me your thought." The Secret Service man did

not know what she meant — telepathy was of course new to him — so she seized his attention and directed it to a certain window in a building a couple of miles away on a hill.

"But they couldn't, from there!"

"But they can. They have a quite efficient engine of destruction — a 'rifle' is their thought. Large, and long, with a very good telescope on it — with cross-hairs. If I scan their minds more precisely you may know the weapon . . . Ah, they think of it as a 'Buford Mark Forty Anti-Aircraft Rifle'."

"A Buford! My God, they can hit any button on her clothes—get her away, quick!" He tried to jump, but could not move.

"As you were," she directed. "There was another Buford there, and another over there." She guided his thought. "Two men to each Buford. There are now six handless men in your hospital room. If you will send men to those three rifle places you will find the Bufords and the hands. Your surgeon will have no difficulty in matching the hands to the men. If any seek to remove either Bufords or hands before your men get there, I will de-hand them, also."

The Secret Service man was completely flabbergasted. Cordeen had told him, with much pounding on his desk and in searing, air-blueing language, what to expect—or, rather, to expect *anything,* no matter what and with no limits whatever—but he hadn't believed it then and simply could not believe it now. God damn it, such things *couldn't* happen. And this beautiful, beautifully-stacked, half-naked girl, who couldn't be a day over twenty-five . . . Even if it had been their leader, Captain Garlock himself . . .

"I am twenty-three of your years old, not twenty five,"

she informed him coldly, "and I will permit no distinction of sex. In your culture the women may still be allowing you men to believe in the fallacy of the superiority of the male, but know right now that I can do anything any man ever born can do, and do it better."

"Oh, I'm . . . I'm sure . . . certainly . . ." Avengord's thought was incoherent.

"If you want me to work with you you'd better start believing right now that there are a lot of things you don't know," Belle went on relentlessly. "Stop believing that just because a thing hasn't already happened on this mudball planet of yours, it can't happen anywhere or anywhen. You do believe, however, whether you want to or not, things you see with your own eyes?"

"Yes. I can *not* be hypnotized."

"I'm very glad you believe that much." Avengord did not notice that she neither confirmed nor denied the truth of his statement. "To that end you will go now into the hospital room and see the bandaging going on. You will see and hear the news broadcast going out as I prepared it."

He went, and came back a badly shaken man.

"But they're sending it out exactly as it happened!" he protested. "They'll all scatter out so fast and far we'll *never* catch them!"

"By no means. You see, the amputees didn't believe that they would lose their hands. Their superiors didn't believe it, either; they assured each other and their underlings that it was just bluff and nonsense. And since they are all even more materialistic and hidebound and unbelieving than you are, they all are now highly confused—at a complete loss."

"You can say *that* again. If I, working with you and

having you pounding it into my head, couldn't more than half believe it . . ."

"So they're now very frightened, as well as confused, and the director of their whole spy system is now violating rule and precedent by sending out messengers to summon his highest agents to confer with him in his secret place."

"If you'll tell me where, I'll get over to my office . . ."

"No. We'll both be in your office in plenty of time. We'll watch Lola get started. It will be highly instructive for you to watch a really capable Operator at work."

President Benton had been introduced, and had in turn finished introducing Lola. The crowd, many thousands strong, was cheering. Lola was stepping into the carefully marked speaker's place.

"You may disconnect these"—she waved a hand at the battery of microphones—"since I do not use speech. Not only do I not know any of your various languages, but no one language would suffice. My thought will go to every person on your world."

"World?" the president asked in surprise. "Surely not behind the Curtains? They'll jam you, I'm afraid."

"My thought, as I shall drive it, will not be stopped," Lola assured him. "Since this world has no telepathy, it has no mind-blocks and I can cover the planet as easily as one mind. Nor does it matter whether it's day or night, or whether anyone is awake or asleep. All will receive my message. Since you wish a record, the cameras may run, although they are neither necessary nor desirable for me. Everyone will see me in his mind, much better than on the surface of any teevee tube."

"And I was going to have her address *Congress!*" the President whispered to General Cordeen.

Then Lola put her whole personality into a smile,

directed apparently not only at each separate individual within sight, but also individually at every person on the globe—and when Brownie Montandon set out to make a production of a smile, it had the impact of a pile-driver. Then came her gently-flowing, friendly thought:

"My name, friends of this world Ormolan, is Lola Montandon. Those of you who are now looking at teevee screens can see my imaged likeness. All of you can see me very much better within your own minds.

"I am not here as an invader in any sense, but only as a citizen of the First Galaxy of our common universe. I have attuned my mind to each of yours in order to give you a message from the United Galaxian Societies.

"There are four of us Galaxians in this Exploration Team. As Galaxians it is our purpose and our duty here to open your minds to certain basic truths, to be of help to you in clearing your minds of fallacies, of lies, and of indefensible prejudices, to the end that you will more rapidly become Galaxians yourselves . . ."

"Okay. This will go on and on. That's enough to give you an idea of what a trained and polished performer can do. What do you think of her, Chief?" Belle deliberately knocked the Secret Service man out of his Lola-induced mood.

"Huh? Oh, yes." Avengord was still groggy. "She's phenomenal—good—I don't mean goody-goody, but sincere and really . . ."

"Yes, but don't fall in love with her. Everybody does and it doesn't do any of them a bit of good. That's her specialty and she's *very* good at it. I told you she's a smooth, smooth worker."

"You can say *that* again. But it isn't an act. She means it and it's true."

"Of course she means it and of course it's true. Otherwise even she, with all her training, couldn't sell such a big bill of goods." Then, in answer to the man's unspoken question, "Yes, we're all different. She's the contactor, the shining example of purity and sweetness and light—in short, the spreader of good old oil. I'm a fighter, myself. Do you think she could actually have de-handed those men? Uh-uh. At the last minute she would have weakened and brought them in whole. My job in this operation is to knock hell out of the ones Lola can't convince, such as those spies you and I are going to interview pretty quick."

"Even they ought to be convinced. I don't see how anybody could help but be."

"Oh no. It'll bounce off like hailstones from a tin roof. The only thing to do to that kind of scum is kill them. If you'll give me a thought as to where your office is we'll hop over and . . ."

Belle and Avengord disappeared from the stand; and, such as Lola's hold, no one on the platform in the throng even noticed that they were gone. They materialized in Avengord's private office—he sitting as usual at his desk, she reclining in ease in a big leather chair.

". . . get to work." Belle's thought had not been interrupted by any passage of time whatever. "What do you want to do first?"

"But I thought you were covering Miss Montandon?"

"I am. Like a blanket. Just as well here as anywhere. I will be, until she gets back to the *Pleiades*. What first?"

"Oh. Well, since I don't know what your limits are— if you have any—you might as well do whatever you think best and I'll watch you do it."

"That's the way to talk. "You're going to get a shock when you see who the Head Man is. George T. Basil."

"*Basil!* I'll say it's a shock!" Avengord steadied,

frowned in concentration. "Could be, though. He would *never* be suspected—but they're very good at that."

"Yeah. His name used to be Baslovkowitz. He was trained for years, then planted. None of this can be proved, since his record is perfect. Born citizen, highest standing in business and social circles. Unlimited entry and top security clearance. Right?"

"Right . . . and getting enough evidence, in such cases as that, is pure, unadulterated hell."

"I suppose I could kill him, after we've recorded everything he knows," Belle suggested.

"No!" he snapped. "Too many people think of us as a strong-arm squad now. Anyway, I'd rather kill him myself than wish the job off onto you—you don't *like* killing, do you?"

"That's the understatement of the century. No civilized person does. In a hot fight, yes; but killing anyone who is helpless to fight back—in cold blood—ugh! It makes me sick in my stomach even to think of it."

"With the way you can read minds, we can get evidence enough to send them all to jail, and that will have to do."

"How about this?" Belle grinned as another solution came to mind. "From those first eight top men, we'll find out a lot of others lower down, and so on, until we have 'em all locked up here. We'll announce that exactly so many spies and agents—giving names, addresses, and facts, of course—got panicky after Lola's address. They fired up their hidden planes and flew back behind the Curtain. Then, when we've scanned their minds and recorded everything you want, I'll back them all, very snugly and carefully, into Sovig's private office. With the world situation what it then will be, he won't dare kill them — he simply won't know what to do."

Avengord did not merely laugh; he roared.

Then, quieting, he began to whistle boyishly, as he had not whistled for many years, as he reached out and flipped the switch of his intercom. "Miss Kimling, come in, please."

The door burst open. "Why it *is* you! But you were on the rostrum just a minute . . . oh!" She saw Belle, and backed, eyes wide, toward the door she had just entered. *"She* was there, too, and it's fifteen *miles* . . ."

"Steady, Fram. I'd like to present you to Prime Operator Belle Bellamy, who is cleaning out the entire Curtain organization for us."

"But how did you . . .?"

"Never mind that. Teleportation. It took her half an hour to pound it into me, and we can't take time to explain anything now. I'll tell everybody everything I know as soon as I can. In the meantime, don't be surprised at anything that happens, and by that I mean *anything*. Such as solid people appearing on this carpet—on that spot right there—instantaneously. I want you to pay close attention to everything your mind receives, put your memory into high gear, listen to everything I record, stop me any time I'm wrong, and be *sure* I get everything we need."

"I don't know exactly what you're talking about, sir, but I'll try."

"Frankly, I don't, either—we'll just have to roll it as we go along. We're ready for George T. Basil now, Miss Bellamy—I hope. Don't jump, Fram."

Basil appeared and Fram jumped. She did not scream, however, and did not run out of the office. The master spy was a big, self-assured, affluent type. He had not the slightest idea of how he had been spirited out of his ultrasecret sub-basement and into this room; but he knew where he was and, after one glance at Belle, he knew why. He decided instantly what to do about it.

"This is an outrage!" he bellowed, hammering with his fist on Avengord's desk. "A stupid, high-handed violation of the rights . . ."

Belle silenced him and straightened him up.

"High-handed? Yes," she admitted quite seriously. "However, from the Galaxian standpoint, you have no rights at all and you are going to be extremely surprised at just how high-handed I am going to be. I am going to read your mind to its very bottom—layer by layer, like peeling an onion—and everything you know and everything you think is going down in Mr. Avengord's Big Black Book."

Belle linked all four minds together and directed the search, making sure that no item, however small, was missed. Avengord recorded every pertinent item. Fram Kimling memorized and correlated and double-checked.

Soon it was done, and Basil, shouting even louder about this last and worst violation of his rights—those of his own private mind—was led away by two men and "put away where he would keep".

"But this *is* a flagrant violation of law . . ." Miss Kimling began.

"You can say *that* again!" her boss gloated. "And if you only knew how tickled I am to do it, after the way they've been kicking *me* around!

"But I wonder . . . are you sure we can get away with it?"

"Certainly," Belle put in. "We Galaxians are doing it, not your government or your Secret Service. We'll start you clean—but it'll be up to you to keep it clean, and that will be no easy job."

"No, it won't; but we'll do it. Come around again, say

in five or six years, and see."

"You know, I might take you up on that? Maybe not this same team, but I've got a notion to tape a recommendation for a re-visit, just to see how you get along. It'd be interesting."

"I wish you would. It might help, too, if everybody thought you'd come back to check. Suppose you could?"

"I've no idea, really. I'd like to, though, and I'll see what I can do. But let's get on with the job. They're all in what you call the 'tank' now. Which one do you want next?"

The work went on. That evening there was of course a reception; and then a ball. And Belle's feet did hurt when she got back to the *Pleiades,* but of course she would not admit the fact—most especially not to Garlock.

Exactly at the expiration of the stipulated seventy-two hours, the Galaxians began to destroy military atomic plants; and, shortly thereafter, the starship's crew was again ready to go.

And James rammed home the red button that would send them—all four wondered—WHERE?

It turned out to be another Hodell-type world; and, even with the high-speed comparator, it took longer to check the charts than it did to make them.

The next planet was similar. So was the next, and the next. The time required for checking grew longer and longer.

"How about cutting out this checking entirely, Clee?" James asked then. "What good does it do? Even if we find a similarity, what could we do about it? We've got enough stuff now to keep a crew of astronomers busy for five years making a tank of it."

"Okay. We're probably so far away now, anyway, that the chance of finding a similarity is vanishingly small.

Keep on taking the shots, though; they'll prove, I think, that the universe is one whole hell of a lot bigger than anybody has ever thought it was. That reminds me—are you getting anywhere on that N-problem? I'm not."

"I'm getting nowhere, fast. You should have been a math prof in a grad school, Clee. You could flunk every advanced student you had with that one. Belle and I together can't feed it to Compy in such shape as to get a definite answer. We think, though, that your guess was right—if we ever stabilize anywhere it will probably be relative to Hodell, not to Tellus. But the cold fact of how far away we must be by this time just scares me to death."

"You and me both. We're a *long* way from home and mother, believe me."

Jumping went on; and, two or three planets later, they encountered an Arpalone Inspector who did not test them for compatibility with the humanity of his world.

"Do not land," the creature said mournfully. "This world is dying, and if you leave the protection of your ship, you too will die."

"But *worlds* don't die," Garlock protested. "People, yes —but worlds?"

"Worlds die. It is the Dilipic. The humans die, too, of course, but it is the world itself that is attacked, not the people. Some of them, in fact, will live through it."

Garlock drove his attention downward and scanned.

"You Arpalones are doing what looks like a mighty good job of fighting. Can't you win?"

"No; it is too late. It was already too late when they first appeared, two days ago. When the Dilipics strike in such small force that none of their—agents?—devices?— whatever they are—can land against our beaming, a world can be saved; but such cases are very few."

"But this thought, 'Dilipic'?" Garlock asked, impatiently. "It is merely a symbol—it doesn't *mean* anything—to me, at least. What are they? Where do they come from?"

"No one knows anything about them, not even their physical shape—if they have any. Nor where they come from, or how they do what they do."

"They can't be very common," Garlock pondered. "We have never heard of them before."

"Fortunately, they are not," the Inspector agreed. "Scarcely one world in five hundred is ever attacked by them—this is the first Dilipic invasion I have seen."

"Oh, you Arpalones don't die with your worlds, then?" Lola asked. She was badly shaken. "But I suppose the Arpales do, of course."

"Practically all of the Arpales will die, of course. Most of us Arpalones will also die, in the battles now going on. Those of us who survive, however, will stay aloft until the rehabilitation fleet arrives, then we will continue our regular work."

"Rehab?" Belle exclaimed. "You mean you can *restore* planets so badly ruined that all the people die?"

"Oh, yes. It is a long and difficult work, but the planet is always repeopled."

"Let's go down," Garlock said. "I want to get all of this on tape."

They went down, over what had been one of that world's largest cities. The air, the stratosphere, and all nearby space was full of battling vessels of all shapes and sizes, ranging from the tremendous globular spaceships of the invaders down to the tiny, one-man jet-fighters of the Arpalones.

The Dilipics were using projectile weapons only—ranging in size, depending on the size of the vessels, from heavy machine-guns up to seventy-five-millimeter quick-firing rifles. They were also launching thousands of guided missiles of fantastic speed and of tremendous explosive power.

The Arpalones were not using anything solid at all. Each defending vessel, depending upon its type and class, carried from four up to a hundred burnished-metal reflectors some four feet in diameter, each with a small black device at its optical center and each pouring out a tight beam of highly effective energy. It was at these reflectors, and particularly at these tiny devices, that the small-arms fire was directed, and the marksmanship of the Dilipics was very good indeed. However, each projector was oscillating irregularly and each fighter-plane was taking evasive action; and, since a few bullet-holes in any reflector did not reduce its efficiency very much, and since the central mechanisms were so small and were moving so erratically, a good three-quarters of the Arpalonian beams were still in action.

There was no doubt at all that those beams were highly effective. Invisible for the most part, whenever one struck a Dilipic ship or plane everything in its path flared almost instantly into vapor and the beam glared incandescently, blindingly white or violet or high blue—never anything lower than blue. Almost everything material, that is; for guns, ammunition, and missiles were not affected. They did not even explode. When whatever fabric it was that supported them was blasted away, all such things simply dropped: simply fell through thousands or hundreds of thousands of feet of air to crash unheeded upon whatever happened to be below.

The invading task force was arranged in a whirling, swirling, almost cylindrical cone, more or less lke an Earthly tornado. The largest vessels were high above the stratosphere; the smallest fighters were close to ground. Each Dilipic unit seemed madly, suicidally determined that nothing would get through that furious wall to interfere with whatever it was that was coming down from space to the ground through the relatively quiet "eye" of the pseudo-hurricane.

On the other hand, the Arpalones were madly, suicidally determined to break through that vortex wall, to get into the "eye," to wreak all possible damage there. Group after group after group of five jet-fighters each came diving in; and, occasionally, the combined blasts of all five made enough of an opening in the wall so that the center fighter could get through. Once inside, each pilot stood his little, stubby-winged craft squarely on her tail, opened his projectors to absolute maximum of power and of spread, and climbed straight up the spout until he was shot down.

And the Arpalones were winning the battle. Larger and larger gaps were being opened in the vortex wall—gaps which became increasingly difficult for the Dilipics to fill. More and more Arpalone fighters were getting inside. They were lasting longer and doing more damage all the time. The tube was growing narrower and narrower.

The four Galaxians perceived all this in seconds. Garlock weighed out and detonated a terrific matter-conversion bomb in the exact center of one of the largest vessels of the attacking fleet. It had no effect. Then he tried a larger one—then another, still heavier. Finally, at over a hundred megatons equivalent, he did get results—of a sort. The invaders' guns, ammunition, and missiles were blown out of the ship and scattered outward for miles in all directions; but the structure of the Dilipic ship itself was not harmed.

Belle had been studying, analyzing, probing the things that were coming down through that hellish tube.

She drove a thought. "Clee! Cut the monkey-business

with those damn firecrackers of yours and look here—pure, solid force, like ball lightning or our Op field, but entirely different! See if you can analyze the stuff."

"Alive?" Garlock asked, as he drove a probe into one of the things—they were furiously-radiating spheres some seven feet in diameter—and began to tune in with the thing, whatever it was, and still following it down.

This particular force-ball happened to hit the top of a six-story building. It was not going very fast—fifteen or twenty miles an hour—but when it struck the roof it did not even slow down. Without any effort at all, apparently, it continued downward through the concrete and steel and glass of the building—and everything in its path became monstrously, sickeningly, revoltingly changed.

"I simply can't stand any more of this," Lola gasped. "If you don't mind, I'm going to go to my room, set all the Gunther blocks it has, and bury my head under a pillow."

"Go ahead, Brownie," James said. "This is too tough for *anybody* to watch. I'd do the same, except I've got to run these cameras."

Lola disappeared.

Garlock and Belle kept on studying. Neither had paid any attention at all to either Lola or James.

Instead of the structural material it had once been, the bore that the thing had traversed was now full of a sparkling, bubbling, writhing, partly-fluid-partly-viscous, obscenely repulsive mass of something unknown and unknowable on Earth—a something which, Garlock now recalled, had been thought of by the Arpalone Inspector as "golop".

As that unstoppable globe descended through office after office, it neither sought out people nor avoided them. Walls, doors, windows, ceilings, floors and rugs, office furniture and office personnel—all alike were absorbed into and made a part of that indescribably horrid brew.

Nor did the track of the globe remain a bore. Instead, it spread. That devil's brew ate into and dissolved everything it touched like a stream of boiling water being poured into a loosely-heaped pile of granulated sugar. By the time the ravening sphere had reached the second floor, the entire roof of the building was gone and the writhing, racing flood of corruption had flowed down the outer walls and across the street, engulfing and transforming sidewalks, people, pavement, poles, wires, automobiles—anything and everything it touched.

The globe went on down, through basement and subbasement, until it reached solid, natural ground. Then, with its top a few inches below the level of natural ground, it came to a full stop and—apparently—did nothing at all. By this time, the ravening flood outside had eaten far into the lower floors of the buildings across the street, as well as along all four sides of the block, and tremendous masses of masonry and steel, their supporting structures devoured, were subsiding, crumbling, and crashing down into the noisome flood of golop—and were being transformed almost as fast as they could fall.

One tremendous mass, weighing hundreds or perhaps thousands of tons, toppled almost as a whole, splashing the stuff in all directions for hundreds of yards. Wherever each splash struck, however, a new center of attack came into being, and the peculiarly disgusting, abhorrent liquidation went on.

"Can you do anything with it, Clee?" Belle demanded.

"Not too much—it's a mess," Garlock replied. "Besides, it wouldn't get us far, I don't think. It'll be more productive to analyze the beams the Arpalones are using to break them up, don't you think?"

Then, for twenty solid minutes, the two Prime Operators worked on those enigmatic beams.

"We can't assemble *that* kind of stuff with our minds," Belle decided then.

"I'll say we can't," Garlock agreed. "Ten megacycles, and cycling only twenty per second." He whistled through his teeth. "My guess is it'd take four months to design and build a generator to put out that kind of stuff. It's worse than our Op field."

"I'm not sure I could *ever* design one," Belle said thoughtfully, "but of course I'm not the engineer you are . . ." Then she could not help adding, ". . . yet."

"No, and you never will be," he said, flatly.

"No? That's what *you* think!" Even in such circumstances as these, Belle Bellamy was eager to carry on her warfare with her Project Chief.

"That's *exactly* what I think—and I'm so close to knowing it for a fact that the difference is indetectible."

Belle managed to restrain an angry outburst; instead, she demanded, "Well, are you just going to sit there and do nothing at all except argue with me?"

"Unless and until I can figure out something effective to do, I'm not going to try to do anything. If you, with your vaunted and flaunted belief in the inherent superiority of the female over the male, can dope out something useful before I do, I'll eat crow and help you do it. As for arguing with you, I'm all done for the moment. Put up or shut up."

Belle gritted her teeth, walked away, and plumped herself down into a chair. She shut her eyes and put every iota of her mind to work on the problem of finding something—*anything*—that could be done to help this doomed world and to show that overbearing jerk of a Garlock that she was a better Operator than he was. Which of the two objectives loomed more important, she herself could not have told.

And Garlock looked around. The air and the sky over the now-vanished city were both clear of Dilipic craft. The surviving Arpalone fighters and other small craft were making no attempt to land, anywhere on the world's surface. Instead, they were flying upward toward, and were being drawn one by one into the bowels of, huge Arpalonian space-fighters. When each such vessel was filled to capacity, it flew upward and set itself into a more or less circular orbit around the planet.

Around and around and around the ruined world the *Pleiades* went . . . recording, observing, charting. Fifty-eight of those atrocious Dilipic vortices had been driven to ground. Every large land-mass surrounded by large bodies of water had been struck once, and only once; from the tremendous area of the largest continent down to the relatively tiny expanses of the largest islands. One land-mass, one vortex. One only.

"What do you suppose *that* means?" James asked. "Afraid of water?"

"Damned if I know. Could be. Let's check . . . mountains, too. Skip us back to where we started—oceans and mountains both fairly close there."

The city had disappeared long since; for hundreds of almost-level square miles there extended a sparkling, seething, writhing expanse of—of what? The edge of that devouring flood had almost reached the foothills, and over that gnawing, dissolving edge the *Pleiades* paused.

Small lakes and ordinary rivers bothered the golop very little if at all. There was perhaps a slightly increased sparkling, a slight stiffening, a little darkening, some freezing and breaking off of solid blocks, but the thing's forward motion was not noticeably slowed down. It drank a fairly large river and a lake one mile wide by ten miles long while the two men watched.

The golop made no attempt to climb either foothills or mountains. It leveled them. It ate into their bases at its own level; the undermined masses, small and large, collapsed into the foul, corrosive semi-liquid and were consumed. Nor was there much raising of the golop's level, even when the highest mountains were reached and miles-high masses of solid rock broke off and toppled. There was *some* raising, of course, but the stuff was fluid enough so that its slope was not apparent to the eye.

Then the *Pleiades* went back, over the place where the city had been and on to what had once been an ocean beach. The original wave of degradation had reached that shore long since, had attacked its sands out into deep water, and there it had been stopped. The corrupt flood was now being reinforced, however, by an ever-rising tide of material that had once been mountains. And the slope, which had not been even noticeable at the mountains or over the plain, was here very evident.

As the rapidly-flowing golop struck water, the water shivered, came to a weirdly unforgettable cold boil, and exploded into drops and streamers and jagged-edged chunks of something that was neither water nor land— nor rock, soil, sand or Satan's unholy brew. Nevertheless, the water won. There was *so* much of it! Each barrel of water that was destroyed was replaced instantly and enthusiastically with no lowering of level or of pressure.

And when water struck the golop, the golop also shivered violently, then sparkled even more violently, then stopped sparkling and turned dark, then froze solid. The frozen surface, however, was neither thick enough nor strong enough to form an effective wall.

Again and again the wave of golop built up high enough

to crack and to shatter that feeble wall; again and again golop and water met in ultimately furious, if insensate, battle. Inch by inch the ocean's shoreline was driven backward toward ocean's depths—but every inch the ocean lost was to its tactical advantage, since the advancing front was by now practically filled with hard, solid, dead blocks of its own substance which it could neither assimilate nor remove from the scene of conflict.

Hence the wall grew ever thicker and more solid, and the advance became slower and slower.

Then, finally, ocean waves of ever-increasing height and violence rolled in against the new-formed shore. What caused those tremendous waves—earthquakes, perhaps, due to the shifting of the mountains masses?—no Tellurian ever knew for sure. Whatever the cause, however, those waves operated to pin the golop down. Whenever and wherever one of those monstrous waves whitecapped in, hurling hundreds of thousands of tons of water inland, the battle-front stabilized then and there.

All over that world the story was the same. Wherever there was water enough, the water won. And the total quantity of water in that world's oceans remained practically unchanged.

"Good! A lot of people escaped," James said, expelling a long-held breath. "Everybody who lives on or could be flown to the smaller islands . . . if they can find enough to eat and if the air isn't poisoned."

"Air's okay—so's the water—and they'll get food, Garlock said. "The Arpalones will handle things, including distribution. What I'm thinking about is how they're going to rehabilitate it. As an engineering project, that's a feat to end all feats."

James nodded vigorous agreement. "Except for the fact that it'll take too many months before they can even start the job, I'd like to stick around and see how they go about it. How does this kind of stuff fit into that theory you're not admitting is a theory?"

"Not worth a damn. However, it's a datum—and, as I've said before and may say again, if we can get *enough* data we can build a theory out of it."

Then it began to rain. For many minutes the clouds had been piling up—black, far-flung, thick and high. Immense bolts of lightning flashed and snapped and crackled; thunder crashed and rolled and rumbled; rain fell, and continued to fall, like a cloudburst. And shortly thereafter —first by square feet and then by acres and then by square miles—the surface of the golop began to die. To die, that is, if it had ever been even partially alive. At least it stopped sparkling, darkened and froze into thick skins . . . which broke up into blocks . . . which in turn sank—thus exposing an ever-renewed surface to the driving, pelting, relentlessly cascading rain.

"Well, I don't know that there's anything to hold us here any longer," Garlock said, finally, "shall we go?"

They went; but it was several days before any of the wanderers really felt like smiling; and Lola did not recover from her depression for over a week.

V

Supper was over, but the four were still at the table, sipping coffee and smoking. During a pause in the casual conversation, James suddenly straightened up.

"I want an official decision, Clee," he said, abruptly. "While we're out of touch with United Worlds you, as captain of the ship and director of the project, are boss—the Lord of Justice, High and Low. The works. Check?"

"On paper, yes—with my decisions subject to appeal and/or review when we get back to Base. In practice, I didn't expect to have to make any very gravid rulings."

"I never thought you'd have to, either, but Belle fed me one with a bone in it, so . . ."

"Just a minute. How official do you want it? Completely formal, screens down and recorded?"

"Not unless we have to. Let's explore it first. As of right now, are we under the Code or not?"

"Of course we are."

"Not necessarily," Belle put in sharply. "Not slavishly to the letter. We're so far away and our chance of getting back is so slight that it should be interpreted in the light of common sense."

Garlock stared at Belle and she stared back, her eyes as clear and innocent as a baby's.

"The Code is neither long enough nor complicated

103

enough to require interpretation," Garlock stated, finally. "It either applies in full and exactly or not at all. It's like being pregnant, Belle—either you are or you aren't."

"The cases aren't comparable," Belle insisted.

"Not precisely, of course, but they *are* analogous. My ruling is that the Code applies, strictly, until I declare the state of Ultimate Contingency. Are you ready, Belle, to abandon the project, find an uninhabited Tellurian world, and begin to populate it?"

"Well, not quite, perhaps."

"Yes or no, please."

"No."

"We are under the Code, then. Go ahead, Jim."

"I broke pairing with Belle and she refused to confirm."

"Certainly I refused. He had no reason to break with me."

"I had plenty of reason!" James snapped. "I'm fed up to here"—he drew his right forefinger across his forehead—"with making so-called love to a woman who can never think of anything except cutting another man's throat."

"You both know that reasons are unnecessary and are not discussed in public," Garlock said flatly. "Now as to confirmation of a break. In simple pairing there is no marriage, no registration, no declaration of intent or of permanence. Thus, legally or logically, there is no obligation. Morally, however, there is always some obligation. Hence, as a matter of urbanity, in cases where no injury exists except as concerns chastity, the Code calls for agreement without rancor. If either party persists in refusal to confirm, and cannot show injury, that party's behavior is declared inurbane. Confirmation is declared and the offending party is ignored."

"Just how would you go about it to ignore Prime Operator Belle Bellamy?"

"You've got a point there, Jim. However, she hasn't persisted very long in her refusal. As a matter of information, Belle, why did you take Jim in the first place?"

"I didn't." She shrugged her shoulders. "It was pure chance. You saw me flip the tenth-piece."

"Am I to ignore the fact that you're one of the best telekineticists living?"

"I don't *have* to control things unless I want to! Can't you conceive of me flipping a coin honestly?"

"No. However, since this is not a screens-down inquiry, I'll give you—orally, at least—the benefit of the doubt. The next step, I presume, is for Lola to break with me. Lola?"

"Well . . . I hate to say this, Clee . . . I thought that mutual consent would be better, but . . ." Lola paused, flushing with embarrassment.

"She feels," James said steadily, "as I do that there should be much more to the sexual relation than merely releasing the biological tensions of two pieces of human machinery."

"I confirm, Lola, of course," Garlock said. Then he went on, partly thinking aloud, partly addressing the group at large. "Ha. Reasons again, and very well put—not off the cuff. Evasions. Flat lies. There's something damned strange here—in sum, indefensible actions based upon unwarranted conclusions drawn from erroneous assumptions. The pattern isn't clear . . . but I won't order screens down until I have to. If the reason had come from Belle . . ."

"*Me?*" Belle flared. "Why from me?"

Ignoring Belle's interruption, Garlock frowned in thought. After a minute or so his face cleared.

"Jim," he said, sharply, "have you been consciously aware of Belle's manipulation?"

"Why, no, of course not. She *couldn't!*"

"Thats *really* a brainstorm, Clee," Belle said. "You'd better turn yourself in for an overhaul."

"Nice scheme, Belle," Garlock said. "I underestimated your power—at least, I didn't consider it carefully enough. And I overestimated your ethics and urbanity."

"What are you talking about?" James asked. "You lost me ten parsecs back."

"Just this. Belle is behind this whole operation, working under a perfectly beautiful smoke-screen."

"I'm afraid the boss is cracking up, kids," Belle said. "Listen to him, if you like, but use your own judgment."

"But nobody could make Jim and me really love each other," Lola argued, "and we really do. It's real love."

"Admitted," Garlock said. "But she could have helped it along—and she's all set to take every possible advantage of the situation thus created."

"I still don't see it," James objected. "Why, she wouldn't even confirm our break. She hasn't yet."

"She would have, at the exactly correct psychological moment; after holding out long enough to put you both under obligation to her. There would have been certain strings attached, too. Her plan was, after switching the pairings—"

"I'd *never* pair with you!" Belle broke in viciously.

"Part of the smoke-screen," Garlock explained. "The re-pairings would give her two lines of attack on me, to be used simultaneously. First, to work on me in bed . . . second, to work on you two, with no holds barred, to form a three-unit team against me. Her charges that I'm losing my grip made a very smart opening lead."

"Do you think I'd *let* her work on me?" James demanded.

"She's a Prime—you wouldn't know anything about it. However, nothing will happen. Nor am I going to let her confuse the real issue. Belle, you are either inside the Code or a free agent outside it. Which?"

"I have made my position clear."

"To me, yes. To Jim and Lola, decidedly unclear."

"Unclear, then. You can *not* coerce me!"

"If you follow the Code, no. If you don't, I can and will. If you make any kind of a pass at Jim from now on, I'll lock you into your room with a Gunther block."

"You wouldn't dare! Besides, you couldn't."

"Don't bet on it," he advised.

After a full minute of silence Garlock's attitude changed suddenly to his usual one of casual friendliness. "Why not let this one drop right here, Belle? I can marry them, with all the official trimmings. Why not let 'em really enjoy their honeymoon?"

"Why not?" Belle's manner changed to match Garlock's and she smiled warmly. "I confirm, Jim. You two are really serious, aren't you? Marriage, declarations, registration, and everything? I wish—I sincerely and really wish you—every happiness possible."

"We really *are* serious," James said, putting his arm around Lola's waist. "And you won't . . . won't interfere?"

"Not a bit. I couldn't, now, even if I wanted to." Belle grinned wryly. "You see, you kids missed the main feature of the show, since you can't know exactly what a Prime Operator is. Especially you can't know what Cleander Simmsworth Garlock really is—he's an out-and-out tiger on wheels. The three of us could have smacked him bow-legged, but of course all chance of that blew up just now. So if you two want to take the big jump you can do it with my blessing as well as Clee's. I'll clear the table."

That small chore taken care of—a quick folding-up of everything into the table-cloth and a heave into the chute did it—Belle set up the recorder.

"Are you both fully certain that you want the full treatment?" Garlock asked.

Both were certain, and Garlock read the brief but solemn marriage lines.

As the newlyweds left the room, Belle turned to Garlock with a quizzical smile. "Are you going to ask me to pair with you, Clee?"

"I certainly am." He grinned back at her. "I owe you that much revenge, at least. But seriously, I'd like it immensely. Look at that mirror—did you ever see a better-matched couple? Will you give me a try, Belle?"

"I will not," she said, emphatically. "I'll take back what I said a while ago—if you were the only man left in the universe, I suppose I *would* pair with you—but as it is, the answer is a definite, resounding, and final 'NO!' "

" 'Definite' and 'resounding,' yes. 'Final,' I won't accept. I'll wait."

"You'll wait a long time then. My door will be locked from now on. Good night, Doctor Garlock; I'm going to bed."

"So am I." He walked with her along the corridor to their rooms, the doors of which were opposite each other. "In view of the Code, locking your door is a meaningless gesture. Mine will remain unlocked. I invite you to come in whenever you like, and assure you formally that no such entry will be regarded as an invasion of privacy."

Without a word she went into her room and closed the

door with a firmness just short of violence. Her lock clicked sharply.

The next morning, after breakfast, James followed Garlock into his room and shut the door.

"Clee, I want to tell you . . . I don't want to get sloppy, but . . ."

"Want to lep it?"

"Hell, no!"

"It's about Brownie, then."

"Yes. I've always liked you immensely. Admired you. Hero, sort of . . ."

"Yeah. I quote. 'Harder than Pharoah's heart.' 'Colder than frozen helium.' 'Ruthless, arrogant, domineering son of a bitch.' "

"Check. And all the others, too. Maybe that's why I've always liked you so much, I don't know. But this thing about Brownie . . ." He paused, then abruptly reached out and shook Garlock's hand firmly. "How could you possibly lay off? Just the strain, if nothing else?"

"A little strain doesn't hurt a man unless he lets it. I've done without for months at a stretch, with it running around loose on all sides of me."

"But she's . . . she's got *everything!*"

"There speaketh the ensorcelled bridegroom. For my taste, she hasn't. She told you, I suppose, when explaining the situation, that I told her she wasn't my type?"

"Yes, but . . ."

"She still isn't. She is one of the two most nearly perfect young women of her race. Her face is beautiful. Her body is an artist's dream. Her mind is one of the very best. Besides all that, she's a damned fine person. But put yourself in my place.

"Here's this paragon we've just described. She had extremely high ideals and she's a virgin, never really aroused.

Also, she's so full of this sickening crap they've been pouring into us—propaganda, rocket-oil, and psychological
gobbledygook—that it's running out of her ears. She's so
stuffed with it that she's going to pair with you, ideals
and virginity be damned, even if it kills her—even though
she's shaking, clear down to her shoes. Also, she is and
always will be scared half to death of you—she thinks
you're some kind of robot. She's a starry-eyed, soft-
headed sissy. A sapadilla. A sucker for a smooth line of
balloon-juice and flapdoodle. No spine; no bottom. Strictly
a pet—you could no more love her, ever, than you could a
half-grown kitten . . ."

"That's a *hell* of a picture!" James broke in savagely.
"Even for such a cold-blooded bastard as you are!"

"People in love can't be objective, is all. If I saw her
through the same set of filters you do, I'd be in love with
her too. So let's see if you can use your brain instead of
your outraged sensibilities to answer a hypothetical question. *If* the foregoing were true, what would *you* do?"

"I'd pass, I guess. I'd have to, if I wanted to look myself in the face in the mirror next morning. But that's such
an *ungodly* cockeyed picture, Clee . . . Still, if that's actually your picture of Brownie, just what kind of a woman
could you love? If any?"

"Belle."

"*Belle?* Belle *Bellamy?* For godsake! That iceberg?
That egomaniac? She's a pure, unalloyed bitch!"

"Right, on all counts. She's also crooked and treacher-
ous. She's a liar by instinct and training. I could add a lot
more. But she's got brains, ability, and guts. She's got the
spine and the bottom and the drive. So just imagine her,
thawed out. Back to back with you when you're surrounded—she wouldn't cave and she wouldn't give. Or
wing and wing—holding the beam come hell or space-

warps. Roll that one around on your tongue, Jim, and give your taste-buds a treat."

"Well, maybe . . . if I've got that much imagination. That's a tough blueprint to read; I can't quite visualize the finished article. However, you're as hard as she is—even harder. You've got more of what it takes. Maybe *you* can make a Christian out of her. If so, you might have something; but I'm damned if I can see exactly what. Whatever it turned out to be, I wouldn't care for any part of if. You could have it all."

"Exactly . . . and you can have Brownie."

"I'm beginning to see. I didn't think you had anything like that in your chilled-steel carcass. And I want to apolo . . ."

"Don't do it. If the time ever comes when *you* go so soft on me as to quit laying it on the line and start sifting out your language . . ." Garlock paused. For one of the very few times in his life, he was at a loss for words. He thrust his hands into his pockets and shrugged his shoulders. "Hell, I don't want to get maudlin, either . . . so . . . well, how many men, do you think, could have gone the route with me on this hellish job without killing me or me killing them?"

"Oh, that's not . . ."

"Lay it on the line, Jim—I know what I am. Only one man could have stood me so well this long. You. One man in six thousand million. Okay—now, how many women could live with me for a year without going crazy?"

"Lots of 'em; but, being masochists, they'd probably drive *you* nuts. And you can't stand 'stupidity'—which, by definition, lets *everybody* out. Nope, it's a tough order to fill."

"Check. She'd have to be strong enough and hard enough not to be afraid of me, by any trace. Able and eager to stand up to me and slug it out. To pin my ears back flat against my skull whenever she thinks I'm off the beam. Do it with skill and precision and nicety, with power and control, yet without doing herself any damage and without changing her basic feeling for me. In short, a female Jim James Nine."

"What? Good God—you think *I'm* like Belle Bellamy?"

"Not by nine thousand megacycles. You're like Belle could be and should be. Like I hope she will be. I'd have to give, too, of course—maybe we can make Christians out of each other. It's quite a dream, I admit, but it'll be Belle or nobody. But I'm not used to slopping over this way—let's go."

"I'm glad you did, Clee—once in a lifetime is good for the soul. I'd say you were in love with her right now —except that if you were, you couldn't possibly dissect her like a specimen on the table, the way you've just been doing. Are you or aren't you?"

"I'll be damned if I know. You and Brownie believe that the poets' concept of love is valid. In fact, you make a case for its validity. I've never believed in it, and don't now . . . but under certain conditions . . . I simply don't know. Ask me again some time say in about a month?"

"That's the surest thing you know. Oh, *brother! This* is a thing I'm going to watch with my eyes out on stalks!"

For the next week, Belle locked her door every night. For another few nights, she did not lock it. Then, one night, she left it ajar. The following evening, the two again walked together to their doors.

"I left my door open last night."

"I know you did."

"Well?"

"And have you scream to high heaven that I opened it? And put me on a tape for wilful inurbanity? For deliberate intersexual invasion of privacy?"

"Blast and damn! You know perfectly well, Clee Garlock, I wouldn't pull such a dirty, lousy trick as that."

"Maybe I should apologize, then, but as a matter of fact I have no idea whatever as to what you wouldn't do." He stared at her, his face hard in thought. "As you probably know, I have had very little to do with women. That little has always been on a logical level. You are such a completely new experience that I can't figure out what makes you tick."

"So you're afraid of me," she said. "Is that it?"

"Close enough."

"And I suppose it's you that cartoonist what's-his-name is using as a model for 'Timorous Timmy'?"

"Since you've guessed it, yes."

"You . . . *weasel!*" She took three quick steps up the corridor, then back. "You say my logic is cockeyed. What system are you using now?"

"I'm trying to develop one to match yours."

"Oh . . . I invited that one, I guess, since I know you aren't afraid of God, man, woman, or devil . . . and you're big enough that you don't have to be proving it all the time." She laughed suddenly, her face softening markedly. "Listen, you big idiot—why don't you ever knock me into an outside loop? If I were you and you were me, I'd've busted me loose from my front teeth long ago."

"Either I know better or I'm afraid to. Anyway, I'm not rocking my boat so far from shore."

"Says you. You're wonderful, Clee—simply priceless. Do you know you're the only man I ever met that I couldn't make fall for me like a rock falling down a cliff? And that the falling is altogether too apt to be the other way?"

"The first, I have suspected. The second is absolute nonsense."

"I *hope* it is . . . I wish I could be as certain of it as you are. You see, Clee, I really expected you to come in, last night, and there really *wasn't* any bone in it. Surely you don't think I'm going to *invite* you into my room, do you?"

"I can't see why not. However, since no valid system of logic seems to apply, I accept your decision as a fact. By the same reasoning—however invalid—if I ask you again you will again refuse. So all that's left, I guess, is for me to drag you into my room by force."

He put his left arm around her and applied a tiny pressure against her side—under which she began to move slowly toward his door.

"You admit that you're using force?" she asked. Her face was unreadable; her mental block was at its fullest force. "That I'm being coerced?"

"Definitely," he agreed. "At least ten dynes of sheer brute force. Not enough to affect a tape, but enough, I hope, to affect you. If it isn't, I'll use more."

"Oh, ten dynes is enough. Just so it's force."

She raised her face toward his and threw both arms around his neck, and Cleander Garlock forgot all about dynes and tapes.

After a time she disengaged one arm, reached out and opened his door. He gathered her up and carried her over the threshold.

A few jumps later they met their first really old Arpalone. This Inspector was so old that his skin, instead of the usual bright, clear cobalt blue, was dull and tending toward gray. The old fellow was strangely garrulous, for a Guardian; he wanted them to pause awhile and gossip.

"Yes, I am lonesome," he admitted. "It has been a long

time since I exchanged thoughts with anyone. You see, no-body has visited this planet—Groobe, its name is—since almost all our humanity was killed, a few periods ago . . ."

"Killed?" Garlock asked sharply. "How? Not Dilipic?"

"Oh, you have seen them? I never have, myself. No, nothing nearly that bad. Merely the Ozobes. The world itself was scarcely harmed at all. Rehabilitation will be a simple matter, so there's no real reason why some of those Engineers . . ."

"The beast!" Lola shot a tight-beam thought at her husband. "Who cares anything about the rock and dirt of a *planet?* It's the *people* that count and his are dead and he's perfectly *complaisant* about it—just *lonesome!*"

"Don't let it throw you, pet," James soothed. "He's an Arpalone, you know, not a sociological anthropologist."

". . . shouldn't come out here and spend a few hours once in a while, but they don't. Too busy with their own business, they say. But while you are physically human, mentally you are not. You're all too . . . too . . . I can't put my thought exactly on it, but . . . more as though you were human fighters, if such a thing could be possible."

"We *are* fighters. Where we come from, most human beings are fighters."

"Oh? I never heard of such a thing. Where can you be from?"

This took much explanation, since the Arpalone had never heard of intergalactic travel. "You are willing, then to fight side by side with us Arpalones against the ene-mies of humanity? You have actually done so, at times, and won?"

"We certainly have."

"I am glad. I am expecting a call for help any time now. Will you please give me enough of your mental pattern, Doctor Garlock, so that I can call you in case of need? Thank you."

"What makes you think you're going to get an S.O.S. so soon? Where from?"

"These Ozobe invasions come in cycles, years apart, but there are always several planets attacked at very nearly the same time. We were the first, this time—so there will be one or two others very shortly."

"Do they always . . . kill all the people?" Lola asked.

"Oh no. Scarcely half of the time. Depends on how many fighters the planet has, and how much outside help can get there soon enough."

"Your call could come from any of the other solar systems in this neighborhood, then?" Garlock asked.

"Yes. There are fifteen inhabited planets within about six light-years of us, and we form a close-knit group."

"What are these Ozobes?"

"Animals. Warm-blooded, but egg-layers, not mammals. Like this—" The Inspector spread in their minds a picture of a creature somewhat like the flying tigers of Hodell, except that the color was black, shading off to iridescent green at the extremities. Also, it was armed with a short and heavy, but very sharp, sting.

"They say that they come from space, but I don't believe it," the old fellow went on. "What would a warm-blood be doing out in space? Besides, they couldn't find anybody to lay their eggs in out there. No, I think they live right here on Groobe somewhere, maybe holed up in caves or something for ten or thirteen years . . . but that wouldn't make sense, either, would it? I just don't know . . ."

Garlock finally broke away from the lonesome Inspector and the *Pleiades* started down.

"That's the most utterly horrible thing I ever heard of

in my life!" Lola burst out. "Like wasps—only worse—
people aren't bugs! Why don't all the planets get together
and develop something to kill every Ozobe in every system of the group?"

"That one has got too many bones in it for me to
answer," James said.

"I'm going to get hold of that Engineer as soon as we
land," Lola said darkly, "and stick a pin into him."

They found the Engineering Office easily enough, in a
snug camp well outside a large city. They grounded the
starship and went out on foot, enjoying contact with solid
ground. The Head Engineer was an Arpalone, too—Engineers were not a separate race, but dwellers on a planet
of extremely high technology—but he did not know anything about space-drives. His specialty was rehabilitation;
he was top boss of a rehab crew . . .

Then Lola pushed Garlock aside and asked her own
questions. Yes, the Ozobes came from space, the Engineers replied. He was sure of it. Yes, they laid eggs in
human bodies. Yes, they probably stayed alive quite
awhile—or might, except for the rehab crew. No, he
didn't *know* what would hatch out—he'd never let one
live that long, but what else *would* hatch except Ozobes?
No, not one; not a single one. If just one ever did, on
any world where he bossed the job, he'd be sent to the
mines for half a year . . .

"Ridiculous!" Lola snapped. "If they *did* come from
space, the adult form would have to be something able
to get back into space, some way or other. *That* is simple, elementary biology. Don't you see that?"

He didn't see it. He didn't care, either. It was none
of his business; he was a rehab man.

Lola ran back to the ship in disgust.

"Something else is even more ridiculous, and *is* your

business," James told the Head Engineer. "Garlock and I are both engineers—top ones. We know definitely that a one-hundred-percent cleanup on such a job as this—millions—simply can't be done. Ever. Under any conditions. Are you lying in your teeth or are you dumb enough to believe it yourself?"

"Neither one," the Engineer insisted stubbornly. "I've wondered, myself, at how I could get them all, but I always do—every time so far. That's why they give me the big job. I'm good at it."

"Oh—Lola's right, Jim," Garlock said. "It's the adult form that hatches—something so different they don't even recognize it. Something able to get into space. Enough survivors to produce the next generation."

"Sure. I'll tell Brownie—she'll be tickled."

"She'll be more than tickled—she'll want to hunt up somebody around here with three brain cells working and give 'em an earful." Then, to the Engineer: "Do you know how they rehab a planet that's been leveled flat by the golop?"

"You've *seen* one? I never have, but of course I've studied it. Slow, but not too difficult. After killing, the stuff weathers down in a few years—wonderful soil it makes, too. What makes it slow is that you have to wait fifty or a hundred years for the mountains to get built up again and for the earthquakes to quit . . ."

"Excuse me, please," Garlock interrupted. "I've got a call—we have to leave, right now."

The call was from the Inspector. The nearest planet, Clamer, was being invaded by the Ozobes and needed all the help it could get.

"Let's go, Jim. Maybe . . ."

"Just a minute!" Lola snapped. She was breathing hard and her eyes were almost shooting sparks as she turned to the old Arpalone and drove a thought so forcibly that he winced.

"Do you so-called 'Guardians of Humanity' give a cockeyed tinker's damn about the humanity you're supposed to be protecting?" she demanded viciously, the thought boring in and twisting. "Or are you just loafing on the job and doing as little as you possibly can without getting fired?"

Belle and Garlock looked at each other and grinned. Jim was surprised and shocked. This woman blowing her top was no Brownie Montandon any of them knew.

The Inspector was not only shocked, but injured and abused. "We do everything we possibly can. If there's any one possible thing we haven't done, even the tiniest . . ."

"There's plenty!" she snapped. "Plain, dumb stupidity, then, it must be. There must be *somebody* around here who has been at least exposed to elementary biology! You should have exterminated these Ozobe vermin ages ago. All you have to do is find out what their life cycle is. How many stages and what they are. How the adults get into space and where they go—" And she went on, in flashing thoughts, to explain in full detail. "Are you smart enough to understand that?"

"Oh, yes. Your thought may be the truth, at that."

"And are you interested enough to find out whose business it would be, and follow through on it?"

"Yes, of course. If it works, I'll be quite famous for suggesting it. I'll give you part of the credit—"

"Keep the credit—just see to it that it gets *done!*" She whirled on James. "This loss of human life is so *appallingly* unnecessary! This time we're going to Clamer, and nowhere else. Push the button, Jim."

"All I can do is set up for it, Brownie. Whether we . . ."

"We'll get there!" she blazed. "It's high time we got a break. *Punch* it! *This* time the ship's going to *Clamer,* if we all have to get out and *push* it there!"

James pushed the button, glanced into his scanner, and froze, eyes staring. They were in the same galaxy!

All three had studied charts of nebular configurations so long and so intensely that recognition of a full-sphere identity was automatic and instantaneous.

Lola, head buried in the scanner, had already checked in with the Port Inspector.

It *is* Clamer!" she shrieked aloud. "I told you it was time for our luck to change, if we pulled hard enough! They're being invaded by Ozobes and they did call for help and they didn't think we could possibly get here this fast and we don't need to be inspected because we're compatible or we couldn't have landed on Groobe!"

For five long minutes Garlock held the starship motionless while he studied the entire situation. Then he drove a probe through the mental shield of the general in charge of the whole defense operation.

"Battle-Cruiser *Pleiades,* Captain Garlock commanding, reporting for duty in response to your S.O.S. received on Groobe.

The Arpalone general, furiously busy as he was, dropped all other business. "But you're *human! You* can't fight!"

"Watch us. You don't know, apparently, that the Ozobe bases are on the far side of your moon. They're bringing their fighters in most of the way in transports."

"Why, they can't be! They're coming in from all directions from deep space!"

"That's what they want you to think. They're built to stand many hours of zero pressure and almost absolute zero cold. Question: if we destroy all their transport, say

120

in three hours, can you handle all the fighters who will be in the air or in nearby space at that time?"

"Very easily. They've hardly started yet. I appoint you Admiral-Pro-Tem Garlock, in command of Space Operations, and will refer to you any other space-fighters who may come, I thank you, sir. Good luck."

The general returned his attention to his boiling office. His mind was seething with questions as to what these not-human beings were, how or if they knew so much, and so on; but he forced them out of his mind and went, quickly and efficiently, back to work. James shot the *Pleiades* up to within about a thousand miles of the moon.

"How long does it take to learn this bombing business, Jim?" Lola asked.

"About fifteen seconds. All you have to do is *want* to. Do you, really?"

"I really do. If I don't do something to help these people. I'll never forgive myself."

James showed her—and, much to her surprise, she found it very easy to do.

The vessels transporting the invading forces were huge, spherical shells equipped with short-range drives—and with nothing else. No accommodations, no facilities, no food, no water, not even any air. Each transport, when filled to the bursting-point with as-yet-docile cargo, darted away, swinging around to approach Clamer from some previously-assigned direction. It did not, however, approach the planet's surface. At about two thousand miles out, great ports opened and the load was dumped out into space, to fall the rest of the way by gravity. Then the empty shell, with only its one pilot aboard, rushed back for another load.

"How heavy shots, Clee?" James asked. He and Lola were getting into their scanners. "Wouldn't take as much as a kiloton equivalent, should it?"

"Half a kilo is plenty, but no use being too fussy about precision out here."

Garlock and Belle were already bombing; James and Lola began. Slow and awkward at first, Lola soon picked up the technique and was firing blast for blast with the others. No more loaded transport vessels left the moon. No empty one, returning toward the moon, reached there. In much less than the three hours Garlock had mentioned, every Ozobian transport craft had been destroyed.

"And now the real job begins," Garlock said, as James dropped the starship down to within a few miles of the moon's surface.

That surface was cratered and jagged, exactly like that of the half always facing Clamer. No sign of activity could be seen by eye, nor anything unusual. Even the immense trapdoors, all closed now, matched exactly their surroundings. Underground, however, activity was violently intense —and, now, confused in the extreme.

"Why, there isn't a single adult anywhere!" Lola exclaimed. "I thought the whole place would be full of 'em!"

"So did I," Belle said. "However, with hindsight, it's plain enough. Their job was done, so they were killed and eaten. Last meal, perhaps."

"I'm afraid so. Whatever they were, they had hands and brains. Just look at those shops and machines!"

"What do we do, Clee?" James asked. "Run a search pattern first?"

"We'll have to, I guess, before we can lay the job out."

It was run and Garlock frowned in thought. "Almost half the moon covered—honeycombed. We'll have to fine-tooth it. Around the periphery first, then spiral in to the center. This moon isn't very big, but even so this is going to be a hell of a long job. Any suggestions, anybody? Jim?"

"The only way, I guess. You can't do it hit-or-miss. I'm damn glad we've got plenty of stuff in our Op field and plenty of hydride for the engines. The horses will all know they've been at work before they get the field filled up again."

"So will you, Junior, believe me . . . Ready, all? Start blasting."

Then, for three hours, the *Pleiades* moved slowly—for her—along a plotted and automatically-controlled course. It was very easy to tell where she had been; the sharply-cut, evenly-spaced, symmetrical pits left by the Galaxians' full-conversion blasts were entirely different from the irregularly-cratered, ages-old original surface.

"Knock off, Brownie," Garlock said then. "Go eat all you can hold and get some sleep. Come back in three hours. Jim, cut our speed to seventy-five percent."

Lola shed her scanner, heaved a tremendous sigh of relief, and disappeared.

Three silent hours later—all three hours were too intensely busy to think of anything except the work in hand —Lola came back.

"Take Belle's swath, Brownie. Okay, Belle, you can lay off. Three hours."

"I'll stay," Belle declared. "Go yourself; or send Jim."

"Don't be any more of a damn fool than you have to. I said beat it."

"And I said I wouldn't. I'm just as good—"

"Chop it off!" Garlock snapped. "It isn't a case of being just as good as. It's a matter of physical reserves. Jim and I have more to draw on for the long shifts than you have. So get the hell out of here or I'll stop the ship and slap you even sillier than you are now."

Belle threw up her head, tossing her shoulder-length green mop in her characteristic gesture of defiance; but after holding Garlock's hard stare for a moment she relaxed and smiled.

"Okay, Clee—and thanks for the kind words."

She disappeared and the work went on.

And finally, when all four were so groggy that they could scarcely think, the job was done and checked. Clamer's moon was as devoid of life as any moon had ever been.

Lola pitched her scanner at its rack and threw herself face-down on a davenport, sobbing uncontrollably. James sat down beside her and soothed her until she quieted down.

"You'd better eat something, dear, and then get a good, long sleep."

"Eat? Why, I couldn't, Jim, not possibly."

"Let her sleep first, I think, Jim," Belle said, and followed with her eyes as Jim picked his wife up and carried her into the corridor.

"We'd better eat *something,* I suppose," Belle said thoughtfully. "I don't feel like eating, either, but I hadn't realized until this minute just how much this had taken out of me, and I'd better start putting it back in . . . She did a wonderful job, Clee, even if she couldn't take it full shift toward the last."

"I'll say she did. I hated like the devil to let her work that way, but . . . you knew I was scared witless every second until we topped off."

Exhausted and haggard as she was, Belle laughed. "I know damn-blasted well you weren't; but I know what you mean. Fighting something you don't know anything about, and can't guess what may happen next, is tough.

Seconds count." Side by side, they strolled toward the alcove.

"I simply didn't think she had it in her," Belle marveled.

"She didn't. She hasn't. It'll take her a week to get back into shape."

"Right. She was going on pure nerve at the last, nothing else . . . but she did a job, and she's so sweet and fine . . . I wonder, Clee if . . . if I've been missing the boat . . ."

"You have *not*." Garlock sent the thought so solidly that Belle jumped. "If you'd just let yourself be, you'd be worth a million of her, just as you stand."

"Oh? You lie in your teeth, Cleander, but I love it. . . . Oh, I don't know what I want to eat—if anything."

"I'll think up yours, too, along with mine."

"Please. Something light, and just a little."

"Yeah. Sit down. Just a light snack—a two-pound steak, rare; a bowl of mushrooms fried in butter; french fries, french dips, salad, and a quart of coffee. The same for me, except more of each. Here we are."

"Why, Clee, I couldn't *possibly* eat half of that . . ." But after a quarter of it was gone, she admitted, "I *am* hungry, at that—simply ravenous."

"That's what I thought. I knew I could, and figured you accordingly."

They ate their meals slowly, enjoying every bite and sip, chatting on a wide variety of subjects as they ate. Neither was aware of the fact that this was the first time they had ever been on really friendly terms, even in bed. And finally every dish and container was empty, almost polished clean.

"One hundred percent capacity—I can still chew, but I can't swallow," Garlock said then, lighting two cigarettes and giving Belle one. "How's that for a masterly job of calibration?"

Belle nodded. "Your ability to estimate the exact capacity of containers is exceeded only by your good looks and by the size of your feet. And now to get some sleep for an indefinite but very long period of time."

Still eminently friendly, the two walked together to their doors. Belle put up a solid block and paused, irresolute, twisting the toe of one slipper into the carpet.

"Clee, I . . . I wonder if . . . " He voice died away.

"I know what you mean." He put his arms around her gently, tenderly, and looked full into her eyes. "I want to tell you something, Belle. You're a woman, not in seven thousand million women, but in that many *planets* full of women. What it takes, you very definitely and very abundantly have got. And you aren't the only one who's tired. I don't need company tonight, either. I'm going to sleep until I wake up, if it takes all day. Or say, if you wake up first, why not punch me and we'll have breakfast together?"

"That's a thought. Do the same for me. Good night, Clee."

"Good night, Belle." He kissed her, as gently as he had been holding her, opened her door, closed it after her, and stepped across the corridor into his own room.

"*What* a man!" Belle breathed to herself, behind the solid screens of her room. "He thought I was too tired, not just scared to death too. What a *man!* Belle Bellamy, you ought to be kicked from here to Tellus . . ." Then she threw back her head, drove a hard little fist into a pillow, and spoke aloud through clenched teeth, "*No,* damn it, I *won't* give in. I *won't* love him. I'll take the project away from him if it's the last thing I ever do in this life!"

She woke up the next day a little before Garlock did,

but not much. When she went into his room he was shaved and fully dressed except for one shoe, which he was putting on.

"Hi, boss! Better we eat, huh? Not only because I'm starving by inches, but if we don't eat pretty quick we'll get only one meal today instead of three. Did you eat your candy bar?"

"Damned right."

She smiled. "In that case, you can kiss me."

He did, still tenderly, and they strolled to and through the Main and into the alcove. James and Lola, the latter looking terribly strained and worn, had already eaten, but joined them in their after-breakfast coffee and cigarettes.

"You've checked, of course," Garlock said. "Everything all right?"

"Absolutely. Even to Lola and her biologists. Everybody's full of joy and gratitude and stuff—as well as information. And we managed to pry ourselves loose without taking up you two trumpet-of-doom sleepers. So we're ready to jump again. I wonder where in *hell* we'll wind up *this* time."

"I'm glad you said that, Jim," Garlock said. "It gives me the nerve to spring a thing on you that I've been mulling around in my mind ever since we landed here."

"Nerve? You?" James asked, incredulously. "Pass the coffee-pot around again, Brownie. If that character there said what I heard him say, this'll make your hair stand straight up on end."

"On our jumps we've had altogether too much power and no control whatever. Consider three things. First, as you all know, I've been trying to figure out a generator that would give us intrinsic control, but I haven't got any farther with it than we did back on Tellus. Second, consider all the jumps we've made except this last one. Every time we've taken off, none of us has had his shield really up. You, Jim, were concentrating on the drive, and so were wide open to it. The rest of us were at least thinking about it, and so were more or less open to it. Not one of us has ever ordered it to take us to any definite place; in fact, I don't believe that any one of us has ever even suggested a destination.

"Third, consider this last jump all by itself. It's the first time we've ever stayed in the same galaxy. It's the first time we've ever gone where we wanted to. And it's the first time—here's the crux—that any of us has been concentrating on any destination at the moment of firing the charge. Brownie was willing the *Pleiades* to this planet so hard that we could all taste it. The rest of us, if not really pushing to get here, were at least not opposed to the idea."

"Are you saying the damn thing's *alive*?" James asked.

"No. I'm saying I don't believe in miracles. I don't believe in coincidence—that concept is as meaningless as that of paradox. I certainly do not believe that we hit this planet by chance against odds of almost infinity to one. So I've been looking for a reason. I found one. It goes against the grain—against everything I've ever believed—but, since it's the only possible explanation, it must be true. The only possible director of the Gunther Drive *must* be the mind."

"Damn it, now you *are* saying that the thing's alive."

"Far from it. It's Brownie who's alive. It was Brownie who got us here. Nothing else—repeat, *nothing* else—makes sense."

James pondered for a full minute. "I wouldn't buy it except for one thing. If you, the hardest-boiled skeptic that ever went unhung, can feed yourself the whole bowl of such a mess as that, I can at least take a taste of it. So go on."

"Okay. You know that we don't know anything really fundamental about either teleportation or the drive. I'm sure now that the drive is simply mechanical teleportation. If you tried to 'port yourself without any idea of where you wanted to go, where do you think you'd land?"

"You might scatter yourself all over space—no, you wouldn't. You wouldn't move, because it wouldn't be teleportation at all. Destination is an integral part of the concept."

"Exactly so—but only because you've been conditioned to it all your life. This thing hasn't been conditioned to anything."

"Like a new-born baby," Lola suggested.

"Life again," James said. "I can't see it—pure luck, even at those odds, makes a lot more sense."

"And to make matters worse," Garlock went on as though neither of them had spoken, "just suppose that a man had four minds instead of one and they weren't working together. Then where would he go?"

This time, James simply whistled; the girls stared, speechless.

"I think we've proved that my school of mathematics was right—the thing was built to operate purely at random. Fotheringham was wrong. However, I missed the point that if control is possible, the controller must be a mind. The idea never occurred to me or anyone working with me. Nor to Fotheringham or anybody else."

"I can't say I'm sold, but it's easy to test and the results can't be any worse. Let's go."

"How would you test it?"

"Same way you would. Only way. First, each one of us alone. Then pairs and threes. Then all four together. Fifteen tests in all. No. Three destinations for each setup—near, medium, and far. Except Tellus, of course; we'd better save that shot until we learn all we can find out. Anybody not in the set should screen up as solidly as he can set his block—eyes shut, even, and concentrating on something else. Check?"

James did not express the thought that Tellus must by now be so far away that no possible effort could reach it; but the thought was nagging at everyone's minds anyway.

"Check. I'll concentrate on a series of transfinite numbers. Belle, you work on the possible number of shades of the color green. Lola, how many different perfumes you can identify by smell? Jim, hit the button."

VI

THE TESTS took much time, and were strictly routine in nature. At ther conclusion, Garlock said:

"First: either Jim alone, or Lola alone, or Jim and Lola together, can hit any destination within any galaxy, but can't go from one galaxy to another.

"Second: either Belle or I, or any combination containing either of us without the other, has no control at all.

"Third: Belle and I together, or any combination containing both of us, can go intergalactic with full control.

"In spite of confession supposedly being good for the soul, I don't like to admit that we've messed things up—do you, Belle?" Garlock's smile was both rueful and forced.

"Not one bit." Belle licked her lips; for the first time since boarding the starship she was acutely embarrassed. "We'll have to admit it, of course. It was all my fault—and it makes me look like a damned stupid juvenile."

"Not at all, since neither of us had any idea. I'll be glad to settle for half the blame."

"Will you please stop talking Sanskrit?" James asked.

"Or lep it, so we two innocent bystanders can understand it?"

"Will do," said Garlock, and he went on in thought: "Remember what I said about this drive not being conditioned to anything? I was wrong. Belle and I have conditioned it, but badly. We've been fighting so much that something or other in that mess down there has become conditioned to her, something else to me. My part will play along with anyone except Belle; hers with anybody except me. Anti-conditioning, you might call it. Anyway, they lay back their ears and balk."

"Oh, hell!" James snorted. "Talk about gobbledegook! You're still saying that that conglomeration of copper and silver and steel and insulation that we built ourselves has got intelligence, and I still don't buy it."

"By no means. Remember, Jim, that both the concept of mechanical teleportation, and that the mind is the only possible controller, are absolutely new. We've got to throw out all previous ideas and start new from scratch. I postulate, as a working hypothesis drawn from original data as modified by these tests, that that particular conglomeration of materials generates at least two fields about the properties of which we know nothing at all. That one of those properties is the tendency to become preferentially resonant with one mind and preferentially non-resonant with another. Clear so far?"

"Dimly." James scowled in thought. "However, it's no harder to swallow than Sanderson's Theory of Teleportation. Or, for that matter, the actual basic coupling between mind and ordinary muscular action. Does that mean we'll have to rebuild half a million credits' worth of . . . no, you and Belle can work it, together."

"I don't know." Garlock paced the floor. "I simply can't see any *possible* mechanism of coupling."

"Subconscious, perhaps," Belle suggested.

"For my money that whole concept is invalid," Garlock said. "It merely changes 'I don't know' to 'I *can't* know,' and I don't want any part of that. However, 'unconscious' could be the answer, and if so, we may have a lever. Belle, are you willing to bury your hatchet for about five minutes—work with me like a partner ought to?"

"I certainly am, Clee. Honestly. Screens down flat, if you say so."

"Halfway's enough, I think—we'll know when we get down there." Her mind joined his and he went on, "Ignore the machines themselves completely. Consider only the fields. Feel around with me—keep tuned!—see if there's anything at all here that we can grab hold of and manipulate, like an Op field except probably very much finer. I'll be completely damned if I can see how this type of Gunther generator can put out a manipulable field, but it must. That's the only—AAAIIII!"

The last was a yell of pure mental agony. Both hands flew to his head, his face turned white, sweat poured, and he slumped down unconscious.

He came to, however, as the other three were stretching him out on a davenport. Belle was mopping his face with a handkerchief.

"What happened, Clee?"

"I found my manipulable field, but a bomb went off in my brain when I straightened it out." He searched his mind anxiously, then smiled. "But no damage done—just the opposite. It opened up a Gunther cell I didn't know I had. Didn't it sock you, too, Belle?"

"No," she said, more than half bitterly. "I must not have one. That makes you a super-Prime, if I may name a new classification."

"Nonsense! Of course you've got it. Unconscious, of

course, like me, but without it you couldn't have conditioned the field. But why——oh, what bit me must have been the one conditioned to me."

"Oh, nice!" Belle exclaimed. "Come on, Clee, let's go get mine!"

"Do you want a bit of knowledge *that* badly, Belle?" Lola asked. "Besides, wait, he isn't strong enough yet."

"Of course he's strong enough. A little knock like that? *Want* it! I'd give my right leg and . . . and almost *anything* for it. It didn't kill him, so it won't kill me."

"There may be an easier way," Garlock said. "I wouldn't wish a jolt like that onto my worst enemy. But that had two hundred kilovolts and four hundred kilogunts behind it. Since I know now where and what the cell is, I think I can connect it up for you without being quite so rough."

"Oh, lovely——come in, quick!"

Garlock went in, and wrought. It took longer——half an hour, in fact——but it was very much easier to take. "What did it feel like, Belle?" Lola asked eagerly. "You winced like he was drilling teeth and struck a couple of nerves."

"No. It was more like being stretched all out of shape. Like having a child, maybe, in a small way. Let's go, Clee!"

They joined up and went. And they got what they were after.

Breaking connection, Belle said, "Thanks a million, Clee; you're tall, solid gold. Do you want to run some more tests, to see which of us is the intergalactic transporter?"

"Not unless you do."

"Who, me? I'll be tickled to death not to. Back to Tellus, then?"

"Tellus, here we come," Garlock said. "Jim, what are

134

the Tellurian figures for exactly five hundred miles up?"

"I'll punch 'em—got 'em in my head." James did so. "Shall Brownie and I set our blocks?"

"No," Belle said. "Nothing can interfere with us now."

"Ready." Garlock sat down in the pilots seat. "Cluster 'round, Belle."

Belle leaned against the back of the seat and put both arms around Garlock's neck. "I'm clustered."

"The spot we're shooting at is exactly over the precise center of the middle blast-pit at Port Gunther. In sync?"

"I'm *exactly* on and locked. Shoot."

"Now, you sheet-iron bucket of nuts and bolts, JUMP!" said Garlock, and snapped the red switch.

Earth lay beneath them. So did Port Gunther.

"Whew!" Garlock's huge sigh held much more of relief than of triumph.

"They did it! We're home!" Lola shrieked; and, breaking into unashamed and unrestrained tears, went into her husband's extended arms.

"Cry ahead, sweet," James said. Then, extending his right hand to Garlock and to Belle: "I was scared to death you couldn't make it except by backtracking. Good going, you two Primes." But his thoughts said vastly more than his words.

Belle's eyes, too, were wet. She looked at Clee and said, "Judging from that sigh of yours, you weren't as sure as you looked, that we could do it the hard way. I was a quivering mass of jelly inside, myself."

"Afterward, you mean. You were solid as Gibralter when I fired the charge. You're the kind of woman a man wants with him when the going's tough. Slide around here a little, so I can get hold of you."

Garlock released Belle—finally—and turned to the pilot, who was just pulling a data-sheet from the computer.

"How far did we miss target, Jim?"

James held up his right hand, thumb and forefinger forming a circle. "You're one point eight seven inches high, and off-center point five three inches to the north northeast by east. I hereby award each of you the bronze medal of Marksman First. Shall I take her down now or do you want to check in from here first?"

"Neither . . . I think. What do *you* say, Belle?"

"Right. Not until you-know-what."

"Check. Until we decide whether or not to let them know just yet that we can handle the ship—and, if we do, how many of our taped reports we turn in and how many we toss down the chute."

"I get it!" James exclaimed, with a spreading grin. "*That,* my dear people, is something I never expected to live long enough to see—our straightlaced Doctor Garlock applying the Bugger Factor to a research problem!"

"I prefer the term 'Monk's Coefficient,' myself," Garlock said, "from the standpoint of mathematical rigor."

"At Polytech we called it 'Finagle's Formula,'" Belle commented. "The most widely applicable operator known."

"Have you three lost your minds?" Lola demanded. "That's nothing to joke about—you wouldn't destroy official reports! All that astronomy and anthropology that nobody ever even dreamed of before? You *couldn't!* Not *possibly!*"

"Each of us knows just as well as you do how much data we have, exactly how new and startling it is; but we've thought ahead farther than you have. None of us likes the idea of destroying it a bit more than you do. We won't, either, without your full, unreserved, whole-hearted consent; nor without your fixed, ironclad, unshakeable determination never to reveal any least bit of it." Garlock's voice was hard and cold.

"That language is far too strong for me. I'd like to be able to go along with you, but on those terms I simply can't."

"I think you can, when you've thought it through. You've met Alonzo P. Ferber, haven't you? Read him?"

"One glimpse; that was all I could stand. He pawed me mentally and wanted to paw me physically, the very first time I ever met him."

"Check. So I'm going to ask you two questions, which you may answer as an anthropologist, as Lola Montandon, as Mrs. James James James the Ninth, as a member of our team, or as any other character you choose to assume. Remembering that Ferber's a Gunther First—and pretends to be an Operator whenever he can get away with it— should he, or anyone like him, *ever* be allowed to visit Hodell? Second question: if there is any possible way for him to get there, can he be made to stay away?"

"Oh . . . Grand Lady Neldine and that perfectly stunning Grand Lady Lemphi they picked out for Jim . . . they're such *nice* people . . . and the Gunther genes . . ." As Lola thought on, her expressive face showed a variety of conflicting emotions before it hardened into decision. "The only possible answer to both questions is no. I subscribe —on the exact terms you stipulated. And you don't believe, Clee, that my thesis had anything to do with my holding out at first?"

"Certainly I don't. Besides . . ."

"What thesis?" Belle asked.

"For my Ph.D. in anthropology. I thought I had it made, but it just went down the chute. And I don't know if any of you realize just how nearly impossible it is to make a really worthwhile original contribution to science in that field."

"As I started to tell you, Brownie," Garlock said, "I don't think you've lost a thing. There's a bigger and better one coming up."

"*What?*"

"He's got a theory," Belle explained. "It's such a weirdie that he won't talk about it to anybody."

"It isn't a theory yet—at least, not ripe enough to pick —but it's something more than a hunch," Garlock said.

"But what could *possibly* make as good a thesis as those extra-galactic tapes?" Lola wailed. "They would have made it a summer breeze."

"More like a hurricane—the hottest thing since doctorate disputations first started," Garlock said. "However, as I started to say twice before, it still will be. Intra-galactic tapes will be just as good. In this case, better."

"W-e-l-l . . . possibly. But we don't have any."

"That's what this conference is about. We can't destroy the stuff we have unless we can replace it with something better. My idea is that we should visit a few—say fifty— Tellus-type planets in this galaxy; the ones closest to Tellus. I'm pretty sure they'll be inhabited by *Homo Sapiens*. There's a chance, of course, that they'll be like Hodell and the others we've seen; in which case I don't see how we can keep Gunther genes confined to Earth. However, I'm pretty sure in my own mind that we'll find them all very much like Tellus, Gunther and all. What would you think of *that* for a thesis, Lola?"

"Oh, wonderful!"

"Okay. Now to get back to whether we want to check in or not. I don't like to duck out without letting them know we can handle this heap—after a fashion, that is; they don't need to know we can *really* handle it—but we've got nothing we can report and Fatso will blow his stack—Oh-oh! Should've remembered Tellus isn't Hodell;

the tri-di's setting up! Belle, you take it. She'd give me Fatso, because he wants to chew me out, but she won't put him on for you. Cut her throat, but good! Brownie, hide somewhere! Jim, set up for Beta Centauri—not Alpha, but Beta—and fast! Give her hell, Belle!" Garlock sent his last thought from behind a davenport, from which hiding-place he could see the tri-di screen and both Belle and James; but anyone on the screen could not see him.

Miss Foster's likeness appeared upon the screen. Chancellor Ferber's secretary was a big woman, but not fat; middle-aged, gray-haired, wearing consciously the aura and the domineering, overbearing expression of a woman who has great power and an even greater drive to exert her authority.

"Why haven't you reported in?" Miss Foster snapped, with a glare that was pure frost. "You arrived thirteen minutes ago. Such delay is inexcusable. Get Garlock."

"Captain Garlock is off-watch; asleep. I, Commander Bellamy, am in charge." Standing stiffly at attention, Belle paused to exchange glares with the woman across the big desk. If Miss Foster's was frost, Commander Bellamy's was helium ice.

"Ready to roll, Jim?" Belle flashed the thought.

"Half a minute yet."

"Any time after I sign off. Pick your own spot." Then aloud on the screen: "I will report to Chancellor Ferber. I will not report to Chancellor Ferber's secretary."

"Doctor James!" Miss Foster's voice was neither as cold nor as steady as it had been. "Bring that ship down at once!"

James made no sign that he had heard the order. Belle stood changelessly stiff. She had not for an instant taken her coldly competent eyes from those of the woman on the ground. Her emotionless, ultra-refrigerated voice went, as ever, directly into the screen.

"I trust that this conversation is being recorded?"

"It certainly is!"

"Good. I want it on record that we, the personnel of the starship *Pleiades,* are not subject to the verbal orders of the Chancellor's secretary. You will now connect me with Chancellor Ferber, please."

"The Chancellor is in conference and is not to be disturbed. I *have* authority to act for him. You will report to me, and do it *right now!*" Foster's voice rose almost to a scream.

"That ground has been covered. Since you have taken it upon yourself to exceed your authority to such an extent as to refuse to connect the officer in command of the *Pleiades* with the Chancellor, I can not report to him either the reasons why we are not landing at this time nor when we expect to return to Tellus. You are advised that we may leave at any instant, just like *that!*" Belle snapped her finger under the imaged nose. "You may inform the Chancellor, or not inform him if you prefer, that our control of the starship *Pleiades* is something less than perfect, I do not know exactly how many seconds longer we will be here. Commander Bellamy signing off. Over and out."

"*Commander* Bellamy, indeed!" Miss Foster was screaming now, in thwarted fury. "You're no more a commander than my lowest office-girl is! Just wait till you get down here, you green-haired—" The set went instantaneously from full volume to zero sound as James drove the red button home.

"Belle, you honey!" Garlock scrambled out from behind the davenport, seized her around the waist, and swung her, feet high in the air, through four full circles before he let her down and kissed her vigorously. "You were *great!* You're the first living human being ever to pull Foster's cork!"

Belle was, however, unusually diffident. "I stuck my neck out a mile—worse, I stuck Clee's out too. I'm sorry, Clee. I had to have some weight to throw around, and I had only a second to think, and that was the first thing that came to me—and after half a minute she made me so *damn* mad that I went entirely too far."

"No . . . just far enough. That was a *perfect* job."

"But she'll never forget that. She knows I'm not a commander. I can laugh at her, of course, but she'll crucify you as soon as we land."

"She just thinks you aren't a commander. The official log will show, though, that after only one day out I discovered that we should all be officers—one captain and three commanders—with pay and perquisites of rank. I'll think up good and sufficient reasons for it between now and the time when I make up the log."

"But you can't! Or can you, really?"

"Well, nobody told me I couldn't, so I'm going to assume the right. Besides, you didn't tell her commander of what, so I'll make it stick, too—see if I don't. Or else I'll tear two or three offices apart finding out why I can't."

"All that may not be necessary," Lola said. "That tape will never be heard. I'll bet she's erased it already."

"Perhaps; but ours isn't going to be erased—it will be heard exactly where it will do the most good."

"I'm awfully glad you don't think we're on the hook. All that's left, then, is that second-in-command business. Both of you know, of course, that that was just window-dressing."

"You were telling the truth and didn't know it," James said, cheerfully. "You've actually been second in command ever since the drive tests."

"I haven't, and I won't. Surely you don't think I'm enough of a heel, Jim, to step on your toes like that?"

"Nothing like that involved. You tell her, Clee."

"Gunther ability is what counts. You're a Prime, Jim's an Operator; so, now that we can handle the heap, you'll have to be second in command whether you like it or not. And any time you can out-Gunther me we'll trade places; and you won't have to take the job away from me— I'll give it to you."

"But . . . no hard feelings, Jim? No reservations? Screens down?"

"None whatever. In fact, I'm relieved. I'm Gunthered for this board here—for that one I'm not. Come in and look; and shake on it."

She looked; and, while they were shaking hands, she flashed a thought at Lola: "Do you know that we've got two of the finest men that ever lived?"

"I've known that for a long time," Lola flashed back, "but you've hardly started to realize what they *really* are."

"Well, shall we start earning our pay and perquisites by getting to work on this planet, which we haven't even looked—wait a minute! We're just about to open up the galaxy, aren't we?"

They were.

"Then there'll have to be some kind of a unifying and correlating authority—a Galactic Council or something— and the quicker it's set up the better, the less confusion and turmoil and jockeying-for-position here'll be. Question: should this authority be political?"

"It should *not!*" James declared. "It takes United Worlds seven solid days of debate to decide whether or not to buy one lead pencil."

"Military—or naval, I suppose it'd be—that's what Clee's driving at," Belle said. "You're priceless, Clee. We're officers of the brand-new Galactic Navy. Subject to civilian control, of course, but the civilians will be the United Galaxian Societies of the Galaxy, and nobody else. *Beautiful,* Clee! There are ten Operators, Jim. Right?"

"Check. Brownie and I are here; the other eight are running the Galaxian Society under Clee. And the whole Society eats right out of his hands."

"I don't know about that, but Belle and I together could swing it, I think," Garlock said.

"I'll say we could!" Belle laughed. "And I simply can't wait to see you kick Fatso's teeth in with *this* one!"

"I don't like the word 'Navy,' " Garlock said. "It's tied definitely to warfare. How about calling it the 'Galactic Service'? Applicable to either war or peace. Brass hats will think of us in terms of war, even though we'll actually work for peace. Any objections?"

There were no objections.

"About the uniforms," Lola said eagerly. "Space-black and star-white, with chromium comets and things on the shoulders . . ."

"To hell with uniforms," Garlock broke in. "Why do women have to go off the deep end on clothes?"

"No, she's right, Clee," James said. "Without a uniform you won't get off the ground, not even with the Society. And you'll be talking to Top Planetary Brass. Also, they're Gunthered plenty—you can feel their OP field clear out here."

"Could be," Garlock conceded. "Okay, you girls dope it out to suit yourselves. But do you think you can stand it, Belle, to wear more than twelve square inches of clothes?"

"Wait till you see it, friend. I've been designing a uniform for myself for positively *years*."

"I can't wait. And you're a captain, of course."

"What? You can't have two cap ... oh, I see. Primes. I appreciate that, Clee. Thanks."

"Hold on, both of you," James said. "You haven't thought this through far enough. Suppose we meet forces already organized? Better start high than low. You've got to be top admiral, Clee."

"Like hell! Suppose we don't find anything at all?"

"You're right, Jim," Belle said. "Clee you talk like a man with a paper nose. It's *you* who's been yowling for two solid years about being ready for anything."

"Correction accepted. Brief me."

"Ranks should be different from those of United Worlds. They should be descriptive, but impressive. Tops could be Galactic Admiral. That's you. Vice Galactic Admiral —me ..."

"Galactic Vice Admiral would be better," Lola said.

"Accepted. Those two we'll make stick come hell or spacewarps. Right?"

Garlock did not reply immediately. "Up to either one of two points," he agreed, finally.

"What points?"

"War, or being out-Gunthered. Top Gunther takes top place—man, woman, bird, beast, fish, or bug-eyed-monster."

"Oh." Belle was staggered for a moment. "No war of course. As to the other . . . I hadn't thought of that."

"There are a lot of things none of us had thought of, but as amended I'll buy it."

"Then several Regional Admirals, each with his Regional Vice Admiral. Then System Admirals and Vices; and World or Planetary—naming the planet, you know—Admirals and Vices. Let the various Galaxian Societies take over from there down. How do you like that?"

"Nice. And formal address, intra-ship, will be Mister and Miss. Jim and Brownie?"

They liked it. "Where do we fit in?" James asked.

"Pick your own spots," Garlock said.

"If we stick to the Solar System we aren't so apt to get bumped by Primes. So you can make me Solar System Admiral and Brownie my Vice."

"Okay. How long will it take you, Belle, to materialize those uniforms?"

"Fifteen seconds longer than it takes the converter to scan us. Lola's color scheme is right, and I've got everything else down to the last curlicue of chrome. Let's go."

They went; and came back into the Main in uniform.

That of the men, while something on the spectacular side, was more or less conventional, with stiff-visored, screened, heavily-chromed caps—but the *women's* uniforms! Slippers, overseas caps, shorts, and jackets—but *what* jackets!

"Well . . ." Garlock said, after examining the two girls speechlessly for a good half minute. "It doesn't look *exactly* like a spray-on job—but if you ever take a deep breath it'll split from here to there."

"Oh, no. The fabric stretches a little, see? Nothing like a sweater, but a similar effect—perhaps a bit more so."

"Quite a bit more so, I'd say. However, since Operators and Primes are automatically stacked like Interplan Towers, I don't suppose your recruits will be unduly perturbed at the exposure. Are we finally ready to go down and get to work?"

"I am," James said. "How do you want to handle it?"

"Run a search pattern. Belle and I will center their Op

field and check on Ops and Primes. You two probe at will."

Around and around the planet, in brief bursts of completely incomprehensible speed, the huge ship darted. The tremendous oceans and six great continents were traversed . . . the ice-caps . . . the frigid, the temperate, and the torrid zones. Wherever she went, powerful and efficient radar scanned and tracked her; wherever she went, excitement seethed.

"Beta Centauri Five," Garlock reported, after a few minutes. "Margonia, they call it. Biggest continent and nation named Nargoda. Capital city Margon; Margon Base is on the coast nearby. Lots of Gunther Firsts. All the real Gunther, though, is clear across the continent. They're building a starship. Fourteen Ops and two Primes —a man and a woman. Deggi Delcamp's a big bruiser, with a god-awful lot of stuff. Ugly as hell, though. He's a bossy type."

"I'm amazed." James played it straight. "I thought all male Primes would be just like you. Timorous Timmies."

"Huh? Oh. . . ." Garlock was taken slightly aback, but went on quickly, "What do you think of your opposite number, Belle?" He smiled broadly and made hour-glass motions with his hands. "I'd thought of trading you in on a new model, but Fao Talaho is no bargain, either—and *nobody's* pushover."

"*Trade!* You *tomcat!*" Belle's nostrils flared. "You know what that bitch tried to do? High-hat *me!*"

"I noticed. When we four get down to business, face to face, there should be some interesting by-products."

"You said it, boss. Primes seem to be *such* nice people." James rolled his eyes upward and steepled his hands. "If you've got all the dope, no use finishing this search pattern."

"Go ahead. Window dressing. Their Brass hasn't any idea of what's going on, any more than ours did."

The search went on until:

"This is it," James reported. "Where? Over Margon Base?"

"Yes. Kick us over there, ten or twelve hundred miles up."

"On the way, boss. Looks like theory is about ripe."

"It isn't much of a theory yet—just that cultural and evolutionary patterns should be more or less homogeneous within galaxies. Until it can explain why so many out-galaxies are just alike it doesn't amount to much. By the way, I'm glad you people insisted on organization and rank and uniforms. The Brass down there is going to take a certain amount of convincing. Take over, Brownie—this is your dish."

"I was afraid of that."

The others watched Lola drive her probe—a diamond-clear, razor-sharp bolt of thought that no Gunther First could possibly either wield or stop—down into the inner-most private office of that immense and far-flung base. Through Lola's inner eyes they saw a tall, trim, handsome, fiftyish man in a resplendent uniform of purple and gold; they watched her brush aside that officer's hard-held mental block.

"I greet you, Supreme Grand Marshal Entlore, Highest Commander of the Armed Forces of Nargoda. This is the starship *Pleiades,* of System Sol, planet Tellus. I am Sol-System Vice-Admiral Lola Montandon. I have with me as guests three of my superior officers of the Galactic Service, including the Galactic Admiral himself. We are making a good-will tour of the Tellus-type planets of this region of space. I request permission to land and information as to your landing conventions. The landing pad—bottom—of the *Pleiades* is flat; sixty feet wide by one hundred twenty feet long. Area loading is approximately eight tons per square foot. Solid, dry ground is perfectly satisfactory. While we land vertically, with little or no shock impact, I prefer not to risk damaging your pavement."

They all felt the Marshal's thoughts race. "Starship! Tellus—Sol, that insignificant, type G dwarf! Interstellar travel a commonplace! A ship *that* size and weight—an organized, uniformed, functioning galaxy-wide navy—and they don't want to *damage* my *pavement!* My God!"

"Good going, Brownie! Kiss her for me, Jim." Garlock flashed the thought.

Entlore, realizing that his every thought was being read, pulled himself together. "I admit that I was shocked, Admiral Montandon. But landing—really, I have nothing to do with landings. They are handled by . . ."

"I realize that, sir; but you realize that no underling could possibly authorize my landing. That is why I always start at the top. Besides, I do not like to waste time on officers of much lower rank than my own, and"—Lola allowed a strong tinge of good humor to creep into her thought— "the bigger they are, the less apt they are to pass the buck."

"You have had experience, I see." The marshal laughed. He *did* have a sense of humor. "While landing here is forbidden—top secret, you know—would my refusal mean much to you?"

"Having made satisfactory contact, I introduce you to Galactic Admiral Garlock. Take over, sir, please."

Entlore winced, for the probe Garlock used then compared to Lola's very much as a diamond drill compares to a piece of soft brass pipe.

"It would mean everything to us," Garlock assured him. "Our mission is a perfectly friendly one. We will have a friendly visit or none. If you do not care for our friend-ship, another nation will."

"That wouldn't do, either, of course." Entlore paused in thought. "It boils down to this: I must either welcome you or destroy you."

"You may try." Garlock grinned in frankly self-satisfied amusement. "However, the best you can do is lithium-hydride fusion missiles in the hundreds-of-megatons range. Firecrackers. Every once in a while a planet has to try a few such things on us before it will believe that we are powerful as well as friendly. Would you like to test our defenses? If so, I will neither take offense nor retaliate."

Supreme Grand Marshal Entlore was floored. "Why . . . er . . . not at all. I read in your mind . . ." He broke off, to quell an invasion into his own private office. "God damn it, keep *still!*" all four "heard" him yell. "I know they ran a search pattern. I know *that,* too. I know *every-thing* about it, I tell you! I'm in full rapport with their Supreme Grand Admiral. There's only the one ship, they're friendly, and I'm inviting them to land here on Margon Base. Give that to the press. Say also that en-trance restrictions to Margon Base will not be relaxed at present. Grand Marshal Holson and ComOff Flurnoy, stay here and tune in. The rest of you get out and *stay* out!"

"Resume command, please, Miss Montandon," Garlock directed, and withdrew his probe from Entlore's mind.

"I thank you, Supreme Grand Marshal Entlore, for your welcome," Lola sent. "I'm sorry that our visits cause so much disturbance, but I suppose it can't be helped. Our Gunther blocks are down. Would you and your two as-sistants like to teleport out here to us, and con us down yourselves?" Lola knew instantly that they could not, and covered deftly for them. "But of course you can't, without knowing a focus spot here in the Main. Shall I tele-port you aboard?"

ComOff Flurnoy's face—she was an attractive, nicely built redhead wearing throat-mike, earphone, and recorder —turned so pale that a faint line of freckles stood out across the bridge of her nose. She very evidently wanted to scream a protest, but would not. Both men, strangely enough, were eager to go. Instantly all three were standing in line on the deep-piled rug of the Main, facing the four Tellurians. Seven bodies came rigidly to attention, seven right hands snapped into two varieties of formal sa-lute. Standing thus, each party studied the other for a couple of seconds.

There was no doubt at all as to which two of the visi-tors the two Nardodian men were studying; but neither of them could quite make up his mind as to which of the black-and-white-clad women to study first or most. The redhead's glance, too, flickered between Belle and Garlock —incredulous envy and equally incredulous admiration.

"At rest, please, fellow-officers," Garlock said.

Lola performed the necessary introductions, adding, "We do not, however, use titles aboardship. Mister and Miss are customary and sufficient."

Behind each row of officers a long davenport appeared; between them a table loaded with food, drinks, cigars and cigarettes.

"Help yourselves," Garlock invited. "We serve neither intoxicants nor drugs, but you should find something there to your taste."

"Indeed we shall, and thank you," Entlore said. "Is there any objection, Mr. Garlock, to Miss Flurnoy trans-mitting information of this meeting and of this ship to our base?"

"None whatever. Send as you please, Miss Flurnoy, or as Mr. Entlore directs."

"I'm glad I didn't quite scare myself out of coming up here," the communications officer said. "This is the biggest and nicest thrill I ever had. Such a thrill I don't know just where to begin." She cocked an eyebrow at her commanding officer.

"As usual. Whatever you think should be sent." Entlore sent her a steadying thought. Then, as the girl settled back with a sandwich in one hand and a tall glass of Chericol in the other, he went on, to Garlock, "She is a very fine and very strong telepath—by our standards, at least."

"By galactic standards also." Garlock had of course been checking. "Accurate, sharp, wide-range, clear-thinking, and fast. Not one of us four could do it any better."

"I thank you, Mr. Garlock," the girl said, with a blush of pleasure—and with scarcely a perceptible pause in her work.

A tour of the ship followed; and as it progressed, the two Nargodian commanders became more and more confused and dismayed.

"But no crew at *all?*" Holson demanded incredulously. "How can a thing like this *possibly* work?"

"It's fully Gunthered," Lola explained. "It works itself. That is, almost all the time. Whenever we land on any planet for the first time, one of us has to control it. Or for any other special job not in its memory banks. When you're ready for us to land I'll show you how we do it."

"Miss Flurnoy, have they cleared the air over Pylon Six?"

"Yes, sir. Clearance came through five minutes ago. They are holding it clear for us."

"Thank you. Miss Montandon, you may land at your convenience."

"Thank you, sir." Lola took the pilot's seat. "This is the scanner. I pull it over my face and head, so. Since I am always in tune with the field . . ."

"What does *that* mean?" Entlore asked, dark foreboding in his mind.

"I was afraid of that. You can't feel an Operator Field. I'm sorry, sir, but that means that you can't handle these forces and never will be able to. Certain Gunther areas of your brain are inoperative. On our scale you are a Gunther First . . ."

"On ours, I'm an Esper Ten, the highest rating in the world—except for a few theoretical crackpots who . . . Excuse me, please, I shouldn't have said that, in view of what I see happening here."

"No offense taken, sir. Those who developed the Gunther Drive were crackpots until they got the first starship out into space. But with this scanner on, I think of where I want to look and I can see it. I then think the ship a few miles sidewise—so—and we are now directly over your Pylon Six. I'm starting down, but I won't go into free fall."

Apparent weight grew less and less until:

"This is about enough for you, Miss Flurnoy?"

"Just," the ComOff agreed, with a gulp. "One pound less and I'm afraid I'll upchuck that lovely lunch I just ate."

"We're going fast enough now. Everyone sitting down? Brace yourselves, please; you'll be about fifty percent overweight for a while."

As bodies settled deeper into cushions Entlore sent Garlock a thought. "We three weigh about five hundred pounds. You lifted us—instantaneously or nearly so, but

I'll pass the question of acceleration for the moment—eleven hundred miles straight up. How did you repeal the Law of Conservation?"

"We didn't. We have fusion engines of twenty million horsepower. Our Operator Field, which has a radius of fifteen thousand miles and is charged to an electrogravitic potential of one hundred thousand gunts, stores energy. Its action is not exactly like that of an electrical condenser or of a storage battery, but is more or less analogous to both. Thus, the energy required to lift you three came from the field, but the amount was so small that it did not lower the potential of the field by any measurable amount. Setting this ship down—call it sixty thousand tons for a thousand miles at one gravity—will increase the field's potential by approximately one-tenth of one gunt. Have you studied paraphysics?"

"No."

Garlock smiled—with a touch of condescension. "Then I can't make even a stab at explaining instantaneous translation to you. I'll just say that there is no acceleration involved, no time lapse. There is no violation of the Law of Conservation, since departure and arrival points are equi-Guntherial. But what I am really interested in is that small group of high espers you mentioned."

"Yes, I inferred that from Miss Montandon's comments." Entlore fell silent and Garlock watched his somber thoughts picture Margon Base and his nation's capital being attacked and destroyed by a fleet of invincible and invulnerable starship like this *Pleiades*.

"You are wrong, sir," Garlock put in quietly. "The Galactic Service has not had, does not and will not have, anything to do with intra-planetary affairs. We have no connection with, and no responsibility to, any world or any group of worlds. We are an arm of the United Galaxian Societies of the Galaxy. Our function is to control space. To forbid, to prevent, to rectify any interplanetary or interstellar aggression. Above all, to prevent, by means of procedures up to and including total destruction of planets if necessary, any attempt whatever to form any multi-world empire."

The three Nargodians gasped, as much at the scope of the thing as at the calmly cold certainty of ability carried by the thought.

"You are transmitting this precisely, Miss Flurnoy?" Entlore asked.

"Precisely, sir—including background, fringes, connotations, and implications; just as he is giving it to us."

"Let us assume that your Nargodian government decides to conquer all the other nations of your planet Margonia. Assume further that it succeeds. We will not object; in fact, ordinarily we will not even be informed of it. If then, however, your government decides that one world is not enough for it to rule and prepares to conquer, or take aggressive action against, any other world, we will be informed and we will step in. First, warning will be given. Second, any and all vessels dispatched on such a mission will be annihilated. Third, if the offense is continued or repeated, trial will be held before the Galactic Council and any sentence imposed will be carried out."

In spite of Garlock's manner and message, both marshals were highly relieved. "You're in plenty of time with us, sir," Entlore said. "We have just sent our first rocket to our nearer moon . . . that is, unless that group of—of espers gets their ship off the ground."

"How far along are they?"

"The ship itself is built, but they are having trouble with their drive. The hull is spherical, and much smaller than this one. It has atomic engines, but no blasts or ion-plates . . . but neither has this one!"

"Exactly; they may be pretty well along. I'd like to get in touch with them as soon as possible. May I borrow a 'talker' like Miss Flurnoy for a few days? You have others, I suppose?"

"Yes, but I'll let you have her; it is of the essence that you have the best one available. Miss Flurnoy?"

"Yes, sir?" Besides reporting, she had been conversing busily with James and Belle.

"Would you like to be assigned to Mr. Garlock for the duration of his stay on Margonia?"

"Oh, *yes,* sir!" she replied, excitedly.

"You are so assigned. Take orders from him or from any designate as though I myself were issuing them."

"Thank you, sir . . . but what limits? and do I transmit to and/or record for you, sir?"

"No limit. These four Galaxians are hereby granted nationwide top clearance. Transmit as usual whatever is permitted."

"Full reporting is not only permitted, but urged," Garlock said. "There is nothing secret about our mission."

As the *Pleiades* landed: "If you will give us your focus spot, Mr. Entlore, we can all 'port to your office and save calling staff cars."

"And cause a revolution?" Entlore laughed. "Apparently you haven't been checking outside."

"Afraid I haven't. I've been thinking."

"Take a look. I got orders from the Cabinet to put guards wherever people absolutely must not go, and open everything else to the public. I *hope* there are enough guards to keep a lane open for us, but I wouldn't bet on it." Garlock was very glad that the military man's stiff formality had disappeared. "You Galaxians took this whole planet by storm while you were still above the stratosphere."

From the *Pleiades* they went to the Administration Building, where an informal reception was held. Thence to the Capitol, where the reception was very formal indeed. Thence to the Grand Ballroom of the city's largest hotel, where a tremendous—and long-winded—banquet was served.

At Garlock's request, all sixteen members of the "crackpot" group—the most active members of the Deep Space Club—had been invited to the banquet. And, even though Garlock was a very busy man, his talker tuned in to each one of the sixteen, tuned them all to Garlock, and in odd moments a great deal of business was done.

After being told most of the story—in tight-beamed thoughts that ComOff Flurnoy could not receive—the whole group was wildly enthusiastic. They would change the name of their club forthwith to THE GALAXIAN SOCIETY OF MARGONIA. They laid plans for a worldwide organization which would have tremendous prestige and tremendous income. They already had a field— Garlock knew about their ship—and they wanted the *Pleiades* to move over to it as soon as possible. Yes, Garlock thought he could do it the following day ... if not, as soon as he could ...

The *Pleiades* had landed at ten o'clock in the forenoon, local time; the banquet did not come to an end until long after midnight. Throughout all this time the four Galaxians carried on, without a slip, the act that all this was, to them, old stuff.

Nargoda's Top Brass, in the limelight for once in a thoroughly pleasant and enjoyable way, allowed as much of their enjoyment to show as was consistant with military dignity.

ComOff Flurnoy, however, made neither physical nor mental secret of the fact that she was having the time of her life.

Garlock told her, as the banquet neared its end, "You don't have to come back to the ship with us if you'd rather go home from here."

"Oh, but I *want* to go back to the ship with you!" she protested. "I'm *assigned* to you for the duration! Surely you can find some little place for me aboard the *Pleiades*? I won't take up hardly any room at all! Honestly, I'll be glad to sleep on the floor, out in the kitchen or anywhere! Besides, I told my folks and all my friends I was living aboard and they're all *insane* with jealousy!"

"Okay, *okay*." Garlock managed finally to choke off the rush of exclamatory thought. She was really a sender. "We've got lots of room, and you're perfectly welcome. It's just that you've put in a lot of overtime today and I thought you'd rather stay at home as usual and work your regular seven-hour day."

"Work? You call this *work?*"

"For me, it most certainly is," Garlock said.

They got back to the starship a little before daylight—through massed crowds all the way. Once in the Main, Belle kicked off her slippers and slumped bonelessly onto a davenport.

"My feet are simply killing me," she moaned, "and I haven't got strength enough left even to think me up a Chericol." A tall glass, tinkling with ice-cubes, appeared in her hand. "Thanks, Clee—you're sweet. But why didn't you make me wear combat boots with an inch of cork sponge inside 'em?"

"Because even my powers are finite. You'd've worn 'em —I don't think."

"Why, of *course* she wouldn't have! the ComOff exclaimed. "And that Grand Marshal Holson—asking you to wear your uniforms all the time you're here so people could *recognize* you. Of all the dim-witted . . . oh, *phogoploot!*" This last, highly idiomatic, thought carried the force of about ten gunts of scorn. The ComOff's still marveling gaze went from Belle to Garlock and back. "With a shape like yours and a build like his you couldn't *help* but be recognized, even all wrapped up in tarps. *Lordy,* I wish I looked like you do!"

"And I've wished, a good many times, that I didn't. . . . Maybe I wouldn't be such a damn fool as to wear shoes like that through such a war as this has been." Belle glared at the offending slippers and they promptly vanished. "Come on, Elta; I'll show you your room. Goodnight, everyone."

The green-haired officer clad in black and white, and the red-haired one in purple and gold, vanished instantaneously; and, a moment later, the Main was empty.

VII

SINCE EVERYONE, including the ebullient ComOff, slept late the following morning, they all had brunch instead of breakfast and lunch. All during the meal Garlock was preoccupied and stern.

"Hold everything for a while, Jim," he said, when everyone had eaten. "Before we move, Belle and I have got to have a conference."

"Not a Fatso Ferber nine-o'clock type, I hope." James frowned in mock reproach and ComOff Flurnoy cocked an eyebrow in surprise. "Monkey-business on company time is only for Big Shots like him; not for small fry such as you."

"Well, it won't be exclusively monkey-business, any-way. While we're gone you might clear with the control tower and take us up into takeoff position. Come on, Belle." He took her by one elbow and led her away.

Inside his room, Garlock checked every Gunther block —a most unusual proceeding. "I was just checking to be sure we're Prime-proof," he said. "I'm not ready for Deggi Delcamp yet. That guy, as you probably noticed, has got one godawful load of stuff."

"Not as much as you have, Clee. Nor as much push behind what he *has* got. And his shield wouldn't make patches for yours."

"Huh? How sure are you of that?"

"I'm positive. I'm the one who *is* going to get bumped, I'm afraid. That Fao Talaho is a hard-hitting, hard-boiled hellcat on wheels."

"I'll be damned. You're wrong. I checked her from stem to gudgeon and you lay over her like a damper field. What's the answer?"

"Oh? Do I? I'm mighty glad . . . Funny, both of us being wrong . . . it must be that it's sex-based differences. We're used to each other, but neither of us has ever felt a Prime of the same sex before, and there must be more difference between Ops and Primes than we realized. Suppose?"

"Could be—I hope. But that doesn't change the fact that we aren't ready. We haven't got enough data. If we start out with this grandiose Galactic Service thing and find only two or three planets Gunthered, we make jack-asses of ourselves. On the other hand, if we start out with a small organization or none, and find a lot of planets, it'll be one continuous cat-fight. On the third hand . . ."

"Three hands, Clee? What are you, an octopus or an Arpalone?"

"Quiet. On the third hand, we've *got* to start somewhere. Any ideas?"

"I never thought of it that way. Hm-m-m-m . . . I see. Damned if we do and blasted if we don't." She thought for a minute, then went on. "We'll have to start without starting, then . . . quite a trick. But how about this? Suppose we take a fast tour, with you and me taking quick peeks, without the peekees ever knowing we've been peeking?"

"That's using the brain, Belle. Let's go."

Then, out in the Main, he said, "Jim, we want to hit a few high spots, as far out as you can reach without losing orientation. Beta Centauri here is pretty bright. Rigel and Canopus are real lanterns. With those three as a grid, you could reach fifteen hundred or two thousand light-years, couldn't you?"

"More than that. That many parsecs, at least."

"Good. Belle and I want to make a fast, random-sampling check of Primes and Ops around here. We'll need five minutes at each planet—quite a ways out. So set up as big a globe as you can and still be dead sure of your locations; then sample it."

"Not enough data. How many samples do you want?"

"As many as we can get in the rest of today. Six or seven hours, say—eight hours max."

Call it seven . . . Brownie on the guns, me on Compy . . . Five minutes for . . . I should be able to lock down the next shot in five . . . one minute extra, for safety factor . . . that'd be ten an hour. Seventy planets enough?"

"That'll be fine."

"Okay. We're practically at Number One now." James and Lola donned their scanners.

"Miss Flurnoy," Garlock said, "you might tell Mr. Entlore that we're . . ."

"Oh, I already have, sir."

"You don't have to come along, of course, if you'd rather stay here."

"Stay here, sir? Why, he' *kill* me! . . . I'm off the air for a minute," she added in a conspiratorial whisper. "Besides, do you think I'd miss a chance to be the first person—and just a girl, too—of a whole world to see other planets of other suns? Unless, of course, you invite Mr. Entlore and Mr. Holson along. They're both simply dying to go, I know, but of course won't admit it."

"You'd be just as well pleased if I didn't?"

"What do you think, sir?"

"We'll be working at top speed and they'd be very much in the way, so they'll get theirs later . . ."

"Ready to roll, Clee," James announced.

"Roll."

"Why, I lost contact!" Miss Flurnoy exclaimed.

"Naturally," Garlock said. "Did you expect to cover a distance it takes light thousands of years to cross? You can record anything you see in the plates. You can talk to Jim or Lola any time they'll let you. Don't bother Miss Bellamy or me from now on."

Garlock and Belle went to work. All four Galaxians worked all day, with half an hour off for lunch. They visited seventy planets and got back to Margonia in time for a very late dinner. ComOff Flurnoy had less than a quarter of one roll of recorder-tape left unused, and the Primes had enough information to start the project they had in mind.

And, shortly after dinner, all five retired.

"In one way, Clee, I'm relieved," Belle mused, "but I can't figure out why all the Primes—the grown-up ones, I mean—on all the worlds are just about the same cantankerous, out-and-out stinkers as you and I are. How does *that* fit into your theory?"

"It doesn't. Too fine a detail. My guess is—at least it seems to me to make sense—it's because we haven't had any competition strong enough to smack us down and make Christians out of us. I don't know what a psychologist would say . . ."

"And I know *exactly* what you'd think of whatever he did say, so you don't need to tell me." Belle laughed and presented her lips to be kissed. "Good night, Clee."

"Good night, Belle."

And the next morning, early, Garlock and Belle teleported themselves—by arrangement and appointment, of course—across almost the full width of a nation and into the private office in which Deggi Delcamp and Fao Talaho awaited them.

For a time which would not have been considered polite in Tellurian social circles the four Primes stood still, each couple facing the other with blocks set tight, studying each other with their eyes. Delcamp was, as Garlock had said, a big bruiser. He was shorter and heavier than the Tellurian. Heavily muscled, splendidly proportioned, he was a man of tremendous physical as well as mental strength. His hair, clipped close all over his head, was blond; his eyes were a clear, keen cold dark blue.

Fao Talaho was a couple of inches shorter than Belle, and a good fifteen pounds heavier. She was in no sense fat, however, nor even plump—actually, she was almost lean. She was wider and thicker than was the Earth-woman, with heavier bones forming a wider and deeper frame. She, too, was beautifully—yes, spectacularly—built. Her hair, fully as thick as Belle's own and worn in a free-falling bob three or four inches longer than Belle's, was bleached almost white. Here eyes were not really speckled, not really mottled, but were regularly *patterned* in lighter and darker shades of hazel. She was, Garlock decided, a really remarkable hunk of woman.

Both Nargodians wore sandals without either socks or stockings. Both were dressed—insofar as they were dressed at all—in yellow. Fao's single garment was of a thin, closely-knitted fabric, elastic and sleek. Above the waist it was neckless, backless, and almost frontless; below, it was a very short, very tight and clinging skirt. Delcamp wore a sleeveless jersey and a pair of almost legless shorts.

Garlock lowered his shield enough to send and to receive a thin layer of superficial thought; Delcamp did the same.

"So far, I like what I see," Garlock said then. "We are well ahead of you, hence I can help you a lot if you want me to and if you want to be friendly about it. If you don't, on either count, we leave now. Fair enough?"

"Fair enough. I, too, like what I have seen so far. We need help, and I appreciate your offer. Thanks, immensely. I can promise full cooperation and friendship for myself and for most of our group; and I assure you that I can and will handle any non-cooperation that may come up."

"Nicely put, Deggi." Garlock smiled broadly and let his guard down to a comfortable lepping level. "I was going to bring that up—the faster it's cleared the better. Belle and I are paired. Some day—unless we kill each other first—we may marry. However, I'm no bargain and she's one-third wildcat, one-third vixen, and one-third cobra. How do you two stand?"

"You took the thought right out of my own mind. Your custom of pairing is not what you call 'urbane' on this world. Nevertheless, Fao and I are paired. We had to. No one else has ever interested either of us; no one else ever will. We should not fight, but we do, furiously. But no matter how vigorously we fly apart, we inevitably fly together again just as fast. No one understands it, but you two are pretty much the same."

"Check. Just one more condition, then, and we can pull those women of ours apart." Belle and Fao were still staring at each other, both still sealed tight. "The first time Fao Talaho starts throwing her weight at me, I'm not going to wait for you to take care of her—I'm going to give her the surprise of her life."

"It'd tickle me silly if it could be done." Delcamp gave a perfectly frank smile. "But the man doesn't live who can do it. How would you go about trying it?"

"Set your block solid."

Delcamp did so, and through that block—the supposedly impenetrable shield of a Prime Operator—Garlock insinuated a probe. He did not crack the screen or break it down by force; he neutralized and counterphased, painlessly and almost imperceptibly, its every component and layer.

"Like this," Garlock said, in the depths of the Margonian's mind.

"My God! You can do *that?*"

"If I tell her, this deep, to play ball or else, do you think she'd need two treatments?"

"She certainly shouldn't. This makes you Galactic Admiral, no question. I'd thought, of course, of trying you out for Top Gunther, but this settles that. We will support you, sir, wholeheartedly—and my heartfelt thanks for coming here."

"I have your permission, then, to give Fao a little discipline when she starts rocking the boat?"

"I wish you would. I'm not too easy to get along with, I admit, but I've tried to meet her a lot more than halfway. She's just too damned cocky for *anybody's* good."

"Check. I wish somebody would come along who could knock hell out of Belle." Then, aloud, "Belle, Delcamp and I have the thing going. Do you want in on it?"

Delcamp spoke to Fao, and the two women slowly and reluctantly lowered their shields to match those of the men.

"Your Galaxian shaking of the hands—handshake, I mean—is very good," Delcamp said, and he and Garlock shook vigorously.

Then the crossed pairs did the same, and lastly the two girls—although neither put much effort into the gesture.

"Snap out of it, Belle!" Garlock sent a tight-beamed thought. "She isn't going to bite you!"

"She's been trying to, damn her, and I'm going to bite her right back—see if I don't."

Garlock called the meeting to order and all four sat down. The Tellurians lit cigarettes and the others—who, to the Earthlings' surprise, also smoked—assembled and lit two peculiar-looking things halfway between pipe and cigarette. And both pairs of smokers, after a few tentative tests, agreed in not liking at all the other's taste in tobacco.

"You know, of course, of the trip we took yesterday?" Garlock asked.

"Yes," Delcamp admitted. "We read ComOff Flurnoy. We know of the seventy planets, but nothing of what you found."

"Okay. Of the seventy planets, all have Op fields and all have two or more Operators; one planet has forty-four of them. Only sixty-one of the planets, however, have Primes old enough for us to detect. Each of these worlds has two, and only two, Primes—one male and one female—and each world the two Primes are of approximately the same age. On fifteen of these worlds the Primes are not yet adult. On the forty-six remaining worlds, the Primes are young adults, from pretty much likes us four down to considerably younger. None of these couples is married-for-family. None of the girls has as yet had a child or is now pregnant.

"Now as to the information circulating all over this planet about us. Part of it is false. Part of it is misleading —to impress the military mind. Thus, the fact is that the *Pleiades,* as far as we know, is the only starship in the whole galaxy. Also, the information is very incomplete, especially as to the all-important fact that we were lost in space for some time before we discovered that the only possible controller of the Gunther Drive is the human mind . . ."

"What?!" And argument raged until Garlock stopped it by declaring that he would prove it in the Margonians' own ship.

Then Garlock and Belle together went on to explain and to describe—not even hinting, of course, that they had ever gone outside the galaxy or had even thought of trying to do so—their concept of what the Galaxian Societies of the Galaxy would and should do; of what the Galaxian Services could, should, and *would* become— the Service to which they both intended to devote their lives. It wasn't even in existence yet, of course. Fao and Deggi were the only other Primes they had ever talked to in their lives. That was why they were so eager to help the Margonians get their ship built. The more starships there were at work, the faster the Service would grow into a really tremendous . . .

(*"Fao's getting ready to blow her top,"* Delcamp flashed Garlock a tight-beamed thought. *"If I were doing it I'd have to start right now."*

"I'll let her work up a full head of steam, then smack her bow-legged."

"Cheers, brother! I hope you can handle her!")

. . . organization. Then, when enough ships were working and enough Galaxian Societies were rolling, there would be the Regional organizations and the Galactic Council . . .

"So, on a one-planet basis and right out of your own little fat head," Fao sneered, "you have set yourself up as Grand High Chief Mogul, and all the rest of us are to crawl up to you on our bellies and kiss your feet?"

"If that's the way you want to express it, yes. However, I don't know how long I personally will be in the pilot's bucket. As I told you, I will enforce the basic tenet that top Gunther is top boss—man, woman, snake, fish, or monster."

"Top Gunther be damned!" Fao blazed. "I don't and won't take orders from *any* man—in hell or in heaven or on this planet or on any other . . ."

"Fao!" Delcamp exclaimed, "Please keep still—*please!*"

"Let her rave," Garlock said coldly. "This is just a three-year-old baby's tantrum. If she keeps it up, I'll give her the damndest jolt she ever got in her life."

Belle tight-beamed a thought to Fao: "If you've got any part of a brain, you'd better start using it. The boy-friend not only plays rough, but he doesn't bluff."

"To hell with that!" Fao rushed on. "We won't have anything to do with your organization—go on back home or anywhere else you want to. We'll finish our own ship and build our own organization and run it to suit ourselves. We'll. . ."

"That's enough of that, you spoiled brat." Garlock penetrated her shield as easily as he had the man's, and held her in lock. "You are *not* going to wreck this project. You will start behaving yourself right now or I'll spread your mind wide open for Belle and Deggi to look at and see exactly what kind of a half-baked egotist you are. If that doesn't work, I'll put you into a Gunther-blocked cell aboard the *Pleiades* and keep you there until the ship is finished and we leave Margonia. How do you want it?"

Fao was shocked as she had never been shocked before. At first she tried viciously to fight; but, finding that useless against the appalling power of the mind holding hers, she stopped struggling and really began to think.

"That's better. You've got what it takes to think with. Go ahead and do it."

And Fao Talaho did have it. Plenty of it. She learned.

"I'll be good," she said, finally. "Honestly. I'm ashamed, really, but after I got started I couldn't stop. But I can now, I'm sure."

"I'm sure you can, too. I know exactly how it is. All us Primes have to get hell knocked out of us before we amount to a whoop in hell. Deggi got his one way, I got mine another, you got yours this way. No, neither of the others know anything about this conversation and they won't. This is strictly between you and me."

"I'm awfully glad of that. And I think I . . . yes, damn you, thanks!"

Garlock released her and, after an embarrassed pause, she said, "I'm sorry, Deggi; and you, too, Belle. I'll try not to act like such a fool any more."

Delcamp and Belle both stared at Garlock; Belle licked her lips.

"No comment," he thought at the man; and, to Belle, "She just took a beating. Will you sheathe your claws and take a lot of pains to be extra nice the rest of the day?"

"Why, surely. I'm *always* nice to anybody who's nice to me."

"Says you," Garlock replied skeptically, and all four went to work as though nothing had happened.

They went through the shops and the almost-finished ship. They studied blueprints. They met all the Operators and discussed generators and fields of force and mathematics and paraphysics and Guntherics. They argued so hotly about mental control that Garlock had James bring the *Pleiades* over to newly-christened Galaxian Field so that he could prove his point then and there.

Entlore and Holson came along this time, as well as the ComOff; and all three were nonplussed and surprised to see each member of the "crackpot" group hurl the huge starship from one solar system to any other one desired, apparently merely by thinking about it. And the "crackpots" were extremely surprised to find themselves hopelessly lost in uncharted galactic wildernesses every time they did not think, definitely and positively, of one specific destination.

Then Garlock took a chance. He had to take it sometime; he might just as well do it now.

"See if you can hit Andromeda, Deggi," he suggested.

While Belle, James, and Lola held their breaths, Delcamp tried. The starship went toward the huge nebula, but stopped at the last suitable planet on the galaxy's rim.

"Can *you* hit Andromeda?" Delcamp asked, more than half jealously, and Belle tensed her muscles.

"Never tried it," Garlock said, easily. "I suppose, though, since you couldn't kick the old girl out of our good old home galaxy, she'll just sit right here for me, too."

He went through the motions and the *Pleiades* did sit right there—which was exactly what he had told her to do. And everybody — even the 'crackpots' — breathed more easily.

And Belle was "nice" to Fao; she didn't use her claws, even once, all day. And, just before quitting time—

"Does he . . . I mean, did he ever . . . well, sort of knock you around?" Fao asked.

"I'll say he hasn't!" Belle's nostrils flared slightly at the mere thought. "I'd stick a knife into him!"

"Oh, I didn't mean physically . . ."

"Through my blocks? A *Prime's* blocks? Don't be ridiculous, Fao!"

"What do you mean, 'ridiculous'?" Fao snapped. "You tried *my* blocks. What did they feel like to you—mosquito netting? What I thought was . . . oh, all he really said was that all Primes had to have hell knocked out of them before they could be any good. That he had had it one way, Deggi another, and me a third. I see—you haven't had yours yet."

"I certainly haven't. And if he ever tries it, I'll . . ."

"Oh, he won't, he couldn't, very well, because after you're married, it would . . ."

"Did he tell you I was going to *marry* him?"

"Of course not. No fringes, even. But who else are you going to marry? If the whole universe was clear full of the finest men imaginable, can you ever conceive of marrying any one of them except him?"

"I'm not going to marry anybody. Ever."

"No? You, with your Prime's mind and your Prime's body, not have any children? And you tell *me* not to be ridiculous?"

That stopped Belle cold, but she wouldn't admit it. Instead: "I don't get it. What did he *do* to you, anyway?"

Fao's block set itself so tight that it took her a full minute to soften it down enough for even the thinnest thought to get through. "That's something nobody will ever know. But anyway, unless . . . unless you find another Prime as strong as he is—and I don't really think there are any, do you?"

"Of course there aren't. There's only one of his class, anywhere. He's it," Belle said, with profound conviction.

"That makes it tough for you. You'll have the toughest job imaginable. The *very* toughest. I know."

"Huh? What job?"

"Since Clee won't do it for you, and since nobody else can, you'll just have to knock hell out of yourself."

And in Garlock's room that night, getting ready for bed, Belle asked suddenly, "Clee, what in hell did you do to Fao Talaho?"

"Nothing much. She's a pretty good one, really."

"Could you do it, whatever it was, to me?"

171

"As the man said when asked if he could play the violin—'I don't know; I never tried it.' "

"Would you, then, if I asked you to?"

"No."

"Why not?"

"Answer that yourself."

"And it was 'nothing much,' it says here in fine print. But I think I know just about what it was. Don't I?"

"I wouldn't be surprised."

"You knocked hell out of yourself, didn't you?"

"I lied to her about that. I'm still trying to."

"So I've got to do it to myself. And I haven't yet?"

"Check. But you're several years younger than I am, you know."

Belle thought it over for a minute, then stubbed out her cigarette and shrugged her shoulders. "No sale. Put it back on the shelf. I like me better the way I am. That is, I *think* I do. . . . In a way, though, I'm sorry, darling."

"Darling? Something new has been added. I wish you really meant that."

"I wish I didn't," Belle said. Ready for bed, she was much more completely and much less revealingly dressed than during her working hours. She slid into bed beside him, pulled the covers up to her chin, and turned off the light by glancing at the switch. "If I thought anything could ever come of it, though, I'd do it if I had to pound myself unconscious with a club. But I wouldn't be here, then, either—I'd scoot into my room so fast my head would spin."

"You wouldn't have to. You wouldn't be here."

"I wouldn't, at that. That's one of the things I like so much about you. But honestly, Clee—seriously, screens-down honestly—can you see any possible future in it?"

"No. Neither of us would give that much. Neither of

us can. And there's nothing one-sided about it; I'm no more fit to be a husband than you are to be a wife. And God help our children—they'd certainly need it."

"We'd never have any. I can't picture us living in marriage for nine months without committing at least mayhem. Why, in just the little time we've been paired, how many times have you thrown me out of this very room, with the fervent hope that I'd drown in deep space before you ever saw me again?"

"At a guess, about the same number of times you've stormed out under your own power, slamming the door so hard it sprung half the seams of the ship."

"That's what I mean. But how come we got off on *this* subject, I wonder? Because when we aren't fighting, like now, it's purely wonderful. So I'll say it again. Good night, darling."

In the dark his lips sought hers and found them. The fervor of her kiss was not only much more intense than any he had ever felt before—it was much, very much more intense than Belle Bellamy had either wanted or intended it to be.

Next morning eight o'clock, the four Tellurians appeared in the office of Margonia's Galaxian Field.

"The first thing to do, Deggi, is to go over in detail your blueprints for the generators and the drive," Garlock said.

"I suppose so. The funny pictures, eh?" Delcamp had learned much, the previous day; his own performance with the *Pleiades* had humbled him markedly.

"By no means, my friend," Garlock said, cheerfully. "While your stuff isn't exactly like ours—it couldn't be, hardly; the field is so big and so new—that alone is no reason for it not to work. James can tell you. He's the Solar System's top engineer. What do you think, Jim?"

"What I saw in the ship yesterday will work. What few

of the prints I saw yesterday will fabricate, and the fabrications will work. The main trouble with this project, it seems to me, is that nobody's building the ship."

"What do you mean by that crack?" Fao blazed.

"Just that. You're a bunch of prima donnas, each doing exactly as he pleases. So some of the stuff is getting done three or four times, in three or four different ways, while a lot of it isn't getting done at all."

"Such as?" Delcamp demanded.

And Fao said, "Well, if you don't like the way we're doing things you can—"

"Just a minute everybody." Lola came in, with a disarming smile. "How much of that is hindsight, Jim? You've built one, you know—and from all accounts, progress wasn't nearly as smooth as your story can be taken to indicate."

"You've got a point there, Lola," Garlock agreed. "We slid back two steps for every three we took forward."

"Well . . . maybe," James admitted.

"So why don't you, Fao and Deggi, put Jim in charge of construction?"

Fao threw back her silvery head and glared, but Delcamp jumped at the chance. "Would you, Jim?"

"Sure—unless Miss Talaho objects."

"She won't." Delcamp's eyes locked with Fao's, and Fao kept still. "Thanks immensely, Jim. And I know what you mean." He went over to a cabinet of wide, flat drawers and brought back a sheaf of drawings—not blueprints, but original drawings in pencil. "Such as this. I haven't even got it designed yet, to say nothing of building it."

James began to leaf through the stack of drawings. They were full of erasures, re-drawings, and such notations as "See sheets 17-B, 21-A, and 27-F." Halfway through the pile he paused, turned backward three sheets, and studied for minutes. Then, holding that one sheet by a corner, he went rapidly through the rest of the stack.

"This is it," he said then, pulling the one sheet out and spreading it flat. "What we call Unit Eight—the heart of the drive." Then, tight-beamed to Garlock:

"This is the thing that you designed *in toto* and that I never could understand any part of. All I did was build it. It must generate those Prime fields."

"Probably," Garlock flashed back. "I didn't understand it any too well myself. How does it look?"

"He isn't even close. He's got only half the constants down, and half of the ones he *has* got down are wrong. Look at this mess here . . ."

"I'll take your word for it. I haven't your affinity for blueprints, you know, nor your eidetic memory for them."

"Do you want me to give him the whole works?"

"We'll have to, I think. Or the ship might not work at all."

"Could be—but how about intergalactic hops?"

"He couldn't do it with the *Pleiades,* so he won't be able to with this. Besides, if we change it in any particular he *might.* You see, I don't know very much more about Unit Eight than you do."

"*That* could be, too." Then, as though just emerging from his concentration on the drawings, James thought at Delcamp and Fao, but on the open, general band.

"A good many errors and a lot of blanks, but in general you're on the right track. I can finish up this drawing in a couple of hours, and we can build the unit in a couple of days. With that in place, the rest of the ship will go fast.

"*If* Miss Talaho wants me to," he concluded, pointedly.

"Oh, I do, Jim—really I do!" At long last, stiff-backed

Fao softened and bent. She seized both his hands. "If you can, it'd be wonderful!"

"Okay. One question. Why are you building your ship so small?"

"Why it's plenty big enough for two," Delcamp said. "For four, in a pinch. Why did you make yours so big? Your main is almost big enough for a convention hall."

"That's what we figured it might have to be at times," Garlock said. "But that's a very minor point. With yours so nearly ready to flit, no change in size is indicated now. But Belle and I have got to have another conference with the legal eagle." He turned to James. "So if you and Browne will 'port whatever you need out of the *Pleiades,* we'll be on our way.

"So long—see you in a few days," he added, and the *Pleiades* vanished to appear instantaneously high above the stratosphere over what was to become the Galaxian Field of Earth.

"Got a minute, Gene?" he sent a thought.

"For you two Primes, as many as you like. We haven't started building or fencing yet, as you suggested, but we have bought all the real estate. So land the ship anywhere out there and I'll send a jeep out after you."

"Thanks, but no jeep. Nobody but you knows that we've really got control of the *Pleiades,* and I want everybody else to keep on thinking it's strictly for the birds. We'll 'port in to your office whenever you say."

"I say now."

In no time at all the two Primes were seated in the private office of Eugene Evans, Head of the Legal Department of the newly reincorporated Galaxian Society of Sol, Inc. Evans was a tall man, slightly thin, slightly stooped, whose thick tri-focals did nothing whatever to hide the keenness of his steel-gray eyes.

"The first thing, Gene," Garlock said, "is this employment contract thing. Have you figured out a way to break it?"

"It can't be broken." The lawyer shook his head.

"What? I thought you top-bracket legal eagles could break anything, if you really tried."

"A good many things, yes, especially if they're long and complicated. The Standard Employment Contract, however, is short, explicit, and iron-clad. The employer can discharge the employee for any number of offenses, including insubordination—which, as a matter of fact, the employer himself is allowed to define. On the other hand, the employee can't quit except for some such fantastic reason as the non-tendering—not non-payment, mind you, but non-*tendering*—of salary."

"I didn't expect that—it kicks us in the teeth before we get started." Garlock got up, lit a cigarette, and prowled about the big room. "Okay. Jim and I will have to get ourselves fired, then."

"Fired!" Belle snorted. "Clee, you talk like a man with foam rubber inside his skull! Who else could run the Project? That is"—her whole manner changed—"he doesn't know I can run it as well as you can—or better—but I could tell him. And maybe you think I wouldn't!"

"You won't have to. Gene, you can start spreading the news that Belle Bellamy is a real, honest-to-God Prime Operator in every respect. That she knows more about Project Gunther than I do and could run it better. Ferber undoubtedly knows that Belle and I have been at loggerheads ever since we first met—spread it thick that we're fighting worse than ever. Which, by the way, is the truth."

"Fighting? Why, you seemed friendly enough . . ."

"Yeah, we can be friendly for about fifteen minutes if we try real hard, as now. The cold fact is, though, that

177

her heart pumps 99% pure potassium cyanide . . ."

"I like *that!*" Belle stormed. She leaped to her feet, her eyes shooting sparks. "All *my* fault! Why, you self-centered, egotistical moron, I could write a book . . ."

"That's enough—let it go—*please!*" Evans pleaded. He jumped up, took each of the combatants by a shoulder, sat them down into the chairs they had vacated, and resumed his own seat. "The demonstration was eminently successful. I'll spread the word, through several channels. Chancellor Ferber will get it all, rest assured."

"And *I'll* get the job!" Belle snapped. "And maybe you think I won't take it!"

"Don't worry, I believe it," came Garlock's thought. "You'd sleep with Ferber to get it. And to keep it you'd go on the sofa whatever mornings he doesn't prefer one of his other girlfriends. Yeah—I don't think."

"Oh?" Belle's body stiffened, her face hardened. "I've heard stories, of course, but I couldn't quite . . . but do you suppose he'd *actually think* . . . why, the bloated, obscene *cockroach!* But surely he can't be *that* stupid—to think he can buy me like so many pounds of calf-liver?"

"He surely is. He does. And it works. That is, if he's ever missed, nobody ever heard of it."

"But how could a man in such a big job *possibly* get away with such foul stuff as that?"

"Because all that SSE is interested in is money, and Alonzo P. Ferber is a tremendously able top executive. In the big black-and-red money books he's always 'way, 'way up in the black."

Belle, even though she was already convinced, glanced questioningly at Evans.

"That's it, Miss Bellamy. That's it, in a precise, if somewhat crude, nutshell."

"That's that, then. But just how, Clee—if he's as smart

as you say he is—do you think you can make him fire you?"

"I don't know — haven't thought about it yet. But I could be pretty insubordinate if I really tried."

"That's the understatement of the century."

"I'll devote the imponderable force of the intellect to the problem and check with you later. Now, Gene, about the proposed Galactic Service, the Council, and so on. What is the reaction? Yours, personally, and others?"

"My personal reaction is immensely favorable; I think it's the greatest advance that humanity has ever made. I've been very cautious, of course, in discussing the matter, or even mentioning it, but the reaction of everyone I *have* sounded—good men; big men in their respective fields— has been as enthusiastic as my own."

"Good. It won't surprise you, probably, to be told that you are to be this system's councillor and—if we can swing it, and I think we can—the first President of the Galactic Council."

Evans was so surprised that it was almost a minute before he could reply coherently. "I *am* surprised—very much so. I thought, of course, that you yourself would . . ."

"Far from it!" Garlock said. "I'm not the type. You are. You're better than anyone else of the Galaxians— which means better than anyone else period. With the possible exception of Lola, and she fits better on our exploration team. Check, Belle?"

"Check. For once, I agree with you without reservation. *That's* a job we can work at all the rest of our lives, and scarcely start it."

"True—indubitably true. I appreciate your confidence in me, and if the vote so fall I will do whatever I can."

"We know you will, and thank *you*. How long will it take to organize? A couple of weeks? And is there anything else we have to cover now?"

"A couple of *weeks!*" Evans was shocked. "You are naive indeed, young man, to think anything of this magnitude can even be *started* in such a short time as that. And yes, there are dozens of matters—hundreds—that should be discussed before I can even start to work intelligently."

So discussions went on and on and on—and it was three days before Garlock and Belle 'ported themselves up into *Pleiades* and the starship displaced itself again to Margonia.

Meanwhile, on Margonia, James James James the Ninth went directly to the heart of his job by leading Lola and Fao into Delcamp's office and setting up its Gunther blocks.

"You said you want me to build your starship. Okay, but I want you both—Fao especially—to realize exactly what that means. I know what to do and how to do it. I can handle your *Operators* and get the job done. However, I can't handle either of you, since you both out-Gunther me, and I'm not going to try to. But there can't be two bosses on any one job, to say nothing of three or seventeen. So either I run the job or I don't. If either of you steps in, I step out and don't come back in. And remember that you're not doing us any favors—it's strictly vice versa."

"Jim!" Lola protested. Fao's hackles were very evidently on the rise; Delcamp's face was hardening. "Don't be so rough, Jim, *please*. That's no way to . . ."

"If you can pretty this up, pet, I'll be glad to have you say it for me. Here's what you have to work on. If I do the job they'll have their starship in a few weeks. The way they've been going, they won't have it in twenty-five years. And the only way to get that bunch out there to really

180

work is to tell each one of them to cooperate or else—and enforce the 'or else'."

"But they'd quit!" Delcamp protested. "They'll *all* quit!"

"With suspension or expulsion from the Society the consequences? Hardly." James said.

"But you wouldn't do that—you couldn't."

"I wouldn't?"

"Of course he wouldn't," Lola put in, soothingly, "except as a very last resort. And, even at worst, Jim could build it almost as easily with common labor. You Primes don't really *have* to have any Operators at all, you know; but all your Operators together would be perfectly helpless without at least one Prime."

"Why?"

"Oh, didn't you know? After the ship is built and the fields are charged and so on, everything has to be activated—the hundred and one things that make it so nearly alive—and that is strictly a Prime's job. Even Jim can't do it."

"I see . . . or, rather, I don't see at all." Fao said thoughtfully. She was no longer either excited or angry. "A few weeks against twenty-five years . . . what do you think of his time estimate, Deg?"

"I hadn't thought it would take nearly that long; but this 'activation' thing scares me. Nothing in my theory even hints at any such thing. So—if there's so much I don't know yet, even in theory, it would take a long time. Maybe I'd never get it."

"Well, anyway, I want our *Celestial Queen* done in weeks, not years," Fao said, extending her hand to James and shaking his vigorously. "So I promise not to interfere a bit. If I feel any such urge coming on, I'll dash home and lock myself up in a closet until it dies. Fair enough?"

Since Fao really meant it, that was fair enough.

For a whole day James did nothing except study blue-prints, going over in detail and practically memorizing every drawing that had been made. He then went over the ship, studying minutely every part, plate, member, machine and instrument that had been installed. He noted what each man and woman was doing and what they intended to do. He went over material on hand and material on order, paying particular attention to times of delivery. He then sent a few—surprisingly few—telegrams.

Finally he called all fourteen Operators together. He told them exactly what the revised situation was and exactly what he was going to do about it. He invited comments.

There was of course a riot of protest; but—in view of what James had said about suspensions and expulsions from the Galaxian Society—not one of them actually quit. Four of them, however, did appeal to Delcamp, considerably to his surprise, to oust the interloper and to put things back where they had been; but they did not get much satisfaction.

"James says that he can finish building this starship in a few weeks," Delcamp told them, flatly. "Specifically, three weeks, if we can get the special stuff made fast enough. Fao and I believe him. Therefore, we have put him in full charge. He will remain in charge unless and until he fails in performance. You are all good friends of Fao's and mine, and we hope that all of you will stay with the project. If, however, we must choose between you—any one of you or all of you—and James, there is no need to tell you what the choice will be."

Wherefore all fourteen went back to work—grudgingly at first and dragging their feet. In a very few hours, however, it became evident to all that James did in fact know what he was doing and that the work was going faster and more smoothly than ever before; whereupon all opposition and all malingering disappeared. They were Operators, and they were all intensely interested in their ship.

Thus, when the *Pleiades* landed beside the now seething *Celestial Queen*, Garlock found James with feet on desk, hands in pockets, and scanner on head—apparently doing nothing at all. Nevertheless, he was a very busy man.

"Hey, Jim!" A soprano shriek of thought emanated from a gorgeous seventeen-year-old blonde. "I can't read this funny-picture; it's been folded too many times. Where does this lead go to?"

"Data insufficient. Careful, Vingie; I'd hate to have to send you back to school."

"Pardon me. Unit six, Sub-Assembly Tee Dash Ni-yun. Terminal Fo-wer. From said terminal, there's a lead—Bee Sub something-or-other—goes somewhere. Where?"

"B sub Four. It goes to Unit Seven, Sub-Assembly Q dash Three, Terminal Two. And watch your insulation—that's a mighty hot lead."

"Okay, I got that. Double Sink Mill Mill; Class Albert Dog Kittens. Thanks, boss!"

"Hi, Jim," Garlock said. Then, to Delcamp: "I see you're rolling."

He's rolling, you mean." Delcamp had not yet recovered fully from a state of near-shock. "So *that's* what an eidetic memory is? He knows every nut, bolt, lead, and coil in the ship!"

"More than that. He's checking every move everybody makes. When they're done, you won't have to just hope everything was put together right—you'll *know* it was."

And Fao sidled over toward Belle. There was something new about the silver-haired girl, Belle decided instantly. The difference was slight—Belle couldn't put her finger on it at first. She seemed—quieter? Softer? More subdued?

No, definitely. More feminine? No; that would be impossible. More . . . more adult? Belle hated to admit it, even to herself, but that was what it was.

"Deg and I got married day before yesterday," Fao confided via tight beam.

"Oh—so you're *pregnant!*"

"Of course. I saw to that the first thing. I knew you'd want to be the first one to know. Oh, isn't it *wonderful?*" She seized Belle's arm and hugged it ecstatically against her side. "Oh, I'm sure it is; and I'm *so* happy for you, Fao!" And it would have taken the mind of a Garlock to perceive anything either false or forced in thought or bearing.

Nevertheless, when Belle went into Garlock's room that night, storm signals were flying high in her almost-topaz eyes.

"Fao Talaho Delcamp is *pregnant!*" she stormed, "and it's all *your* fault!"

"Oh no," he demurred, trying to snap her out of her world. It was Deggi."

"You know very well what I meant, Clee Garlock! If you hadn't given her that treatment she'd have kept on fighting with him and they wouldn't have been married and had any children for positively *years*. So now she'll have the first double-Prime baby and it ought to be *mine*. I'm older than she is—our group is 'way ahead of theirs— we have the first and *only* starship—and then you do *that*. And you wouldn't give *me* that treatment. Oh, no—just to *her!* I'd like to strangle you to death with my own bare hands!"

"What a *hell* of a logic!" Garlock had been trying to keep his own temper in leash, but the leash was slipping. "Assume I tried to work on you—assume I succeeded— what would you be? What would I have? What age do you think this is—that of the Vikings? When SOP in getting a wife was to beat her unconscious with a club and drag her into the longboat by her hair? Hardly, I do not want and will not have a conquered woman. Nor a spoiled-rotten, mentally-retarded brat . . ."

"You unbearably, conceited jerk! Why, I'd rather . . ."

Get out! And *this* time, *stay* out!"

Belle got out—and if door and frame had not been built of super-steel, both would have been wrecked by the blast of energy she loosed in closing the door behind her.

In her own room, with Gunther blocks full on, she threw herself face down on the bed and cried as she had not cried since she was a child.

And finally, without even taking off her clothes, she cried herself to sleep.

VIII

NEXT MORNING, early, Belle tapped lightly on Garlock's door.

"Come in."

She did so. "Have you had your coffee?"

"Yes."

"So have I."

Neither Belle nor Garlock had recovered; both faces showed strain and drain.

"I think we'd better break this up," she said quietly.

"Check. We'll have to, if we expect to get any work done."

Belle could not conceal her surprise.

"Oh, not for the reason you think," Garlock went on, quickly. "Your record as a man-killer is still one hundred point zero zero zero percent. I've been in love with you ever since we paired. Before that, even."

"Like hell" she snorted inelegantly. "Why, I . . ."

"Keep still a minute. And I'm not going to fight with you again. Ever. I'm not going to touch you again until I can control myself a lot better than I could last night."

"Oh? That was mostly my fault, of course. But in love? Oh no—I've seen men in love. You aren't, and I couldn't make you be, not with the best I could do. Not even in bed."

"Perhaps I'm an atypical case. I'm not raving about your perfect body—you already know what that's like. Nor about your mind, which is the only one I know of as good as my own. Maybe I'm in love with what I think you ought to be . . . or what I hope you will be. Anyway, I'm in love with *something* connected with you—and no other woman alive. Shall we go eat?"

"Okay; let's."

They joined Lola and James at the table; and if either noticed anything out of the ordinary, neither made any sign.

And after breakfast, out in the Main—

"About three weeks, Jim, you think?" Garlock asked.

"Give or take a couple of days, yes."

"And Belle and I would just be in the way—at least until time to show Deggi about the activation. And all those Primes to organize . . . We'd better leave you here, don't you think, and get going?"

"I'll buy that."

Lola and James moved a few personal belongings planetside; Garlock and Belle shot the *Pleiades* across a vast gulf of space to one of the planets they had scanned to fleetingly on their preliminary survey. Its name was, both remembered, Lizoria; its two Primes were named Rezdo Semolo and Mirea Mitala—male and female, respectively.

After sending down a very brief and perfunctory request for audience—which was in effect a declaration of intent and nothing else—Garlock and Belle teleported themselves down into Semolo's office, where both Lizorian Primes were.

Both got up out of peculiar-looking chairs to face their visitors. Both were tall and peculiarly thin—not the thinness of emaciation, but that of bodily structure.

187

"On them it looks good," Belle tight-beamed to Garlock. Both moved fast and with exquisite control; both were extraordinarily graceful. "Snaky" was Belle's thought of the woman; "sinuous" was Garlock's of the man. Both were completely hairless, of body and of head—not by nature, but via electric-shaver clipping. Both wore sandals. The man wore shorts and a shirt-like garment of nylon or its like; the woman wore just enough ribbons and bands to hold a hundred thousand credits' worth of jewels in place. She appeared to be about twenty years—Tellurian equivalent—old; he was probably three or four years older.

"We did not invite you in and we do not want you here," Semolo said coldly. "So get out, both of you. If you don't, when I count three I'll throw you out, and I won't be too careful about how many of your bones I break. One . . . Two . . ."

"Pipe down, Rezdo!" the girl exclaimed. "They have something we haven't, or they wouldn't be here. Whatever it is, we want it."

"Oh, let him try, Miss Mitala," Garlock said, through her hard-held block, in the depth of her mind. "He won't hurt us a bit and it may do him some good. While he's wasting effort I'll compare notes with my partner here, Galactic Vice-Admiral Belle Bellamy. I'm glad to see that one of you has at least part of a brain."

". . . Three!" Semolo did his best, with everything he had, without even attracting Garlock's attention. He then tried to leap at the intruder physically, despite the latter's tremendous advantage in weight and muscle, but found that he could not move.

Then, through Belle's solidly-set blocks, Garlock asked, "How are you coming? Getting anywhere?"

"My God!" came Belle's mental shriek. "What—how

188

can—but no, you *didn't* give *that* to Fao, surely!"

"I 'llsay I didn't—nor to Delcamp. But you're going to need it, I'm thinking."

"But *can* you? Even if you *would*—and I'm just beginning to realize how big a man you really are—can that kind of stuff be taught? I probably haven't got the brain-cells it takes to handle it."

"I'm not sure, but I've reworked our Prime Fields into one and made a few other changes. Theoretically, it ought to work. Shall I come in and try it?"

"Don't be an idiot, darling. *Of course!*"

As impersonally as a surgeon exploring an organ. Garlock went into Belle's mind. "Tune to the field . . . that's it —fine! Then—I'll do it real slow, and watch me close— you do it like so . . . get it?"

"Oh, lovely!" Belle breathed excitedly. "Got it!"

"Then this . . . and this . . . and there you are. You can try it on me, if you like."

"Oh no. No sale. I don't need practice and I'd like to preserve the beautiful illusion that maybe I *could* crack *your* shield if I wanted to. No, I'll work on Miss Snake-Hips here—but say, I'll bet there's a bone in it. *You* can block even that, can't you?"

"Yes. The block works like this." He showed her. "It takes full mastery of the Prime Field, but I see you've got that."

"Oh, wonderful! Thanks, Clee darling. But do you actually mean to say that I can now block you or any other Prime out completely?"

"You're going too far. Me, yes—but don't forget that there very well may be people—or things—as far ahead of us as we are ahead of pointer pups."

"Hah! Like hell! I just *know,* Clee, that you're the absolute tops of the whole universe."

189

"Well, we can dream, of course," Garlock withdrew his mind from Belle's and turned his attention to the now quiet Semolo. "Well, my overconfident and contumacious young squirt, are you done horsing around or do you want to keep it up until you addle completely what few brains you have?"

The Lizorian made no reply; he merely glared.

"The trouble with you half-baked, juvenile Primes is that you know too damned much that isn't true. As an old Tellurian saying hath it, you're 'too big for your britches'.

"Thus, simply because you have lived a few years on a single planet and haven't met anyone able to slap you down, you've sold yourself on the idea that there's nobody, anywhere, who can. You're wrong—in fact, you couldn't be wronger.

"What, actually, have you done? What, actually, have you got? Practically nothing. You haven't even started a starship; you've scarcely started making plans. You realize dimly that the theory is not in any of the books, that you'll have to dig it out for yourself, but that is *work*. So you're still just posing and throwing your weight around.

"As a matter of fact, you're merely a drop in a—not in a tubful, but a lake. There are thousands of millions of planets, and thousands of millions of Prime Operators. Most of them are probably a lot stronger than you are; many of them may be stronger than my partner and I are. I am not at all certain that you will pass even the first screening; but since you are without question a Prime Operator, I will deliver the message we came to deliver. Miss Mitala, do you want to listen or shall we drive it into you, too?"

"I want to listen to anyone or anything who has a working starship and who can do what you have just done."

"Very well." And Garlock told the general-distribution version of the story of the Galactic Service.

"Quite interesting," Semolo said loftily, at its end. Whether or not I would be interested depends, of course, on whether there's a position high enough . . ."

"I doubt very much if there's one low enough," Garlock cut in sharply. "However, since it's part of my job, I'll get in touch with you later."

Back in the Main—"What a jerk!" Belle exclaimed. "I simply marvel at your forbearance, Clee. You should have turned him inside out and hung him up to dry—especially behind the ears!" Then, suddenly, she giggled. "But do you know what I did?"

"I can guess. A couple of shots in the arm?"

"Right Next time he pitches into her she'll slap his ears right off!"

"Fine. But let's hop to Number Two—here it is."

"Oh, yes," came a smooth, clear, diamond-sharp thought in reply to Garlock's introductory call. "This world, as you have perceived, is Falne. I am indeed Baver 14WD27, my companion Prime is indeed Glarre 12WD91. You are, we perceive, Bearers of the Truth; of great skill and of high advancement. Your visit here will, I am sure, be of immense benefit to us and possibly, I hope, of some small benefit to you. We will both be delighted to have you 'port yourselves to us immediately."

The Tellurians did so—to be attacked on the instant by a blast of force the like of which neither had even imagined. The two Falnian Primes, capable operators both, had built up their highest possible potentials and had launched both terrific bolts without any hint of warning.

Belle's mind, however, was already fused with Garlock's. Their combined blocks were instantaneous in action; their counterthrust very nearly so. Both Falnians staggered backward until they were stopped by the room's wall.

"Ah, yes," Garlock said then. "You are indeed, in a small and feeble way, Seekers After the Truth; of which we are indeed Bearers. Lesser Bearers, perhaps, but still Bearers. You will indeed profit greatly from our visit. You err, however, in thinking that we may in any respect profit from you. You have nothing whatever that we have not had for long. Now let us, if you please, take a few seconds of time to get acquainted, each with the other."

"That, indeed, is the logical and seemly thing to do." Both Falnians straightened up and stepped forward— neither arrogantly nor apologetically, but quite as though nothing at all out of the ordinary had taken place.

Each pair studied the other. Physically, the two pairs were surprisingly alike. Baver was almost as big as Garlock and almost as heavily muscled. Glarre could have been cast in Belle's own mold.

With that, however, all resemblance ceased.

Both Falnians were naked. The man wore only a belt and pouch in lieu of pockets; the woman only a leather carryall slung from one shoulder—big enough, Garlock thought, to hold a week's supplies for an Explorer Scout.

His hair was thick, bushy, unkempt; sun-bleached to a nondescript blend of pale colors. Hers—long, heavy, meticulously middle-parted and dressed—was a startling two-tone job. To the right of the part it was a searingly-brilliant red; to the left, an equally brilliant royal blue.

His skin was deeply tanned. The color of hers was completely masked by a bizarrely spectacular overlay of designs done in semi-indelible, multi-colored dyes.

"Ah, you are worthy indeed of receiving an increment of Truth. Hear, then, the message we bring." And again Garlock told the story.

"We thank you, sir and madam, from our hearts. We will accept with joy your help in finishing our ship; we will do all that in us lies to further the cause of the Galactic Service. Until a day, then?"

"Until a day." Then, to Belle, "Okay—ready? Go!"

And again in the Main:

"What a pair *they* turned out to be! Clee, that simply scared me witless!"

"It was a shock, all right." Garlock jammed his hands into his pockets and prowled about the room, his face a black scowl of concentration.

Finally he pulled himself out of the brown study and said, "I've been trying to think if there's any other thing, however slight, that I have and you haven't. There isn't. You've got it all. You're just as fast as I am, just as sharp and as accurate—and, since we now draw on the same field, just as strong."

"Why, Clee! You're worrying about *me?* You've done altogether too much for me, already."

"Anything I can do I've got to do . . . Well, shall we go?"

"We shall."

They visited four more planets that day. And after supper that night, standing in the corridor between their doors, Belle began to soften her shield, as though to send a thought. Almost instantly, however, she changed her mind and snapped it back up to full power.

"Good night, Clee," she said.

"Good night, Belle."

And each went into his own room.

The next day they worked nine planets, and the day after that they worked ten. They ate supper in friendly fashion; then strolled together across the Main to a davenport.

"It's funny," Belle said thoughtfully, "having this tremendous ship all to ourselves. To have a private conference right out here in the Main . . . or is it?"

He triggered the shields; she watched him do it. "It is now," he assured her.

"Prime-proof? Not ordinary Gunther blocks?"

"Yes. Two hundred kilovolts and four hundred kilogunts, backed by all the stuff of the Prime and Op fields and the full power of the engines. I told you I made some changes."

"Private enough, I guess . . . What a mess those Primes are! And we'll have to make the rounds twice more—when we alert 'em and when we pick 'em up."

"Not necessarily. This new setup ought to give us a galaxy-wide reach. Let's try Semolo, on Lizoria, shall we?"

"Okay, darling—let's." *"Darling?"*

"Yes. You said you weren't going to fight with me any more. Okay—I'm not going to try to lick you any more until after I've licked myself. I'm locked tight—you may fire when ready."

They fired—and hit the mark dead center. Toplofty and arrogant and belligerent as ever, the Lizorian Prime took the call. "I thought all the time you wanted something. Well, I neither want nor need . . ."

"Cut it, you unlicked cub, until you can begin to use that half-liter of golop you call a brain," Garlock said harshly. "We're just trying out a new ultra-communicator. Thanks for your help."

On the fourth day they worked eleven planets; the fifth day saw the forty-sixth planet done and the immediate job finished. All during supper it was very evident that Belle had something unpleasant on her mind.

After eating, she went out into the Main and slumped down on a davenport. Garlock followed her. A cigarette leaped out of a closed box and into place between her lips. It came alight. She smoked it slowly, without relish, almost as though she did not know that she was smoking.

"Might as well get it out of your system, Belle," Garlock said aloud. "What are you thinking about at the moment?"

Belle exhaled; the half-smoked butt vanished. "At the moment I was thinking about Gunther blocks. Specifically, their total inability to cope with that new Prime probe of yours." She stared at him, narrow-eyed. "It goes through them just like nothing at all." She paused, and eyed him questioningly.

"No comment."

"And yet you gave it to me. Freely. Of your own accord. Even before I needed it. Why?"

"Still no comment."

"You'd better comment, Clee, before I blow my top."

"There is such a thing as urbanity."

"I've heard of it, yes; even though you never did believe I ever had any. But it doesn't apply in this case. You *talk* a good game of urbanity, but your brand of it would never carry you *that* far. . . ."

She paused. He remained silent. She went on:

"Of course, it does put a lot of pressure on me to develop myself."

"I'm glad you used the word 'develop' instead of 'treatment'."

"Oh, sometimes—at rare intervals—I'm not exactly dumb. But you *must* have known what a horrible risk you took in making me as powerful as you are."

"Some, perhaps, but very definitely less risky than *not* doing it."

"Damn it, getting information out of you is harder than pulling teeth the old way. Clee Garlock, I want to know *why!*"

"Very well." Garlock's jaw set. "You've had it in mind all along that this is some kind of a lark; that you and I are Gunther tops of the universe. Or did that belief weaken a bit when we met Baver 14WD27 and his lady-love?"

"Well, perhaps—a little. However, the probability is becoming greater with every planet we visit. After all, *some* race has to be tops. Why *shouldn't* it be us?"

"What a *hell* of a logic—excuse me, please. Skip it."

"Oh, you really *meant* it when you said you weren't going to fight with me any more?"

"I'm going to try not to. Now, remembering that I don't consider your premise valid, just suppose that when we visit some planet some day, you get your mind burned out and I don't—solely because I had something I could have given you and wouldn't. What then?"

"Oh. I thought that was what you . . . but suppose that I can't . . ."

"We won't suppose anything of the kind. But that wasn't all that was on your mind. Nor most."

"How true. Those Primes—the women. Honestly, Clee, I never *imagined* such a bunch of exhibitionistic, obnoxious, swell-headed, spoiled-rotten *bitches* in my whole life. And every day it was borne in on me more and more that I'm exactly like the rest of them."

Garlock was wise enough to say nothing, and Belle went on:

"I've been talking a good game of licking myself, but this time I'm going to *do* it."

She jumped up and doubled her fists. "If you can do it, I can," she declared. "Like the ancient song—'Anything you can do I can do better; I can do anything better than you.'" She tried to be jaunty, but the jauntiness did not ring quite true.

"That's an unfortunate quotation, I'm afraid. The trouble is, I haven't."

"Huh? Don't be an idiot, Clee. You certainly have—what else do you suppose put me so far down in the dumps?"

"In that case, you *certainly* will. So come on up out of the dumps."

"Okay—I certainly will. But for a woman who's been talking so big, I feel low in my mind. A good-night kiss, Clee darling? Just one; and just a little one, at that?"

There were more than one, and none of them was very little. Eventually, however, the two stood, arms still around each other, in the corridor between their doors.

"But kissing's as far as it goes, isn't it," Belle said. The remark was not a question; nor was it quite a statement.

"That's right."

"So good night, darling."

"Good night."

And when they next saw each other, at the breakfast table, Belle was apparently her usual dauntless self.

"Hi, darling; sit down," she said gaily. "Your breakfast is on the table."

They ate in silence for a few minutes; then her hand crept tentatively across the table. He pressed it warmly. "You look great, Belle. Out of the dumps?"

"Pretty much—in most ways. One way, though, I'm in deeper than ever. You see, I know exactly what you did to Fao Talaho—and why neither you nor anybody else could do it to me. Or if they could, what would happen if they did."

"I was hoping you would. I couldn't very well tell you, before, but . . ."

"Of course not. I see that."

". . . the fact is that Fao, and all the others we've met, are young enough, unformed enough—yes, damn it, *weak* enough—to bend. But you are tremendously strong, and twelve numbers Rockwell harder than a diamond. You wouldn't bend. If enough stress could be applied—and that's decidedly questionable—you'd break. I can't figure it. You're a little older, of course, but certainly not enough to . . ."

"How about the fact that I've been banging myself for eight years against Cleander Garlock, the top Prime of the universe? That might have something to do with it, don't you think?"

"Indefensible conclusions drawn from insufficient data," Garlock countered. "That's just what I've been talking about. No matter how we got the way we are, though, the fact is that you and I have got to fight our own battles and bury our own dead."

"Check. Like having a baby, but worse. There's nothing anybody else can do—even you—except maybe hold my hand, like now."

"That's about it. But speaking of holding hands, would it help if we paired again?"

Belle studied the question for two full minutes; her fine eyes clouded. Then she shook her head. "No. I'd enjoy it too much, and you'd . . . well, it would . . ."

"What?"

"Oh, physically, of course; but that isn't enough, or good enough, now. You see, I know what your personal code is. It's unbelievable, almost—I never heard of one like it, except maybe a priest or two—but I admire you tremendously for it. You would never, willingly, pair with a woman you really loved. That was why you were so glad to break ours off. You can't deny it."

"I won't try to deny it. But you can't bluff me, Belle, so please quit trying. Basically, your code is the same as mine. Why else did you initiate our break?"

Her block went on solid, and Garlock said hastily,

aloud, "Excuse it, please. Cancel, I've just said, and know as an empirical fact, that you've got to do the job alone—but I can't seem to help putting my foot in it by blundering in anyway. Let's get to work, shall we?"

"What at? Interview the Primes, I'd say—tell them to hold themselves in readiness to attend . . ."

"On very short notice . . ."

"Yes. To attend the big meeting on Tellus. We'll have to make a schedule. It shouldn't be held until after Fao and to make a schedule. It shouldn't be held until after Fao and Deg get their ship built—it *can't* be held, of course, until after you and Jim are out of SSE. Have you got *that* figured out yet?"

"Pretty much." He told her his plan.

Belle listened, then burst into laughter. "So *I'm* in it, too? Wonderful!"

"You have to be. If we make him mad enough he'll fire you, too."

"Without hiring me first? He couldn't."

"He could—very easily. He doesn't know one-tenth of one percent of his people. If we work it right he'll assume that you're one of us wage-slaves, too. Lola, too, for that matter."

"Careful, Clee. You and I think this is funny, but Lola wouldn't. She'd be shocked to her sweet little core, and she'd louse up the whole idea. So be very sure she doesn't get in on it."

"I guess you're right. . . . Well, shall we go out and insult our touchy young friend Semolo? Ready . . . go!"

"Oh it's *you* again. I tell you . . ." the Lizorian began.

"You will tell me nothing. You will listen. Link your mind to Mitala's." The fused Tellurian minds enforced the order. "In about two weeks the Primes of many worlds will meet in person on Tellus. Arrange your affairs so that on ten minutes' notice you can both leave Lizoria for Tellus aboard our starship, the *Pleiades*. That is all."

"He'll come, too," Belle chortled.

"You couldn't keep him away," Garlock agreed.

On the next planet, Falne, the procedure was a little different. The information was the same, but—"One word of warning," Garlock added. "It is to be a meeting of minds, not a contest to set up a pecking-order. If you try any such business you will be disciplined—sharply and in public."

"Suppose that, under such conditions, we refuse to attend the meeting?"

"That is your right. There is no coercion whatever. Whether or not you come will depend upon whether or not you two are in reality Seekers after Truth. Until a day."

And so it went. Planet after planet. On not one of those worlds had any Prime changed his thinking. Not one was really interested in the Galactic Service as an instrument for the good of all mankind. There were almost as many attitudes as there were Primes; but all were essentially self-centered and selfish.

"That tears it, Belle—busts it wide open. The two of us together can do either job—that is, either be top boss and run the thing or put in full time beating some sense into those hard, thick skulls. We can't do both."

"On paper, we should," Belle said, thoughtfully. "You're Galactic Admiral; I'm your Vice. One job apiece. But we're *not* going to be separated. Besides . . ."

"Two minds are much better than one," he said.

Belle laughed. "That settles that. The Garlock-Bellamy fusion is Galactic Admiral—so we need a good Vice. Who? Deggi and Fao? They're cooperative and idealistic enough, but . . . Oh, I don't know exactly what it is they lack. Do you?"

"No; I can't put it into words, or thoughts. Probably the concept is too new for pigeonholing. It isn't exactly strength or hardness or toughness or resilience or brisance —maybe a combination of all five. What we need is a pair like us but better."

"There *aren't* any."

"Don't be too sure." Belle glanced at him in surprise and he went on: "Not that we've seen, no. But each of those worlds centers a volume of space containing thousands of planets. Including the Tellurian and the Margonian, we now have forty-eight regions defined. Let's run a very fast search-pattern of Region Forty-Nine and see what we come up with."

"All right—but suppose we do find somebody who out-Guthers us?"

"I'd a lot rather have it that way than the way it is now. I'll do the hopping, you the checking. Here's the first one—what do you read?"

"No good."

"And this one?"

"The same."

"And this?"

"Ditto."

Until, finally: "Clee, just how long are you going to keep this up?"

"Until we find something or run out of time for the meeting. Belle, I really *want* to find somebody who amounts to something."

"So do I, really, so go ahead."

But they did not run out of time. At planet number four-hundred-something Belle suddenly emitted a shriek— vocally as well as mentally.

"Clee! Hold it! There's something here, I think!"

"I'm sure there is, and I'm gladder to see you two people than can possibly be expressed."

Belle whirled; so did Garlock. A man stood in the middle of the Main—a man shaped very much like Garlock, but with long, badly-tousled fiery-red hair and a bushy wilderness of fiery-red whiskers.

"Please excuse this intrusion, Admiral—or should it be plural? Improper address, I'm sure, but your joint tenure is a concept so new and so vast that I am not yet able to grasp it fully—but you are working at such high speed that I had to do something drastic. You will, I trust, remain here long enough to discuss certain matters with my wife and me?"

"We'll be very glad to."

"Thank you. I will return, then, more decorously, and bring her along. One moment." He disappeared.

"Wife!" Belle exclaimed, more than half in dismay. "Then they must be . . ."

"Yeah." The thought of a wife did not bother Garlock at all. "Talk about *power!* And *speed!* To get all that stuff and 'port up here in a fraction of a second? There's a guy who is what a Prime Operator ought to be!"

In a few seconds the man reappeared, accompanied by a woman who was very obviously pregnant—eight months or so. Like the man, she was dressed in tight-fitting coveralls. Her hair, however—it was a natural red, too—was cut to a uniform length of eight inches, and each hair individually stood out, perfectly straight and perfectly perpendicular to the element of the scalp from which it sprang.

"Friends Belle and Clee of Tellus, I present Therea, my wife . . . and Alsyne, myself . . . of this planet Thaker.

202

We have numbers, too, but they are never used among friends."

Acknowledgments were made and a few minutes of conversation ensued, during which the two couples studied each other.

"This looks mighty good to me," Garlock said then. "Shall we go screens half-down, Alsyne, and cry in each other's beer?"

In thirty seconds of flashing communication each became thoroughly informed. Those minds could send, and could receive, an incredibly vast amount of information in an incredibly brief space of time.

"Your ship should work and doesn't," Garlock said. "Show me, in detail."

Alsyne showed him.

"Oh, I see. You didn't work out quite all the theory. It has to be activated. Like this. . . ." Garlock showed Alsyne.

"I see. Thanks." Alsyne disappeared and was gone for some ten minutes. He reappeared, grinning hugely behind his flaming wilderness of beard. "It works perfectly— for which our heartfelt thanks. And now that my mind is at complete peace with the universe, we will consider the utterly fascinating subject of your proposed Galactic Service. You two Tellurians, immature although you are, have made two tremendous contributions to the advancement of the Scheme of Things—three, if you count this starship, which is comparatively unimportant—each of such import that no human mind can foresee any fraction of its consequences. First, your Prime Field, the probe and its screen . . ."

"Clee!" Belle drove the thought. "You *didn't* give him *that,* surely!"

"Tut-tut, my child," Therea soothed her. "You are

alarming yourself about nothing."

"The only trouble with you two youngsters is that you aren't quite—very nearly, of course, but very definitely not quite—grown up." Alsyne smiled again . . . not only with mouth and eyes, but with his whole hairy face. "To the mature mind there is no such thing as status. Each knows what he can do best and does it as a matter of course.

"Second, the unimaginably important contribution of the ability to combine two dissimilar but intimately compatible minds into one tremendously effective fusion. While Therea and I have had only a few moments to play with it, we realize some of its possibilities. Thus, since she is a Doctor of the Humanities . . ."

"Oh," Belle interrupted. *"That's* why you knew what I was thinking about, even though I tight-beamed the thought and my screens were tight?"

"Exactly so. But to continue. With her sympathy and empathy, and my driving force and so on, the job of licking these young Primes into shape is precisely right for us. It is a truly delicious thought.

"You two, on the other hand, have much that we lack. Breadth and depth and scope of imagination and of vision; yet almost incredible will-power and stamina and resolve . . ."

"That's the word I was trying to think of—will-power!" Belle flashed a thought at Garlock.

". . . qualities virtually always mutually exclusive; but the combination of which makes your fusion uniquely qualified to lead and direct this new and magnificent movement. But Therea and I have been idle and frustrated far too long. We can be of most use, at the moment, on Margonia, working with the Fao-Deggi unit. Therefore, with renewed deep thanks, we go."

Man and wife disappeared; and, then seconds later, the Thakern starship vanished from its world.

"Well, what do you think of that?" Belle gasped. "I was actually afraid to think, even behind a Prime screen. I don't know *yet* whether I want to kiss 'em or kill 'em."

"I do. That guy is really a Prime, Belle. He's older, bigger, and a lot better than I am."

"Oh no," she said positively. "Older, yes. More mature —you *baby*, you!" She laughed. "If he hadn't included you in that crack I'd've stabbed him, so help me, even though it wasn't true. He said himself it's *you* who has got what it takes to lead and direct, not him."

"The *two* of us, not just me."

"Right—the two of us, now and forever. Anyway, he wants us to, and we want to, so everything's lovely—so let's get to work on Fatso and his Foster. I think we ought to have some fun for a change and that'll be a lot. When do we want to hit him?"

"Any day Monday through Friday. Nine-fifteen A.M. Eastern Daylight Time. Plus or minus one minute."

"Nice! Catch him in *flagrante delicto*. Lovely!"

On a Wednesday morning, then, at twelve minutes past nine EDT, the *Pleiades* hung poised high over the Chancellory of Solar System Enterprises, Incorporated.

"Remember, Belle!" Garlock was pacing the Main. "To keep 'em staggering we'll have to land slugging and beat 'em to every punch. You did a wonderful job on her last time, and it's been eating on her ever since. She's probably been rehearsing in front of a mirror just how she's going to tear you apart next time and just how she's going to spit out the pieces. Last time, you were cold, stiff, rigidly formal, and polite. So this time it'll be me, and I'll be hot and bothered, dirty, low, coarse, lewd, and very, very rough."

Belle threw back her head and laughed. "Rough? Yes. Vicious contemptuous, or ugly; yes. A master of profanity; yes. But low or dirty or coarse or lewd, Clee? Or any one of the four, to say nothing of them all? Oh no. Ferber's a filthy beast, of coarse; but even he knows you're one of the cleanest men that ever lived. They'd *know* it was an act."

"Not unless I give 'em time to think—or unless you do, before he fires Jim—in which case we'll lose the game anyway. But how about you? If I can knock 'em too groggy to think, can you carry on hard enough to keep 'em that way?"

"Oh, just watch me! I never tried anything like that, but I'll guarantee to be just as low, dirty, coarse, lewd, and crude as you are. Probably more so, because in this particular case it'll be fun. You see, you're a man—you can't possibly despise and detest that slimy Ferber either in the same way or as much as I do."

"This ought to be good. Cut the rope, Jim."

Even before the starship came to rest, Garlock drove a probe into the *sanctum sanctorum* of the Chancellory—an utterly unheard-of act of insolence.

"Foster! This is the *Pleiades* coming in. Garlock calling. Hot up the tri-di and the recorder, and put Fatso on—and snap into it!"

"Why, I . . . you . . ."

"Stop stuttering and come to life, you halfwit! Gimme Ferber and hurry it up! This ship's trickier'n hell!"

"Why, you . . . I never . . ." Ferber's outraged First Secretary could scarcely talk. "He . . . he is . . ."

"I know, babe, I know—'Chancellor Ferber is in conference and can not be disturbed,'" he mimicked. "What is it this time? Has he got a naked file-clerk on the davenport because you're getting too old and fat to do a good job on him any more? Listen, you worn-out battle-axe—didn't you get your tits far enough into the wringer when you tangled with Belle Bellamy? This is *me,* not her, and I haven't got time to waste on you, or any of the rest of Fat Stuff's sofa-partners. Put him on now—but *quick*—or I'll 'port down there and slap 'em clear off. Now *jump!"*

Belle, seated cross-legged on the floor, was rocking back and forth with both hands jammed into her mouth. James was standing up, gesticulating fervently with hands clasped high above his head. Lola, who had not been completely informed, was staring in wide-eyed, horrified amazement.

The tri-di tank brightened up, Chancellor Ferber's image appeared. He was disheveled, surprised, and angry; but Garlock gave him no chance to speak.

"Well, Fatso—at last! Where the *hell* have you been all morning? I want some stuff, just as fast as God will let you get it together." And he began to read off, as fast as he could talk, a long list of highly technical items.

Ferber tried for many seconds to break in, and Garlock finally allowed him to do so.

"Are you crazy, Garlock?" he shouted. "What in hell's name are you bothering *me* with *that* stuff for? You know better than that—make out your requisitions and send them through regular channels!"

"Channels, hell!" Garlock shouted back. "Hasn't it got through your four-inch-thick skull yet that I'm in a hurry? I don't want this stuff week after next; I want it day before yesterday—this damned junk-heap is apt to fall apart any second. So quit goggling and slobbering at me, you slimy fat toad, and get that three hundredweight of suet into action—*hump* yourself!"

"You . . . you . . . Why, I was never so insulted . . ."

"Insulted? You?" Garlock out-roared him. "Listen, Fatso. If I ever really set out to insult you, you'll know it—it'll blister all the plastic off the walls. All I'm trying to do now is to get you off that fat butt of yours and get some action. Tell that woman on the sofa to put her clothes back on and get to hell out!"

"Woman!" Ferber yelled, pounding his desk. "There's no woman here, you God damned insubordinate son of a . . ."

"The hell there isn't!" Garlock yelled louder and pounded harder. "It's nine-seventeen—and besides, I'm a Prime, not a lousy dumb low First, like you. So put the filthy pictures and nasty pamphlets back in the drawer. Start rounding up this stuff—but *fast*— or I'll come down there and take your job away from you and do it myself —and for your own greasy hide's sake you'd better believe I'm not just blowing wind, either."

"You'll *what?*" Ferber screamed. "YOU'RE FIRED!"

"*You* fire *me?*" Garlock mimicked the scream. "And make it stick? You'd better write that one up for the funnies. Why, you lard-brain, you couldn't fire a cap-pistol."

"Foster!" Ferber yelled. "Terminate Garlock as of now. Insubordination, misconduct, abuse of position, incompetence, malfeasance—everything else you can think of— blacklist him all over the system!"

At the word "fired" Belle had leaped to her feet and had stopped laughing.

"Miss Bellamy!" Ferber snapped.

"Yes, sir?" she answered, sweetly.

"You are hereby promoted to Head of the . . ."

"Oh, yeah?" Belle said, her voice fairly reeking with contempt. "You filthy slob—you unprincipled, lascivious, lecherous *hitler!* Have you got the unmitigated gall to take *me* for a whore? To think you can add *me* to your collection of boot-licking, round-heeled tramps?

"Me? Take *you* on? No, thanks. Just looking at you with your corset and all your clothes on makes me sick at the stomach—if I actually had to *touch* your sloppy carcass I'd vomit all over the floor. Oh no! Instead of promoting me you can take the job I've got now and stick it!"

"You're fired and blacklisted, too!"

"How nice! You know, I don't know of *anything* I'd rather have happen to me?"

"Get James on there. You, James . . ."

"You don't need to fire me, you fathead," James said contemptuously. "I've already quit—the exact second you fired Clee."

"No you didn't!" Ferber screamed. "Resignation not accepted. You're *fired.* Dishonorably discharged—blacklisted everywhere—you'll *never* get another job—*anywhere!* And here's your slip, too!" Miss Foster was very fast on the machines.

James 'ported his slip up into the *Pleiades,* just as Garlock and Belle had done with theirs, and disappeared with it as they had; reappearing almost instantly.

"Montandon!"

"Chancellor Ferber, are you completely out of your mind? You can't discharge either Miss Bellamy or me."

"I can't?" he gloated. "Why not?"

"Because neither of us is employed. By anybody."

"That's right, Fatso," Belle jeered. "We just came along. Just to keep the boys company. It's lonesome, you know, 'way out in deep space."

Miss Foster ripped a half-filled-out termination form out of her machine and hurled it into a waste-basket. Ferber's jaw dropped and his eyes stared glassily, but he rallied quickly.

"I can blacklist her, though, and maybe you think I won't. Belle Bellamy will never get another job in this whole solar system as long as she lives, except through me! Maybe I'll hire her some day, for something, and maybe I won't. Are you listening, Bellamy?"

"Not only listening, I'm reveling in every word." Belle laughed derisively. "I hate to shatter such wonderful dreams—or do I? You see, the *Pleiades* really works, and the Galaxians own her in fee simple and lock, stock, and barrel. You wouldn't have any part of her, remember? Insisted on payment for every nut, wire, and service? Now, they want to hire us four for a big operation with this starship. Since you only loaned Garlock and James to them, you might have made some legal trouble on that score, but now that you've fired them both—and in such *conclusive* language!—we're all set. So when you blacklist us with the Society, *please* let me know—I want to take a tri-di in technicolor of you doing it!"

"I'll see about that!" Ferber stormed. "We'll have an injunction out in an hour!"

"Go ahead," Garlock said, with a wide grin. "Have fun —the Galaxians have lawyers too, you know. One thing Belle forgot. Just in case you recover consciousness some time and want to steal our termination papers back— especially Belle's; what a howler *that* was!—don't try it. They're in a Gunther-blocked safe."

Then, as comprehension began to dawn on Ferber's face:

The *Pleiades* disappeared.

IX

THE *Pleiades* landed on Margonia's Galaxian Field, where the Tellurians found the project running smoothly, a little ahead of schedule. Delcamp and Fao were working at their fast and efficient pace, but the hairy pair from Thaker seemed to be, literally, everywhere at once.

"Hi, Belle." Fao 'ported up and shook hands warmly. "I thought I was going to have the first double-Prime baby, until *she* appeared on the scene."

"Didn't it make you mad? I'd've been furious."

"Maybe a little at first, but not after I'd talked with her for half a minute. She'd never even thought of that angle. Besides she thinks the whole galaxy is fairly crawling with double-Primes."

"That's funny—so does Clee. But there are other things —strictly not angles—that she hasn't thought of, too. If those coveralls were half an inch tighter they'd choke her to death. You'd think she'd . . ."

"What?" Fao interrupted. *"You* should scream—oh, that ridiculous Tellurian prud—"

"It *isn't* ridiculous!" Belle snapped. "And it isn't pur-dishness, either—not with me, anyway. It's just that"—she ran an indicative glance over Fao's trim flanks and hard, flat abdomen—"it spoils your figure. It's only temporary, of course, but . . ."

"*Spoils* it! Why, how *utterly* idiotic! Why, it's magnificent! Just as soon as it starts to show on me, Belle, I'm going to start wearing only half as many clothes as I've got on now."

"You couldn't." Belle eyed the other girl's bathing-suit-like garment. Except for being blue instead of yellow, it was the same as the one she had worn before.

"Hey, you two!" came Delcamp's hail. "How about getting some work done?"

With six Prime Operators on the job the work went on very rapidly, yet without error. The *Celestial Queen* was finished, tested, and found perfect, one full day ahead of James' most optimistic estimate for construction alone. The six Primes conferred.

"Do you want us to help you pick up the other Primes?" Delcamp asked. "Your Main, big as it is, will be crowded, and we have three ships here now instead of one."

"I don't think so . . . no," Garlock decided. "We told 'em we'd do it, and in the *Pleiades,* so we'd better. Unless, Alsyne, you don't agree?"

"I agree. The point, while of course minor, is very well taken. We and our Operators—we brought six along; experts in their various fields—can serve best by working on Tellus with its Galaxian Society in getting ready for the meeting."

"Oh, of course," Fao said. "Probably Deg and I should do the same thing?"

"That would be our thought." The two Thakerns were thinking—and lepping—in fusion. "However," they went on carefully, "it must not be and is not our intent to sway you in any action or decision. While not all of you four, perhaps, are as yet fully mature, not one of you should be subjected to any additional exterior stresses."

"I hope you don't think that way about *all* Primes," Garlock said grimly. "I'm going to smack some of those kids down so hard that their shirt-tails will roll up their backs like window shades."

"If you find such action either necessary or desirable, we will join you quite happily in it. We go."

The four remaining Primes looked at each other in puzzled surprise.

"What do you think about *that?*" Garlock asked finally, of no one in particular.

"I don't understand them," Fao said, "but they're mighty nice people."

Belle nibbled at her lower lip. "Clee, do you suppose we're going off on the wrong foot with uniforms and admirals and things? That with really adult Primes running things the Galactic Service would run itself? No bosses or anything?"

Garlock frowned heavily. "I hope not. Or do I? Anyway, not enough data yet to make speculation profitable. But I wonder, Miss Bellamy, if it would be considered an unjustifiable attempt to sway you in any action or decision if I were to suggest that if we're going to be busy tomorrow morning then we ought to get some sleep right now."

"Considering the source, as well as and/or in connection with the admittedly extreme provocation"—Belle straightened up into a regal pose—"you may say, Mister Garlock, without fear of successful contradiction, that in this instance no umbrage will be taken, at least for the moment." She broke the pose and smiled. "So goodnight, all."

Belle was still sunny and gay when the *Pleiades* reached Lizoria; Garlock was inwardly happy and outwardly content. Semolo, however, was his usual intransigent self. In fact, if it had not been for Mirea Mitala, and the fact that she—metaphorically—did pin Semolo's ears back, Garlock would not have taken him aboard at all.

Thus, after loading on only one pair of Primes, that auspiciously-beginning day had lost some of its luster; and as the day wore on it got no better fast. Baver of Falne had not learned anything, either—only Garlock's intervention saved the cocky and obstreperous Semolo from a mental blast that would have knocked him out cold.

Then there were Onthave and Lerthe of Crenna; Korl and Kirl of Gleer; Parleof and Ginseona of Pasquerone; Atnim and Sotara of Flandoon; and eighty others. Very few of them were as bad as Semolo; some of them, particularly the Pasqueronians and the Gleerans, were almost as good as Delcamp and Fao.

This was the first time that any pair of them had ever come physically close to any other Prime. Many of them had not really believed that any Primes abler than themselves existed. The *Pleiades* was crowded, and Garlock and Belle were not giving to any of them the deference and consideration and submissive respect which each considered his unique due.

Therefore the undertaking was neither easy nor pleasant, and both Tellurians were tremendously relieved when, the last pair picked up, they flashed the starship back to Tellus and Delcamp, Fao, and the Thakerns 'ported themselves aboard.

"Give me your attention, please," Garlock said crisply. Then, after a moment, "Any and all who are not tuned to me in five seconds will be returned immediately to their home planets and will lose all contact with this group. . . .

"That's better. For some of you this has been a very long day. For all of you it has been a very trying day. You were all informed previously as to what we had in mind.

However, since you are young and callow, and were thoroughly convinced of your own omniscience and omnipotence, it is natural enough that you derived little or no benefit from that information. You are now facing reality, not your own fantasies.

"Each pair of you has been assigned a suite of rooms in Galaxian Hall. Each suite is furnished appropriately; each is fully Gunthered for self-service.

"This meeting has not been announced to the public and, at least for the present, will not be. Therefore none of you will attempt to communicate with anyone outside Galaxian Hall. Anyone making any such attempt will be surprised.

"The meeting will open at eight o'clock tomorrow morning in the auditorium. The Thakerns and the Margonians will now inform you as to your quarters." There was a moment of flashing thought. "Dismissed."

At one second before eight o'clock the auditorium was empty. At eight o'clock, ninety-eight human beings appeared in it—six on the stage, the rest occupying the first few rows of seats.

"Good morning, everybody," Garlock said pleasantly. "Everyone being rested, fed, and having had some time in which to consider the changed reality faced by us all, I hope and am inclined to believe that we can attain friendship and accord. We will spend the next hour in becoming acquainted with each other. We will walk around, not teleport. We will meet each other physically, as well as mentally. We will learn each other's forms of greeting and we will use them. This meeting is adjourned until nine o'clock—or, rather, the meeting will begin then."

For several minutes no one moved. All blocks were locked at maximum. Each Prime used only his eyes.

Physically, it was a scene of almost overpowering perfection. The men were, without exception, handsome, strong, and magnificently male. The women, from heroically-framed Fao Talaho to surprisingly slender Mirea Mitala, all were arrestingly beautiful, breathtakingly proportioned, spectacularly female.

Clothing varied from complete absence to almost complete coverage, with a bewildering variety of intermediate conditions. Color was rampant.

Hair—or lack of it—was also an individual and highly variant matter. Some of the women, like Belle and Fao, were content with one solid but unnatural shade. One shaven head—Mirea Mitala's—was deeply tanned, but unadorned, even though the rest of her body was almost covered by precious stones. Another was decorated with geometrical and esoteric designs in eye-searing colors. A third supported a structure—it could not possibly be called a hat—of spun metal and gems.

Among the medium- and long-hairs there were two-, three-, and multi-toned jobs galore. Some of the color-combinations were harmonious; some were sharply contrasting, such as black and white; some looked as though their wearers had used the most violently-clashing colors they could find.

The prize-winner, however, was Therea of Thaker's enormous, inexplicable mop; and it was that phenomenon that first broke the ice.

The girl with the decorated scalp had been glancing questioningly at neighbor after neighbor, only to be met by uncompromising stares. Finally, however, her gaze met another as interested as her own. This second girl, whose coiffure was a high-piled confection of black, white, yellow, red, blue, and green, half-masted her screen and said:

"Oh, thanks Jethay of Lodie-Yann. I'm glad everybody isn't going to stay locked up all day. I'm Ginseona of

Pasquerone. They call me 'Jin' whenever they want to call me anything printable. And *this*"—she dug a knuckle into her companion's short ribs, whereupon he jumped, whirled around, lowered his screen, and grinned—"is my . . . the boyfriend, Parleof. Also of Pasquerone, of course. Par, both Jethay and I . . ."

"Call me 'Jet'—everybody does," Jethay said . . . almost shyly, for a Prime.

"Both Jet and I have been wondering about that woman's hair—over there. How could you possibly give a head of hair a static charge of fifty or a hundred kilovolts and not have it leak off?"

"You couldn't, unless it was a perfectly-insulated wig . . . but it looks as though she did, at that. . . ." Parleof paused in thought.

"Maybe Byuk would have an idea or two." And Jet uttered aloud a dozen or so crackling syllables that sounded as if they could have been ladylike profanity. Whatever they were, Byuk jumped, too, and tuned in with the other three.

"Oh, it's quite easy, really," Therea said then. "Look." Her mass of hair cascaded gracefully down around her neck and shoulders. "Look again." Each hair stood fiercely out all by itself, exactly as before. "All you young people will learn much more difficult and much more important things before this meeting is over. I can not tell you how glad I am that so many of you are here."

And so it went, all over the auditorium. Once cracked, the ice broke up fast.

Fao and Delcamp worked hard; so did Belle and Garlock. Alsyne was a potent force indeed—his abounding vitality and his tremendous smile broke down barriers that logic could not affect. And Therea worked near-miracles, did more than the other five combined. Her sympathy, her empathy, her understanding and feeling, were as great as Lola's own, but her operative ability was much greater than Lola's.

Thus, when half of the hour was gone, Garlock heaved a profound sigh of relief. He wouldn't have half the trouble he had expected—it was not going to be a riot. And when he called the meeting to order he was more pleasant and friendly than Belle had ever seen him before.

"While I am calling this meeting to order, it is only in the widest possible sense that I am its presiding officer, for we have as yet no organization by the delegated authority of which any man or any woman has any right to preside. Yesterday I ruled by force, simply because I am stronger than any one of you or any pair of you. Today, in the light of the developments of the last hour, that rule is done; except, perhaps, for one or two isolated and non-representative cases which may develop today. By this time tomorrow, I hope that we will be forever done with the law of claw and fang. For, as a much abler man has said—'To the really mature mind, the concept of status is completely invalid.' "

"He's putting that as a direct quote, Alsyne, and it isn't." Belle lanced the thought.

"He thinks it is," Alsyne flashed back. *"That is the way his mathematician's mind recorded it."*

"This meeting is informal, preliminary, exploratory—a meeting of minds from which, we hope, a useful and workable organization can be developed. Since you all know what we think it basically should be, there is no need to repeat it.

"I must now say something that a few of you will construe as a threat. You are all Prime Operators. Each pair of you is the highest development of a planet, perhaps of a solar system. You can learn if you will. You can cooperate if you will. Any couple here who refuses to learn, and hence to cooperate, will be returned to their native planet and will have no further contact with this group.

"I now turn this meeting over to our first moderators: Alsyne and Therea of Thaker, the oldest and ablest Prime Operators of us all."

"Thank you, Garlock of Tellus. One correction, however, if you please. I who speak am neither this man nor this woman standing here, but both. I am the Prime Unit of Thaker. For brevity, and for the purposes of this meeting only, I could be called simply 'Thaker'. Before calling for general discussion I wish to call particular attention to two points, neither of which has been sufficiently emphasized.

"First, the purpose of a Prime Operator is to serve, not to rule. Thus, no Prime should be or will be 'boss' of anything, except possibly of his own starship.

"Second, since we have no data we do not know what form the proposed Galactic Service will assume. One thing, however, is sure. Whatever power of enforcement or of punishment it may have will derive, not from its Primes, but from the fact that it will be an arm of the Galactic Council, which will be composed of Operators only. No Prime will be eligible for membership."

Thaker went on to explain how each pair could obtain instruction and assistance in many projects, including starships. How each pair would, when they were mature enough, be coached in the use of certain abilities they did not as yet have. He suggested procedures and techniques to be employed in the opening up of each pair's volume of space. He then asked for question and comments.

Semolo was the first. "If I'm a good little boy, and do exactly as I'm told, and take over the region you tell me to and not the one I want to, what assurance have I that some other Prime, just because he's a year older than I am, won't come along and take it away from me?"

"Your question is meaningless," Thaker replied. "Since you will not 'take over,' or 'have,' or 'own,' any region, it cannot be 'taken away' from you."

"Then I will . . ." Semolo began.

"You will keep still!" came a clear, incisive thought, just as Garlock was getting ready to intervene. Miss Mitala then switched from thought, which everyone there could understand, and launched a ten-second blast of furious speech. Semolo wilted and the girl went on in thought: "He'll be good—or else."

A girl demanded recognition and got it. "Semolo's right. What's the use of being Primes if we can't get any good out of it? We're the strongest people of our respective worlds. I say we're bosses and should keep on being bosses."

Garlock got ready to shut her up, then paused, holding his fire.

"Ah, yes, friend Garlock, you are maturing fast," came Thaker's thought; and, in answer to Garlock's surprise, he went on, "This situation will, I think, be self-adjusting; just as will be those in the as yet unexplored regions of space."

The girl kept on. "I, at least, am going to keep on bossing my own planet, milking it just as I . . ."

Her companion had been trying to crack her shield. Failing in that, he stepped in close and tapped her— solidly, but with carefully-measuring force—behind the ear. Before she could fall, he 'ported her back up into their quarters. "This happens all the time," he explained to the group at large. "Carry on."

Discussion went on, with less and less acrimony, all the rest of the day. And the next day, and the next. Then, argument having reached the point of diminishing returns, the three starships took the forty-six couples home.

The six Primes went into Evans' office, where the lawyer was deeply engaged with Gerald Banks, the Galaxians' Public Relations Chief. Banks was holding his head in both hands.

"Garlock, maybe *you* can tell me," Banks demanded. "How much of this stuff, if any, can I publish? And if so, *how?*"

"Nothing," Garlock said, flatly.

"What do you think, Thaker?" Belle asked. "You're smarter than we are."

"What Thaker thinks has no bearing," Garlock said.

Belle, Fao, and Delcamp all began to protest at once, but they were silenced by Thaker himself.

"Garlock is right. My people are not your people; I know not at all how your people think or what they will or will not believe. I go."

"Then that lets Deg and me out, too." Fao said with a grin, "so we'll leave that baby on your laps. We go, too."

Garlock smiled quizzically at Belle. "Well . . . you grabbed the ball—what are you going to do with it?"

"Nothing, I guess . . ." Belle thought for a minute. "We couldn't stuff any part of that down the throat of a simple-minded six-year-old. We haven't really *got* anything, anyway. Time enough, I think, when we have six or seven hundred planets in each region, instead of only one planet. Maybe we'll know something by then. Does that make sense?"

"It does to me," Garlock said, and the others agreed.

"That Thakern 'we go' business sounds rough at first, but it's contagious. Fao and Deggi caught it, and I feel like I'm coming down with it myself. How about you, Clee?"

"We go," Belle and Garlock said in unison, and vanished.

Aboard the *Pleiades,* the next few days passed quietly enough. James set up, in the starship's memory banks, a sequence to mass produce instruction tapes and blueprints. Garlock and Belle began systematically exploring the Tellurian Region. Now, however, their technique was different. If either Prime of any world was not enthusiastic about the project—

"Very well; think it over," they would say. "We will get in touch with you again in about a year." And the starship would go on to the next planet.

On Earth, however, things became less and less tranquil with every day that passed. For, in deciding not to publish anything, Garlock had not considered at all the basic function and the tremendous ability, power, and scope of The Press. And Galaxian Hall had never before been closed to the public, not for any hour of any day of any year of its existence. A non-profit organization, dependent upon the public for its tremendous income, the Galaxian Society had always courted that public in every possible ethical way.

Thus, in the first hour of closure, a bored reporter came out, read the smoothly-phrased notice, and lepped it in to the desk. It might be worth half an inch, he figured.

Later in the day, however, the world's most sensitive news-nose began to itch. Did, or did not, this quiet, unannounced closing smell ever-so-slightly of cheese? Wherefore Benjamin Bundy, the newscaster who had covered the starship's maiden flight, went out himself to look the thing over. He found the whole field closed. Not only closed, but Gunther-blocked impenetrably tight. He studied the announcement, his sixth sense—the born newsman's sense for news—probing every word.

"Regret . . . research . . . of such extreme delicacy . . . vibration . . . temperature control . . . one one-hundredth of one degree Centigrade . . ."

He sought out his long-time acquaintance Banks, finding him in a temporary office half a block away from the Hall. "What's the story, Jerry?" he asked. "The *real* story. I mean."

"You know as much about it as I do, Ben. Garlock and James don't waste time trying to detail me on that kind of business, you know."

This should have satisfied any newshawk, but Bundy's nose still itched. He mulled things over for a minute, then probed, finding that he could read nothing except Banks' outermost, most superficial thoughts.

"Well . . . maybe . . . but . . ." Then Bundy plunged. "All you have to do, Jerry, is tell me screens-half-down that your damn story is true."

"That's the one thing I can't do," Banks admitted; and Bundy could not detect that any part of his sheepishness was feigned. "You're just too damned smart, Ben."

"Oh—one of *those* things?"

"Yup. I told Evans it might not work."

That should have satisfied the reporter, but it didn't. "Now it doesn't smell just a trifle cheesy; it stinks like rotten fish. You won't go screens-down on that one, either."

"No comment."

"Ha!" Bundy said. "*This* must be a *story!* So big that Gerald Banks, the top press-agent of all time, actually doesn't *want* publicity! The starship works—this lack-of-control stuff is the bunk—from here to another star in nothing flat—Garlock's back, and he's brought—what *have* you got in there, Jerry?"

"The only way I can tell you is in confidence, for Evans' release. I'd like to, Ben, believe me, but I can't."

"Confidence, hell! Do you think we won't get it?"

"In that case, no comment." The interview ended and the siege began.

Newshounds and detectives questioned and peered and probed. They dug into morgues, tabulating and classifying. They recalled and taped and sifted all the gossip they had heard. They got a picture of sorts, but it was maddeningly confusing and incomplete. And, since it was certain that inter-systemic matters were involved, they could not extrapolate—any guess was far too apt to be wrong. Thus nothing went on the air or appeared in print; and, although the surface remained calm, The Press seethed to its depths.

Wherefore haggard Banks and harried Evans greeted Garlock with a good deal of joy when the four wanderers came back to spend the weekend on Earth.

"I'll talk to 'em," Garlock decided, after the long story had been told. "Have somebody get hold of Bundy and ask him to come out."

"Get hold of him!" Banks snorted. "He's here. Twenty-four hours a day. Eating sandwiches and cat-napping on chairs in the lobby. All you have to do is unseal that door."

Garlock flung the door wide. Bundy rushed in, followed by a more-or-less steady stream of some fifty other top-bracket newspeople, both men and women.

"Well, Garlock, perhaps *you* will give us some screens-down facts?" Bundy asked angrily.

"I'll give you *all* the screens-down—"

"Clee—you can't!" Belle and all the Operators protested at once.

Ignoring the objections, Garlock cut his shield to half

and gave the whole group a true account of everything that had happened in the galaxy. Then, while they were all too stunned to speak, a grin of saturnine amusement spread over his dark, five-o'clock-shadowed face.

"You pests insisted on grabbing the ball," he said. "Now let's see you run with it."

Bundy came out of his trance. *"What* a story!" he yelled. "We'll plaster it . . ."

"Yeah," Garlock said dryly. *"What* a story. Exactly."

"Oh." Bundy deflated suddenly. "You'll have to prove it—demonstrate it—of course."

"Of course? You tickle me. Not only do I not have to prove it, I won't. I won't even confirm it."

Bundy glared at Garlock, then whirled on Banks. "If you don't give me this in shape to use, you'll never get another line or mention anywhere!"

"Oh, no?" For the first time in his professional life Banks gloated, openly and avidly. "From now on, my friend, who is in the saddle? Who is going to come to whom?"

When the fuming newsmen had gone, Garlock said, "It'll leak, of course."

"Of course," Banks agreed. " 'It is rumored . . .' and 'from a usually reliable source . . .' and so on. Nothing definite, but each one of them will want to put out the first and biggest."

"That's what I figured. It'll have to break sometime and I thought easing it out would be best. . . . But wait a minute." He thought for two solid minutes. "We're going to need a lot of money, and we're just about broke, aren't we?" This thought was addressed to Frank Macey, the Galaxians' treasurer.

"Worse than broke—much worse."

"I could loan you a couple of credits, Frank," Belle said

brightly. "But go ahead, Clee."

"People like to be sidewalk superintendents. Suppose they could watch the construction of an outpost so far away that nobody ever dreamed of getting there. Could you do anything with that, Jerry?"

"Could I!" Banks said, and whistled.

"That's the first good idea any one of you crackpots has had for five years," Macey said suddenly. "But wouldn't transportation of material and so on present problems?"

"No; just buying it," Garlock said soberly. "Or, rather, paying for it."

"No trouble there . . ."

"What?" Belle exclaimed. " 'No trouble, it says here in fine print? How the old skinflint has changed—instead of screaming his head off about spending money he's actually *offering* to. Frank, I'll loan you *three* credits!"

"Quiet, the menfolks are talking business. Look, Clee. We'll use the *Pleiades* at first, while we're building a regular transport. A hundred passengers per trip, one thousand credits one way . . ."

"Wow!" Belle said. "Our ex-skinflint is now a barefaced, legally-protected robber."

"By no means, Belle," Evans said. "How much would that be per mile?"

"Say ten round trips per day. That would be twenty million a day gross for a small ship not intended for passenger service. When we get ships built . . . and the extras . . ." The money-man went into a financial revel of his own.

"Lots of extras," Banks agreed. "And oh, *brother,* what a public-relations dream of heaven!"

"Maybe I'm dumb," Garlock broke in, "but just what are you going to use for money to get started?"

"The minute we confirm any part of the story, the credit of the Galaxian Society will jump from X-O to AA-A1."

"Oh. So Belle and I will have to lose our *Pleiades* for awhile. I don't like that, but we do need the money . . . but we *can* have her for this coming week?"

"Of course."

"So maybe we'd better break the story now, instead of letting it leak."

"*Can* you, after what you just told them?"

"Sure I can." He set his mind and searched. "Bundy, this is Garlock . . ."

"So what am I supposed to do—burst into tears of joy?"

"Save it. I changed my mind. You can break it as fast and as hard as you like. I'll play along."

"Yeah? Why the switch? What's the angle?"

"Strictly commercial. Get it from Banks."

"And you'll—personally—go on my hour with it?"

"Yes. Also, we'll demonstrate—take you to any star-system in the galaxy. You and all the rest of the news-hawks who were here and any fifty VIP's you want to invite. Tomorrow morning."

"You, personally, in the *Pleiades?*" Bundy insisted.

"Better than that. The other two starships, too. You've got them—particularly those four Primes—clearly in mind?"

"Not exactly, there was so much of it. Refresh my memory a bit, okay?" Garlock did so. "Thanks, pal, for the scoop. I'll crash it right now, and follow up with Banks. 'Bye!"

"Think you can deliver on that, Clee?" Banks asked.

"Sure. Both Deggi and Alsyne will need a lot of extra money, fast. They'll play along."

They did; and that three-starship tour—which visited twenty solar systems instead of one—was the most sensational thing old Earth had ever spawned.

Belle and Garlock did not spend that weekend on Earth. "We go," they said, as soon as the *Pleiades* was empty of pressmen, and they took James and Lola along. "If we *never* see another such brawl as this is going to be," Belle told Banks, who was basking in glory and entreating them to stay on for the show, "it will be exactly twenty minutes too soon."

Thus it came about that Earth's first four deep-spacemen were completely out of reach when unexpected developments began.

Alonzo P. Ferber was one of the VIP's on Bundy's personally conducted tour of the stars. He was a very able executive, with an extremely keen profit-sense. This new thing simply reeked of money. SSE would have to get in on it.

Ferber was not thin-skinned; where money was concerned it would never even occur to him to cherish grudges or to retain animosities. Wherefore SSE's purchasing department suggested to the Galaxian Society that negotiations be opened concerning licenses, franchises, royalties, and so on. These suggestions were politely but firmly brushed off. Then emissaries were sent, of ever-increasing caliber and weight. Next, Ferber himself tried the tri-di; and finally he came in person.

Rebuffed, he made such legally-sound threats that Evans and Macey agreed to a meeting—stating flatly, however, that no commitments could possibly be made without the knowledge and approval of the Society's president, Cleander Garlock. Thus, at the meeting, the Galaxians made only two statements that were even approximately definite. One was that Garlock would probably return to Earth during the afternoon or evening of the following Friday; the other that they would take the matter up with Garlock as soon as they could.

After that meeting Macey was unperturbed, but Evans was a deeply worried man.

"You, see," he explained, "the real crux wasn't even mentioned."

"No. What is it, then?"

"Operators, Primes, and the practically nonexistent laws pertaining to their . . . what? Labor? Skill? Genius? For instance, could Garlock be forced to do whatever it is that he does? On the other hand, if Ferber offered Belle Bellamy five million credits a year to 'work' for SSE, is there anything we could do about it?"

"Oh. I thought all there was to it was that you'd delay 'em for a year or so and that'd be it."

"Far from it. To date I have listed fifty-eight points for which, as far as we can learn, there are no precedents." And the lawyer called a meeting of his staff.

For Belle and Garlock, the week went quickly. On Friday afternoon, high above Earth's Galaxian Field, Garlock said, more than half regretfully, "No more fun. Back to the desk. Back to the salt-mines." James frowned in puzzlement. "Why the sob-and-moan routine, Clee, from a guy who's going to be monarch of all he surveys?"

"His conscience aches him," Belle explained. "This monarching business is tough if you haven't thought up how to monarch it, and he hasn't. Have you, Clee?"

"No." Garlock smiled slightly. "I've been busy."

"You better start to," she advised darkly. "You aren't busy now, and we've got about an hour. We better confer—I'll make like a slave-driver."

"Conferring with slave-drivers is the fondest thing I am of," Garlock said.

They 'ported into his room and he set the blocks. His attitude changed instantly. "Nice act, Belle. What was it all about?"

"That theory of yours. Your predictions are too uncannily accurate to be guesswork, and the more times you dead-center the bullseye the worse scared I get. I really want to know, Clee."

"Okay. It isn't complete—I need a lot more data—but I'll show you what I have. It's fairly strong medicine and it comes in big chunks."

"It would have to—it covers the whole macrocosmic universe doesn't it?"

"Yes. I'll start with the striking fact that, on every out-galaxy planet we visited, the human beings were *Homo Sapiens* to N decimal places—fertile with each other and, according to expert testimony, with us. All planets had humanoid 'guardians,' the Arpalones and Arpales. Some, but not all, had one or more non-human, more-or-less-intelligent races, such as the Fumapties, the Lemarts, the Sencors, and so on. These other races never seemed to fight each other, but both races of Guardians fought any and all of them, on sight and to the death. What do those facts mean to you?"

"Nothing beyond face value. I've gnawed at them and others—'nibbled' might be a better word—but I haven't been able to come up with anything."

"I have." He unrolled a sheet of drafting paper covered with diagrams, symbols, and equations. "But before I go into this stuff, consider the human body. How many red cells are there in your blood stream?"

"Billions, I suppose."

"And there are billions of human beings on billions of planets, each having red blood cells identical, as far as we know, with yours and mine. Also white cells. Also, sometimes, various kinds of pathogenic microorganisms, such as staphs, streps, viruses, spiros, and so on.

"Okay. My thought is that the Lemarts, Ozobes, and the like are analogous to disease-producing organisms. We saw the full range of effects—from none at all up to death itself."

"But the Ozobes and so on died, too."

"How long do disease germs live in a human body after they've killed it?"

"But that horrible Dilipic—the golop. They don't seem to fit."

"Try that on for size as cancer. Also, the Arpalones typed us before they'd let us land on any planet. Why didn't we blast them out of the way and land anyway?"

"Why, we didn't want to. It wasn't worthwhile."

"We couldn't. Psychic block. And if we had, we would have died. Different blood-types don't mix."

"So you and I are merely two red cells in the bloodstream of a super-galactic super-monster? Like hell!" she snorted. "That chestnut was propounded a thousand years ago. Are you trying to take me for a ride on *that* old sawhorse?"

"That's the attitude I had at first. So now we're ready for the chart." He pointed to a group of symbols. "We start with symbolic logic; manipulating like so to get this." There was a long mathematical dissertation, a mind-to-mind, rigorous, point-by-point proof.

"Q.E.D." Garlock concluded.

"I see your math, and if I believed half of it I'd be scared witless. Those few pieces fit, but they're scattered around in vast areas of blackness and you're just jumping around between them. And how about our own galaxy, the most important piece of all? It's different, and we're different, mentally. That wrecks your whole theory."

"No. I told you I need a lot more data. Also, beyond a certain point the analogy appears to get looser."

"*Appears* to! It's as loose as it can get!"

"Think a minute. Is it actually loose, or are we getting up into concepts that no human mind can grasp?"

"Oh . . . You're quite a salesman, Clee, but I'm still not buying."

"Our galaxy is a bit of specialized tissue—part of a gang-lion, maybe. Over here, see? I'll have to leave it dangling until we find some more like it."

"I see. But anyway, you haven't a tenth's worth of real material on that whole sheet. Feed everything you have there into a computer and it'd just laugh at you."

"Sure it would. The great advantage of the human brain is its ability to arrive at valid conclusions from incomplete data."

"The brain of a Newton or an Einstein, yes." Belle thought for a minute, then grinned at him impishly. "Now watch the brain of a Bellamy perform. Get into high gear, brain . . . I wish I knew something about biochemical embryology; but I read somewhere that ova are sterile, so our galaxy is an ovum. Therefore our super-monster is a female—which accounts for and explains rigorously the long-known truth that women always have been, are now, and always will be vastly superior to men in every quality, aspect, and . . ."

"Hold it!" Garlock snapped. His face hardened into intense concentration. Then: "Do you think you're kidding, Belle?"

"Why of *course* I'm kidding . . ."

"Look here, then." He picked up a pencil and filled in blank after blank after blank. "I'm making one unjustifiable assumption—that the *Pleiades* is the first intergalactic starship. The super-being is a female, and she is just becoming pregnant . . ."

"Nonsense! There are no blood cells in a sperm, and I don't think there are any in an ovum."

"I didn't mention either sperm or ovum. The analogy is so loose here that it holds only in the broadest, most general terms. The actual process of reproduction is unknowable. But wherever we went, we changed things. Not only by what we actually did, but also as a catalyst—no . . ."

"No, not a catalyst. A hormone."

"Exactly. Each of these changes would cause others, and so on. An infinite series. Calling the first three terms alpha, beta, and gamma, we operate like this . . ." Garlock's pencil was flying now. "Following me?"

"On your tail." Belle was breathing hard; as the blank spaces became fewer and fewer her face began to turn white.

"From this we get that . . . and *that* makes the whole bracket tie into the same conclusion I had before. So, except for that one assumption, it's solid."

"My God, Clee!" Belle studied the chart. "I mentioned Newton and Einstein . . . add to that 'the brain of a Garlock, better than either.'" Then seeing his reaction, she said, "You're blushing. I didn't think . . ."

"Cut the comedy. You know I couldn't carry either of their hats to a dog-fight."

"And I would *never* have believed that you were basically modest."

"I said cut out the kidding, Belle."

"I'm deadly serious. A brain that could do *that*"—she waved at the chart— ". . . well, even *I* am not enough of a heel to belittle one of the most tremendous intuitions ever achieved by man. Not that I like it. It's horrible. It denies mankind everything that made him come up from the slime—everything that made him man."

"Not at all. Nothing is changed, in man's own frame of reference. It merely takes our thinking one step farther. That step, of course, isn't easy."

"That is the understatement of all time. What it will *do*, though, is set up an inferiority complex that would wipe out the whole human race."

"There might be some slight tendency. Also, since my basic assumption can't be justified, the whole thing may be fallacious. So I'm not going to publish it." He glanced at the chart and it vanished.

"Clee!" Belle stared, almost goggle-eyed. "With your name?" The tremendous splash . . . I see. You're really grown up."

"Not all the way, probably; but pretty nearly—I hope."

"But some of the . . . not exactly corollaries, but . . ." Belle's face, which had regained some of its color, began again to pale.

"Which one of the many?"

"The most shattering one, to me, concerns intelligence. If it *is* true that our vaunted mentality is only that of one blood cell compared to that of a whole brain . . . and that intelligence is banked, level upon level . . . well, it's simply mind-wrecking. I've been trying madly not to think of that concept at all, but I can't put it off much longer."

"Now's as good a time as any. Probe. I'll hold your hand."

"You'd better hold more of me than that, I think."

"I'll do even that, in a good cause." He put his arms around her and held her close. "Go ahead. Face it. All the way down and all the way up. You've got what it takes. You'll come back sane and it'll never bother you again."

She closed her eyes, put her head on his shoulder. Her every muscle went tense.

Neither of them ever knew how long they stood there, close-clasped and motionless in silence; but finally her muscles loosened. She lifted her head; raised her brimming eyes.

"All the way down?" he asked.

"To almost a geometrical point."

"And all the way up?"

"I touched the fringe of infinity."

"Intelligence all the way?"

"All the way. I couldn't understand any of them, of course, but I looked each one squarely in the eye."

"Good girl. And you're still sane."

"As much so as ever . . . more so, maybe." She disengaged herself, sat down on the bed, lit a cigarette and smoked half of it. Then she stood up. "Clee, if anything in the whole universe ever knocked hell out of anything, that did out of me. I'm going to do something that will take about ten minutes. Will you wait right here?"

"Of course. Take all the time you want."

When she came back Garlock leaped to his feet and stared speechlessly. Belle's hair was now its natural deep, rich chestnut, her lipstick was red, her nails were bare, and she wore a white shirt and an almost-knee length crimson skirt.

"Here's what I'm going to do," she said quietly. "I'm going to be a plain, ordinary brownette. I'm going to marry you as soon as we land—registered permanent family. I'm going to have six kids and spoil them rotten. In short, I have grown up—at least partly."

"Plain?" he managed to say, finally. "Ordinary? You? Yes—like a super-nova going off under a man's feet!" With a visible effort, Garlock pulled himself together. "I don't need to tell you what a surprise this is, and can't tell you what it means to me. But you never have said you love me. Hadn't you better?"

"I'm afraid to. Our next kiss will be different. I'd spoil all this nice new makeup." She tried to grin in her old-time fashion, but failed. She sobered, then, and went on with a completely new intensity. "Listen, Clee. I'm all done—forever—with lying and pretending to you. I love you so much that . . . well, there simply aren't any thoughts. And when I think of how I acted, it hurts— God, how it hurts! I don't see how you can love me at all. I'd take a miracle."

"Miracles happen, then." He put both arms around her, very gently. "For the first time in my life I'm cutting my screens to zero. Come in!"

"What?" For a moment she was unable to believe the thought. Then, cutting her own shield, she went fully into his mind. "Oh, I didn't dare hope you could possibly feel . . . oh, this is wonderful, Clee—simply *wonderful!*"

As the two fully-opened minds met and joined she threw both arms around him and their embrace tightened as though their bodies were trying to become as nearly one as were their minds. Finally she pulled herself away and put up a solid block.

"What a mess!" she said, shakily. "Lipstick all *over* you . . ."

"Why words, sweetheart? That was perfect."

"Oh, it was . . . but wide open, with such a mind as yours . . ." She paused, then came back to normal almost with a snap. ". . . But say; I'll bet that's what Therea and Alsyne were doing. That 'fusion' thing. We'll practice it tonight."

He pondered briefly. "Sure it was."

"But he said they learned it from us. How could he

have, when we . . . Oh, we did, of course, in moments of high stress . . . but we didn't actually know it . . ." She paused.

"We wouldn't admit it, you mean, even to ourselves."

"Maybe; and of course it never occurred to us that it could be done for more than a microsecond at a time. Or that two people could ever, possibly, *live* that way."

"Or what a life it would be. So let's chop this and get back to you and me."

"Okay, let's," she agreed, but in a severely practical tone. "You've got lipstick even on your shirt. So change it and I'll go put on a new face and bring over some stuff and clean you up."

While she cleaned, she talked. "I told you our next kiss would be different, but I had no idea . . . wow! *That* will be as much different, too, I'm sure . . . hmmmm?" Again she pressed herself against him—this time in a somewhat different fashion.

"Stop that, you little devil, or I'll . . ." His arms came up of themselves, but he forced them back down. ". . . No I won't. We'll save that for tonight, too."

"I'll behave myself!" She laughed, pure joy in voice, eyes, and smile. "I bet myself you wouldn't and I won! You're tall, solid gold, Clee darling—the absolute top."

"Thanks, sweetheart. I wish that were true," he said, soberly. "But I can't help wondering if two such hellions as you and I are can make a go of marriage—no, cancel that. We'll do it—all we have to figure out is how."

"I know what you mean. Not at first—it'll be purely wonderful then. After five years, say, when the glamor has worn off and I've had three of our six children and two of them are in bed sick and I'm all frazzled out and you're strung up tight as a bowstring with overwork and . . ."

"Hold it! No. If we can live together six months—or even six weeks—without killing each other, we'll have it made. It's at first that it'll be rugged. No matter how rugged it gets, though, we'll know one thing for sure. We couldn't live apart. That'll give us enough leverage. Right?"

"Yes," she laughed. "I'll take care of any and all situations, whatever they are, that arise in the first six months. You'll be responsible for the next sixty years. That's a perfectly fair and equitable division of responsibility. Now kiss me and we'll go."

When Garlock cut the Gunther blocks, however, James' thought came instantly in: "Been trying to get you for twenty minutes."

"And in a couple of seconds he brought Garlock and Belle up to date. ". . . So Fatso's been waiting in Evans' office. He's throwing fits all over the place and Evans and Macey are both going quietly mad."

"He'll have to wait," Garlock decided instantly. "No matter how many fits he has, no such decision is going to be made until there's enough of a Galactic Council to make it."

"Well, you'll have to tell him that yourself. In person."

"I'll do just that, and tell him so he'll stay told."

"Okay, but hurry—"

Belle and Garlock 'ported out into the Main, arms around each other like a couple of college freshmen.

Both James and Lola stared thunderstruck at them.

"*Belle!*" Lola shrieked. "*Why—Belle—Bellamy!*"

"*What* goes *on* here?" James demanded.

"Nothing much," Garlock replied, although he blushed almost as deeply as Belle did. "Cut the rope, Jim, and let the old bucket drop."

ACE SCIENCE FICTION SPECIALS

Just $1.25 each

#1—From the Legend of Biel Staton

#2—Red Tide Tarzan & Chapman

#3—Endless Voyage Bradley

#4—The Invincible Lem

#5—Growing Up In Tier 3000 Gotschalk

#6—Challenge the Hellmaker Richmond

#7—Tournament of Thorns Swann

#8—Fifth Head of Cerberse Wolfe

Available wherever paperbacks are sold or use this coupon.

64A